CW01511268

Here in My Heart

By Jo Fletcher

2025

Butterworth Books is a different breed of publishing house. It's a home for Indies, for independent authors who take great pride in their work and produce top quality books for readers who deserve the best. Professional editing, professional cover design, professional proof reading, professional book production—you get the idea. As Individual as the Indie authors we're proud to work with, we're Butterworths and we're *different*.

Authors currently publishing with us:

E.V. Bancroft
Valden Bush
Addison M Conley
Jo Fletcher (JL Fletcher)
Helena Harte
Lee Haven
Karen Klyne
Sydney Lear
AJ Mason
Ally McGuire
James Merrick
Robyn Nyx (RJ Nyx)
JP Preston
Simon Smalley
JJ Taylor
Brey Willows

For more information visit www.butterworthbooks.co.uk

HERE IN MY HEART © 2025 by Jo Fletcher
All rights reserved.

This trade paperback is published by Butterworth Books, UK

This is a work of fiction: names, characters, and incidents are the product of the author's imagination or are used fictitiously. Any resemblance to actual persons, living or dead, business establishments, events, or locales is entirely coincidental.

This book, or parts thereof, may not be reproduced in any form without express permission, and no part of this book may be used in any manner for the purpose of training artificial intelligence technologies or systems.

CATALOGING INFORMATION
ISBN: 978-1-915009-97-5
CREDITS
Editor: Nicci Robinson
Jacket Design: Global Wordsmiths
Production Design: Global Wordsmiths
Cover Design: Hird Creates

Acknowledgements

Writing wouldn't be nearly as much fun without my author buddy Iona Kane. Thanks for sticking with me through the highs and lows of this one. And the highs and lows of life, generally.

Big kisses to my little family for giving me space to write. I love that we can make time for each other and our passions. Even if we have thirty-four passions between us...

This novel came to life at a writing retreat in Spain during the autumn of 2024. Thanks to Global Wordsmiths and my editor, Nicci, for helping me to crystallise Sylvie's story and for smoothing the rough edges of my early drafts.

Writing can be a solitary sport, so I do love spending time with like-minded authors who make me laugh til I cry. You know who you are.

Thanks especially to my author friends Lee Haven and Sue Still, who gave me a space to share my ideas and insecurities about this book. Their feedback and insight has been so valuable.

I've wanted to write Sylvie's story since she made her first, spiky appearance in *Here You Are*. But I was blown away by how many people told me they loved her as a character. I'm grateful to all the readers who have shared their thoughts with me in messages of support and reviews. Thank you for reading my books.

Big thanks particularly to those loud and proud cheerleaders who've been there since the start: Louise, Jodi, Nikki. Helen D for bringing me cans of pop at Pride events: you're the roadie that every sapphic author needs.

Finally, thanks to my lovely mum and dad for encouraging me to study in the south of France back in the 1990s. If I hadn't had that amazing experience, I wouldn't have lived in Montpellier. Sylvie might have had to stay in Paris, and she might never have met her favourite Californian. Phew!

This book contains some detail of self-harm with a tertiary character.

Dedication

To everyone who loved Sylvie so much,
I had to write her story.

To the love of my life, R,
who loves me despite my quirks. IYKYK

Chapter One

SYLVIE BOUCHER WIPED THE sweat from her brow and peeled her sticky thigh from the chair. The late September spike in temperature had surprised none of her southern French neighbors, but she'd already packed away her summer clothes, ready for the new term to begin.

Isabelle de Causier shifted under the parasol, draped in white linen. "Your move, Professor Boucher."

"I'm so hot," said Sylvie, envying her friend's effortless style and poise.

"Damn right." Isa raised her eyebrow with a hint of her typical mischief. "Too hot to be spending all these nights alone."

"I mean, I'm sweating from every orifice." Sylvie nudged her black queen into the sight line of Isa's king and dabbed the moisture from her lip. She wafted the menu, creating no breeze at all. How did this city carry on in such sweltering temperatures?

The waiter danced across the town square with a sixth sense for who needed his attention. He stopped at a table with a couple engrossed in one another as if the bustling around them didn't exist. Sylvie dismissed the pulling sensation in her gut. Aside from a full-on job and the odd game of chess, her time in the south had so far been pretty unadventurous. And quite lonely.

"Damn it." Sylvie had missed the sly maneuver which had lost her the advantage. "Always ten steps ahead, you fox."

"Foxy. I like that." Isa's contagious laugh attracted the attention of the neighboring tables.

Sylvie dismissed the flirtation. Isa was nothing more than a new friend. God knows she'd needed one when she arrived in

Montpellier hoping to break the glass ceiling of academia.

"Can you believe the summer is over? It's devastating." Isa sipped her cool rosé. "Another year of herding students through the halls again. Yuck."

Sylvie shrugged. "Another merry-go-round of ignorance and calamity." She puffed warm air across her top lip. "I'm looking forward to the autumn. This heat is unbearable. When will it cool down?"

"Just in time for reading week, I suspect. You've another month yet." Isa moved her knight to take Sylvie's queen. "At least we have the beach. Paris must be awful in the summer."

Sylvie peeked over her oversized sunglasses. "Real Parisians don't stay for the summer."

"Makes sense." Isa patted her sundress. "Are you taking on the new classes this term?"

"Paul asked me." Sylvie scowled, recalling the strained conversation before the end of last semester. "But he's more concerned with me finishing my book."

"Mais oui. Mon amie, the published professor. How many books have you written now?"

"Soon to be five." Sylvie frowned, the seed of doubt stirring inside. "If I can get to work."

"I have every faith in you. You're a winner at life, Sylvie." Isa took the king with a flourish. "Except in chess. Checkmate."

The waiter appeared from nowhere and relieved them of their empty glasses. "Can I get you another?"

"I shouldn't really. I have some work to do." Sylvie tapped a cigarette on the cast iron table and made to leave, dismissing the waiter with a nod.

"Oh, come on, you may as well settle in for the afternoon." Isa adjusted her wide-brimmed sun hat and held out her hand. "We're playing in the sunshine with fine wine flowing. I'll make a southerner of you yet."

The beautiful white stone of the old buildings flanked them on four sides. Relaxed locals weaved through the cafés on their gentle meander across town. It was nothing like the grey business of a September in Paris. On days like these, Sylvie wondered whether she could make this city her forever home. "I'm not so sure. Another year rounding up eighteen-year-olds and I might have a change of heart."

"It's your heart that's the problem. I think you left a piece of it back in Paris."

The memory of her last kiss flooded Sylvie's mind. Paris had been warm and crowded that day, but the kiss had been cold and empty. She and Armelle dated for a few weeks, but it was nothing serious. Armelle had grown clingy and intolerable, eventually giving Sylvie an ultimatum: all in or call it. Sylvie hadn't given it a second thought. She had no desire to overcomplicate life with co-dependence on another human, and with no relationship and a stalled career, there really had been a diminishing list of things keeping her in the capital.

Two months later, she'd seen the chance for a transfer to Montpellier and the promise of a new start. "No, my heart is very much here, along with the rest of me. I left Paris for the taste of something new and that's what I got." Sort of. The past year had been more of a simple entrée than a full plat du jour, but she was hopeful that promotion was on the menu this year. With that came status and connections. She yearned for international travel and the chance to share her work with a global audience.

Another couple walked past: two stylish women hand in hand. Sylvie met Isa's stare. "Okay, so I haven't quite nailed a love life, but casual dating isn't for me."

"You can't expect some intellectual beauty to come walking into your lecture room and throw themselves at your feet. You might need to do some of the leg work. You should put yourself out there."

Sylvie cringed. She'd say the same to her single friends. "I don't want to bare my soul on the internet."

"Your soul has nothing to do with it. It's your smile people are interested in, among other things."

Sylvie's cheeks flared with heat. "Such as?"

Isa's laugh rang out. "Your fine wit."

Sylvie didn't feel very witty right now, or attractive. Sweat pooled at her armpits, and she regretted the choice of fibers this morning.

"Seriously, just have some fun," Isa said. "Try not to close down every possibility, and you never know who might walk into your life when you least expect it."

"I'll think about it. For now, I need shade and water. Until next time." She kissed Isa three times on the cheeks and turned into the glare of the sun.

Seeking out the narrowest, shadiest streets, Sylvie strolled slowly to exert the least amount of energy possible. A hush fell over the city as Sunday afternoon stretched toward the evening, and everyone enjoyed the lull before the storm of the nightlife. This place rarely stilled. There was always someone enjoying themselves somewhere. But on a Sunday, or early in the morning before dawn, Sylvie found time to catch her breath.

She paused at the Place St Roch and sat on the steps of the church, in the welcome shadow of the tall, impressive building. She looked up to the drawn shutters of her apartment, grateful she'd had the foresight to block out the afternoon sun and save herself from a stifling return home.

She'd slowed down here, in the heat of the south. It was nothing like the frenetic pace she'd kept up in Paris. Sometimes, she even had time to hear her thoughts and wonder. What did she want now she'd accepted a permanent job at the university? Was the city home? Except Isa and a couple of colleagues, there was no one to come home to. No one to share her day with.

Her mind drifted to her parents' smallholding along the coast near Sète. Each year that passed, they worked their little plot together, turning another vegetable bed over to rest. She smiled, the taste of her mother's cassoulet stirring in her memory.

She'd visit as soon as she could. Isa was right: the summer had passed all too quickly, and she wasn't quite ready for the return to a timetable which meant her balmy late nights would be curtailed until at least the reading week.

"Sylvie, I'll see you tonight?" Colette waved from her café across the square.

"Maybe. Save me something nice just in case." She smiled. The prettiest around, Colette's place was nestled between a launderette and a crêperie, its bottle-green doors flanked by hanging baskets of little flowers tumbling down the stone wall.

"Okay, come down when you wake up from your nap." Colette washed down another table ready for the evening service. She worked like a horse, all day and night.

"I will do. It's been a hard day at the office." Sylvie laughed and shrugged off the post-wine haze. The guilt of not making progress on her book lingered like the smell of rainy drains. She hadn't worked hard enough this summer. The sands of time had fallen through her hands as she'd laid on the beach at Palavas, the waves lapping gently at the Mediterranean shore. But she'd be back at it tomorrow, and nothing was going to get in the way of keeping that publishing advance.

This year, she'd be more productive than ever and show the university bigwigs that she deserved her place at the top table. She'd earned it. Hadn't she?

Chapter Two

ADELAIDE POOLE STARED INTO her twin's eyes, her knee twitching with guilt. "What have I forgotten?"

Stephanie frowned her familiar frown: a sign that Ade had fallen short again. "Dad just messaged to say he sent a package to the hotel in Paris. Did you not tell them we were leaving today?"

"Okay, did you really ask me to, or did you infer it and expect me to read your mind? Because either way, no, I didn't tell Dad we were leaving Paris."

Steph tsked. "I told you that Dad and Pops would be worried about us if they didn't know exactly where we were."

Ade blinked and nodded, remembering the conversation they'd had back home. "Well, that's not asking me to do it. That's telling me about their feelings." She stiffened under Steph's glare. "You couldn't have told them yourself?"

"Are you for real? I had a million things to remember before this trip. You couldn't handle one simple task?"

Ade wriggled against the seat of the train, the fabric scratching her back even though she'd worn two layers for the journey. She stared at the table, blocking the noise from the nearby passengers.

"Ade? Are you listening?" Steph tapped her shoulder.

The thirty-minute head start from their rent-a-womb had really given Steph the edge. Ade was always catching up, trying to work out which conversation to prioritize or which tab in her overloaded brain to close. It was a truth she'd long since accepted: she was the weak link in their family chain. Despite her dads' constant love and support, somehow, she managed to screw up. A lot.

Ade blinked against the harsh sunlight and tuned into the

rumble of the train car against the tracks. She hadn't eaten since the Gare de Lyon and her head pounded.

"We'll be there soon, and we can grab a bite," Stephanie said with a gentle nudge.

Ade bounced her knee out of time with the train's jog along the track. The apprehension of starting her new life in the South of France gnawed deep in her abdomen. She'd been in her comfort zone at the Northern Californian college, which had shielded her from the realities of adulting for the last six years.

But she could only blame herself for the upheaval of spending a year abroad. She'd spent far too long with her head down in the lab and had attracted the unwanted attention of her supervisors. Looking after her marine animals wasn't enough, they'd said; she had to take on other duties. Peopling. Mentoring students. All the things she'd avoided since graduation.

She rubbed dust from the train's window and revealed the horizon. The dry landscape of southern France reminded her a little of California. Not that she'd been further than the Monterey city limits that often. Places she didn't know confused her, so she did her best to avoid that.

The train slowed as they neared the university town of Montpellier. The window framed a patchwork of graffiti art, stocky condos, and concrete overhangs, before Ade glimpsed the city's historic glory. The balconies grew taller and more ornate, and with age came beauty. Excitement fluttered in her stomach, combining with the acidic worry she'd been cultivating since they'd flown out of San Francisco on Wednesday.

"You okay there, Ady-baby?"

She cringed at her sister's use of their family nickname. "This place looks kind of cool. What do you think?"

Stephanie beamed. "I think it'll be the making of you." The announcement of their arrival pierced Ade's ears, and she cowered into the seat.

Steph rose to collect their bags. "You have your cell? Passport?

Check around you."

"Okay, Dad." Ade huffed. She'd catalogued everything she'd brought and knew its exact position.

"I'm just being careful, honey. You don't want to be lost in a strange place without your documents. I have no idea what the French police would make of that."

Ade patted her pockets. "I'm good. Let's go." Stepping onto the platform, the evening heat hit her cheeks, and her shirt clung to her back beneath her oversized bag. "It's hotter than home."

"You'll get used to it." Steph led the way with the confidence of a seasoned traveler and checked them into a nearby hotel.

In their air-conditioned room, Ade peeled off a layer of clothes and collapsed on one of the beds, her heavy limbs exhausted from the day's efforts. She scanned the room for essentials. The door and window locked. *Adequate.* The air-conditioning unit was a little loud for her liking, but she'd manage.

"I've turned on the shower. How about you jump in first, and I'll get us a cold drink from the bar?" Steph scooped up Ade's discarded clothes from the floor. "Please take a shower. Otherwise, you'll get into something, and it'll be midnight by the time we eat."

Ade grunted. She could do without Steph bossing her around but chose to comply rather than stand her ground. In the small bathroom, she wiped down the surface and laid out her products. It was nothing like what she was used to at home, and she breathed through the discomfort, while her skin crawled.

Under the lukewarm jet, she closed her eyes. The journey had taken its toll on her, but the pent-up adrenaline of starting a new life quivered just beneath the surface. She was tired, for sure, but there was no way she'd sleep with the nervous excitement flowing through her veins right now.

Back in Monterey, she'd stuck a pin in life. With the mounting pressures from her supervisors to be more of a "people person," she'd accepted the rotation into the pastoral care team just to shut them up for a while. She secretly hoped that taking care of the animals would take up more of her time than mentoring the amateur biologists she'd accompanied to Europe.

She closed off the shower and wrapped herself in a towel before opening the door just enough to let the steam out of the tiny room.

Steph held two champagne flutes in her hand. "Do you want to hit a couple of bars tonight?"

Ade groaned. Steph clearly wanted to start her gap year already. Whether Ade liked it or not, she'd be dragged along for the ride. What she really wanted was to tuck herself under the white cotton sheets of the hotel bed, scroll through her cell for a couple of hours, and get some rest.

***

Ade might've vomited over the realtor's shoes if Stephanie hadn't opened the window to take in the view. Thank God for fresh air and personal space. Her stomach lurched with all the force of a pirate-ship ride at the carnival. It would be awful to spoil the crimson leather of those fancy shoes. They looked French, but how would she know? Ade had no clue what was typical in this strange new country.

"I like your shoes." She realized by the scrunch of the woman's eyebrows that she'd spoken the words out loud. The interminable monologue that played on a loop inside her mind every minute of the day sometimes escaped for air.

"They're gorgeous, aren't they? Let's go check out the kitchen." Steph pulled a face behind the realtor's back and led the way to the so-called kitchen, which turned out to be nothing more than a sink and a stovetop in the minuscule living area.

Back in Monterey, Ade and Stephanie lived in the annex of their parents' plus-sized condo. They weren't mega-rich by any means. But they were comfortable, and their California proportions dwarfed this tiny old-town apartment. Ade stared at the gaping hole in the ceiling. It matched one around the pipes coming out of the wooden floors. Black voids out of which anything could appear. Maybe she could keep a pet rat.

"You okay?" Stephanie bumped her elbow. "Tell me what you're thinking."

Ade recalled her dad's final words of advice at the airport a few days prior: *"Think before you speak and try not to offend anyone."* He'd cupped her cheeks and forced her to look at him. Then he'd kissed the tip of her nose and enveloped her in an uncharacteristic bear hug. Steph had dawdled in the tearful embrace of Pops, while they both swiped at their damp cheeks and promised to call when they could.

"This is better than everything we've seen today," Ade said, which was neither a lie nor offensive...she hoped.

Steph cracked a smile and moved out of the realtor's earshot. "With a bit of a polishing, I think this'll do fine. That last place was a total dive."

"I can't afford anything better." The paycheck bump she was promised by the faculty would be eaten up in no time at this rate.

"Unless you sub-let, I guess," Steph said.

"No way." The idea of sharing a space with strangers was off the cards. Ade had only managed to co-habit with one person since conception. "I can't have people in my space. It's bad enough at work."

"I know, honey. I was just kidding." Stephanie laughed. "Dad and Pops will send you some cash if you need it."

"No, I don't think so." Ade swallowed the taste of white wine that persisted on her tastebuds. Last night's dinner had turned into drinks and despite Ade's protests, Steph had made some new friends, and they'd finished up at a club. The only reason she stuck around was because going back to the hotel was impossible on her own: she hadn't had the chance to map the route yet.

The realtor's heels sounded against the boards.

Ade inhaled the woman's impatience as if it were a strong scent.

"Do we need to do something right now?" The options exploded like fireworks in Ade's mind. She didn't want to offend the realtor or embarrass Steph.

"You don't have to rush." Steph touched her sleeve, as if she knew that the situation was sending her sideways. "We can always look around again tomorrow."

Dragging ourselves around for another day? No, thanks. Endless real estate windows, half-translated, broken conversations, and a maddening midday heat had made for a miserable first day in her new city. "Can we just take the apartment?" Ade asked.

"Of course," the realtor said, clapping her hands with a finality. "You'll need to follow me down to the office to sort out some paperwork."

The next hour proved to be the most tedious of the whole day. Ade found herself on the ground floor of a tall office block trying to focus on something that wouldn't hurt her head.

She stared ahead, avoiding the overflowing filing cabinets. She shut her eyes, only for the brown stain of a coffee ring to appear on the back of her eyelids. The whirling blades of a fan did nothing more than send papers flying and disperse the stench of stale sweat around the room.

The realtor peered above a pair of scarlet spectacles. "Who will sign the lease for you, Mademoiselle...Poole?"

Ade wondered if she had eyewear to match all her footwear.

"Adelaide will sign it," Steph said. "We can pay the deposit today."

Ade nodded beside her sister, grateful to avoid taking the lead.

"You will need a French guarantor," the realtor said.

"A what now?" Steph asked.

"Someone who lives in France to co-sign the lease with you. It is the way these things are done here."

Steph shuffled in her seat. "I'm sorry, I don't understand. My sister and I are both adults. We can pay rent up front if that's what the issue is."

There was much gesticulating from the back office as the realtor sought a second opinion.

"Some air," Ade said. "I need some air."

"Sure thing. I'll sort this out and come get you." Steph twisted the cap of her water bottle.

Ade paced the sidewalk, staying close enough to the shop window to keep Steph in her eyeline. She stepped over the dog mess and gum and studiously avoided the cracks in the pavements. The screech of tires and roar of engines filled her ears while exhaust fumes invaded her nostrils. She counted to ten, just like Pops had taught her. Would she ever settle and adjust to the new smells and sounds? A rattle of foreign words distracted her across the road. She looked back at Steph, and she was still there.

This morning on the way back from the club, the rising sun had bathed the city's rooftops in an amber glow as the street cleaners washed down the sins of the night. She'd liked the cleaners. They'd been loud but effective.

Stephanie poked her head through the office door. "Okay, we're all done here."

"Do you need me? I don't feel that well."

"You need to sign some papers." Steph held the door open. "It's your studio, not mine."

Ade's shoulders stiffened as she stepped inside. Why couldn't her sister stay with her a little longer? Soon enough, she'd be all alone in this strange city, starting a new job with a bunch of new people she'd no doubt annoy in her first week.

All their first days had been done as a duo: kindergarten, middle school, high school. They'd been hand in hand through every milestone: major to minor. Would Ade fall apart without the glue that held her together?

Ade didn't want Steph to leave, but that had been the deal. She'd come with her to France and go on traveling through Europe, which had been her sister's dream since they'd been in high school. A little part of Ade wished that Stephanie would be charmed by this little French city and stay for longer. Maybe even the whole year.

But the chance of that, based on the last twenty-four hours, was pretty slim. Ade had proven herself to be the perennial family burden, someone to be coaxed along, second-guessed, and occasionally rescued from the jaws of disaster.

Stephanie had done more than discharge her sisterly duty; it was time for her own adventures, leaving Ade to her own devices. What would life look like then? Ade cleared her throat. It did her no good to run off too far into the future. The echo of her pop's advice rang in her ears: *"Stay here in the moment, kiddo, and deal with what's in front of you."* She drew her pen across the page, signing her name. If only she had the certainty of that scrawl of black ink.

Chapter Three

"OUT OF THE WAY, please. This isn't a common room; it's a corridor." Sylvie held her head high past the freshers' orientation, hoping to set the tone for the coming academic year. She turned into the relative peace of her classroom and set down her tower of books. She'd need to get used to the weight of her various tomes after a summer carrying nothing but sunscreen and a beach towel.

The Post-it note on her screen curled up at the corner. She looked away, not needing the reminder that the international placement students and their mentor would arrive today. It had been a last-minute addition to her responsibilities, and she'd hoped in vain that Paul would have arranged something else by the start of term.

Sadly, she remained burdened with the extra load. She sighed. Would she ever climb high enough up the steep academic ladder to deserve her own oak-paneled office and a clear schedule? Other professors set their working hours. Christ, some even turned up midway through a semester. If she cared less, maybe she could too. As it was, she was stuck in a dated classroom with a list as long as her arm of additional leadership tasks.

A stocky young man cleared his throat at the door. "Bonjour. Hello," he said, gingerly making his way in.

"International group?" Sylvie glanced at the clock, assuring herself of the time.

"Yes, ma'am. Are we in the right place?" He dithered, along with his friends hugging the door frame.

"Absolutely. If this is where you've been sent. Come in and sit down." Sylvie considered the group as they entered, seeking out their leader. They were five of the most unlikely specimens, sporting a range of casual wear so unlike the fashions that usually graced the catwalk of her classroom. Science graduates from California, here to study the marine life off the coast, Paul had said, when he mentioned it before the summer break. She tried, unsuccessfully, to recall any further details. "Which one of you is the group leader?" Sylvie asked. The stocky boy shuffled under her scrutiny and didn't reply. "Hello?" Sylvie didn't doubt her English and refused to repeat such a basic question to her new academic hopefuls. "Alors, you've made it all the way across the ocean to begin your studies here: at least one of you must know who is in charge."

"She's not here yet, ma'am," one of the girls said as she inspected her nails.

"Sit down." She wrote her name on the board. "My name is Professor Sylvie Boucher, and I am a specialist in European Feminism. Please introduce yourselves."

The five of them looked at each other, wide-eyed and mute.

"Monsieur..." Sylvie pointed to Mr. Stocky at the end of the row. "Would you like to go first?"

"My name is Greg Shannon," he said.

"And you are from..." Sylvie circled her hands, as if the winding motion might illicit more detail from her shy audience. *Mon dieu.*

"I'm part of the marine conservation program at the University of California in Monterey. We're here for our year abroad."

And so it went. Four more forgettable introductions from a quintet of post-acne young adults trying to convince themselves that they weren't homesick for peanut butter and jelly sandwiches.

The door creaked, disturbing the awkward moment of silence. A flame-haired, tall woman froze in the frame, scanning the room, her eyes wild with uncertainty. She tilted her head toward Sylvie, clearly identifying her as the authority. "I'm..."

Unwilling to put the latecomer out of her misery, Sylvie held the stillness for several beats.

"I'm Adelaide Poole. I'm so sorry I'm late."

"I thought we were lacking a program leader. Please, sit down," said Sylvie.

Adelaide seemed to contemplate the seating arrangements for much longer than was necessary before taking a seat next to a sporty-looking, broad-shouldered young man.

Sylvie shook her head, despairing at what had landed in her lap this year. Between this and the pressures of her timetable, she was never going to get her book published. "Now you're here, we can conclude our introductions."

Silence reigned.

"Adelaide Poole? Can you introduce yourself?"

"Oh, I'm sorry." She wriggled in her seat and fiddled with the spinning ring on her thumb. "My name is Ade Poole. I'm in my final year of a PhD at Monterey. I've been asked to chaperone these folks, but I don't really have any experience in this kind of thing."

"How reassuring." Sylvie handed each student a binder. "These are your induction folders. They contain details of the university campus, how to join the library, the access code to the Wi-Fi, timetables—" Sylvie looked up at the class of jet-lagged Americans. "I don't need to explain everything. You're not children."

Ade raised her hand as if she was about to argue.

"Miss Poole?"

"Thanks." Ade avoided eye contact with the students. "I have a guidance sheet which you can all add to your folders. It includes the timetable for my student counselling sessions and my cell number in case you need to get hold of me."

"Useful." Sylvie nodded. "Thank you, Ade."

Six pairs of eyes stared at her, seeking direction.

"Let's leave it there. My office hours are posted on my door, should you need me. I hope that won't be necessary. Until next time," Sylvie said, closing her notebook with finality.

Chairs scraped across her classroom floor. Ade gathered her belongings and made for the exit, looking more eager than any of the students to escape Sylvie's further examination.

***

"How could you?" Sylvie stormed into her boss's office without knocking, the frustration of the last half an hour whipping around her like a strong gale.

"Sylvie, Sylvie," Paul said, as he looked up from his desk. "I've been expecting you to drop in. I just made fresh coffee by chance. Would you like one?"

"Your Colombian beans aren't enough to calm me down this time. What were you thinking sending me a group of Americans unable to string a sentence?"

He offered Sylvie the armchair: a sign of his relative seniority at the university. "Someone has to take care of them."

"Give them to Richard. He has nothing to do other than tidy his bookcases."

Paul laughed.

"Well?" she asked.

"Richard is old and becoming more useless with each semester. He doesn't have the energy to run around after an international cohort."

"At least find them someone in the sciences." Sylvie sighed. *I can't deal with that troop of misfits for a whole year.* "How do you expect me to supervise marine biologists? The closest I get to the ocean is teaching *The Waves.*"

He raised his eyebrow. "Perhaps the marine scientists will be of some value to your exploration of setting in early twentieth-century literature? Push those boundaries you've been telling me about."

"I'm not here for your amusement, Paul. What are you going to do about it?"

"There's nothing I can do for you, my dearest Sylvie. We talked about this before the summer. It's not about the subject specifically; it's just pastoral care. They could be a bunch of trainee chefs or budding filmmakers. It makes no difference. You need to ramp up your supervision hours before you can take on any more responsibility here."

The penny dropped, along with Sylvie's stomach. "Are you telling me that this is a condition of any future promotion?"

"I am simply saying that you're a junior professor now. When you come to the next opportunity, you'll need to demonstrate two things to any academic board: that you've published a successful commentary on the juxtaposition between French and English literary feminists," he sipped the piping hot coffee and smiled, "and a bulging portfolio of leadership evidence. Take the chance to build your case."

This fucking guy. "The so-called mentor they've sent couldn't even get out of bed on time," Sylvie said through gritted teeth.

"Give her a break, perhaps?" His grin widened.

"I don't give people breaks. There's no time for breaks if they're serious about what they're doing."

"There lies your problem, my dear. We're in the privileged position of being paid to foster people's potential. They will always have flaws which need addressing. Our job is to nurture improvement."

"Or perfection." Sylvie tipped her chin in defiance.

"Ah. That's where you and I differ. I simply seek improvement. Perfection is a curse. Polishing something until it shines only makes your hand ache. I try to avoid it."

Sylvie pursed her lips. Of course he avoided pain; he was the king of delegation. They could quarrel over their academic purpose all day. She and Paul had enjoyed hours of intellectual debate, but that's not what she was there for now. She had to change tack if she was going to walk out of his office with fewer burdens and more free periods. She'd have to meet him in his meandering world of rationale, rather than rely on her straight-talking reason. "Perhaps this requires a collective response? I'm not the only professor at my level, and I wouldn't wish to deny any of the others the opportunity to excel. It's a chance for Jean, or André, or even Matthieu, is it not?" She was fed up with sucking up the extra load while her male colleagues swanned about the faculty enjoying liberty and fraternity, while she was desperate for equality.

Paul steepled his fingers. "It's decided. The Americans are your babies this year. Congratulations on your new arrivals."

Sylvie groaned with all the drama of a two-year old denied another cookie.

"There's more." Paul leaned in. "The pastoral supervisor who needs a new alarm clock will also need some extra support, because she's new to all this. The Monterey team suggested regular coaching sessions. I have every faith in you to bring her on."

"Sure. I'll squeeze those between my teaching timetable and my editing all-nighters."

Paul nodded. "It'll be a productive year for you. I can feel it in my bones."

Sylvie's bones already ached with fresh defeat. This year was going to be an impossible juggling act. She wouldn't mind if the international cohort had been full of energy and ambition, but this morning's session had proved the exact opposite. Adelaide Poole certainly lacked the driving force of a pastoral care leader, and Sylvie couldn't get sucked into coaching a PhD student into leadership. It was all a waste of her energy, especially when she had a book to publish. But how could she spend as little time as possible babysitting the Americans without Paul noticing? And how would she spend time on her real purpose this year: securing the promotion that she'd moved south for?

Chapter Four

"The bubbles are trying to escape." Ade scraped her shoe against the tiled floor of the laundromat.

"Will you stop staring at the machine and come help me fold this laundry?" Steph fought the tangled mess of T-shirts, pants, and socks which had emerged en masse from the dryer. "How have we worn so many clothes in a week?"

"The heat is making us sweat," Ade said, "and you said we couldn't wear clothes that had started to smell."

Steph closed her eyes and took a deep breath, before reaching inside the drum for another jumbled pile.

"Sorry. Did I state the obvious again?" Ade asked.

Emerging from her heap of clothes, Steph shot her sister a smile. A familiar warmth flowed over Ade, but it wasn't enough to figure out her understanding of the world.

"A little, honey, but don't you worry. You're right. It's been a hot, dusty week of traveling, but this load should get us back on track." Steph folded the last of the socks and turned to a second machine, still in mid-cycle. "I need to get all this dry by tomorrow to pack up."

Dread crept into Ade's chest. Fending for herself was daunting. She'd never had to do it before. Both her dads had been ever-present, along with Stephanie. They sat on the bench seat, and Ade resumed her watch. The soap suds whirled around the machine, as if they were trying to escape through the window. "When will you be back?"

"I've posted my itinerary on your fridge, so you always know where I am. Tomorrow, I'm heading to Perpignan and then onto Barcelona. There's a cool town I want to hit up along the coast.

Everyone's talking about its gay vibes."

The bubbles gathered in the fold of the machine door, thickening, concentrating. "Then where are you going?" Ade asked, desperate to soak up as much reassuring detail as possible.

"I'd like to head south while it's still warm enough. I've come all this way, why not soak up some sun? Then I hope to make it to Lisbon before I come back here for Thanksgiving. I'll keep you posted Ady-baby, and you can call me anytime you need me."

"Sure." Ade began to spin the loose ring on her thumb in time with the rotation of the washing machine. Steph held her hand, calming the panic which had risen into her throat.

"It'll be okay, Ade. You can do this." Steph smiled. "Just focus on what's in front of you. Don't race into the future."

"Sure," Ade said. "Because we don't know what's going to happen." *Except I'll be alone.*

Steph stood to inspect the display panel. "Five minutes, and we'll be done here." She wandered to the messy noticeboard and unpinned a black and white flyer. "Look at this: music in the square tonight. It's right here around the corner. Do you want to go?"

Ade peered at the advertisement. Classical strings in Place St Anne. Harmless enough. She couldn't imagine it getting too crowded in that tiny square. She hadn't seen many people walking past her apartment in the last few days. "Okay. Sounds nice, let's go."

"Great." Steph jogged on the spot. "I love it when I don't have to convince you."

Ade basked in the beam of her sister's contentment for as long as she could. Sometimes, the fleeting glimpse of Steph's happiness brought her more joy than anything else in her world. Once the last machine had finished, Steph packed their pile of fresh clothes, and they headed out. The violin strings lilted across the square as Ade sidestepped a gathering crowd. Steph strode on and claimed a table at the church steps. She tucked her unwieldy laundry bag out of sight. The sun had begun to set in the late September sky, casting a pink glow across the city's rooftops and creating a tall silhouette of the church spire.

"Want a beer? We may as well settle in," Steph whispered.

Ade nodded, not wanting to disturb the grace and tranquility they'd stumbled into in the square. *Her* square. She marveled at how, in a few short days, she'd gone from tourist to resident in one of the most charming little areas of the city. Sure, her fifth-floor apartment was rough around its edges and in need of some serious maintenance. But sitting here tonight, with a string ensemble blending unknown but undeniable melodies, it was simply beautiful.

As the sun set, people settled on the church steps, with a single familiar figure in the crowd: Professor Sylvie Boucher. Ade fiddled with her thumb ring, deciding whether to re-introduce herself. *It would be weird. She probably won't even recognize me.* Too late, she'd stared for too long in the professor's direction and was now in the grip of a blinking competition with her supervisor.

"What are you doing, Ade? You look super awkward." Steph turned to meet the subject of Ade's gaze.

There was a gap in the harmony, and a round of applause scattered across the square. Sylvie rose to approach them. Ade could hardly breathe. She'd had no idea what to say at the beginning of the week in the classroom, never mind here in a social space.

"Hello again." Sylvie raised a glass of pale wine in her direction.

Her cheeks blushed with the warm evening air, and tonight, her smile reached her eyes. Ade hadn't noticed the crease of her smile back in the classroom, but now she was transfixed by how the upturn of her lips made her eyes glimmer in the falling light.

"Ade, please introduce us." Steph extended her hand anyway. "I'm Stephanie Poole, Ade's twin sister."

"Delighted to meet you. I'm Sylvie Boucher, one of Adelaide's colleagues at the university."

"It's Ade," she said, looking to Steph and mirroring her body language. Ade's neurons popped like corn as she deciphered Sylvie and Steph's expressions. What were they saying without words? She froze, paralyzed by the frustration of trying to read too many signals at once.

Steph leaned in. "She prefers to be called Ade. Adelaide is a little too old-fashioned for her. Our dads named her after one of our great-grandmothers."

"And it's too feminine," Ade said, desperate for Sylvie to see something beyond her flawed presentation to the world. "I just prefer Ade. It's better, somehow." She'd left their last encounter with an unsettling suspicion that she hadn't made the best impression. It wasn't something she could pin down, but Sylvie frowned just as she had back in the classroom.

"I see." Sylvie tapped her toe on the flagstones. "Ade suits you."

"I don't really think of myself as fitting in boxes," said Ade, finally getting a grip of what Sylvie meant.

"I can imagine." Sylvie tilted her head, her blond bob of hair catching the last rays of the sun. "Do you mind if I join you?"

Ade studied the line of Sylvie's jaw, entranced by the journey from her earlobe to her chin.

Steph cleared her throat. "Don't wait for an invitation from my sister. Hospitality isn't her strong suit."

"How do you find the music?" Sylvie asked.

"We saw a flyer in the laundromat," Ade said.

Sylvie tipped her head, and her frown deepened, the silence stretching between them. Ade took a breath, gifting her a couple of seconds to process what was happening.

"It's wonderful, isn't it? I had no idea what to expect." Steph gestured to the waiter for more drinks. "We were just doing our laundry and were on our way back to the apartment."

"You're renting locally?" Sylvie raised her eyebrow.

"Up there." Ade pointed to her building. "We found an apartment on the fifth floor. It's eighty-four steps."

Steph leaned in. "I'm heading to Spain tomorrow for a little tour of my own."

"Really?" Sylvie asked.

"A gap year," said Steph. "I can't wait."

"Are you on your way to professorship, like your sister?"

"I don't quite have the academic brain that Ade does." Steph laughed, nudging Ade's elbow. "I'm more of a people person. I graduated in nursing, and I've got an internship to get back to when I'm done. But I always said I'd love to travel before I finally settle into full-time work. When Ade was heading to Europe, it seemed like a win-win to settle her in and head off from here."

"So, you're leaving your sister to her day job while you enjoy the student life for a little longer. How about you, Ade, you didn't fancy hosteling through Europe?"

"I like the idea of traveling, but I'm not a fan of unpredictability or lack of routine. Plus, I have a job to do." Ade rubbed the edge of the table.

Sylvie's hair bounced as she nodded. "Very conscientious of you."

"I didn't have a choice." Ade folded her arms, resentment bubbling up in her stomach.

"And why's that?"

"My boss said if I didn't do it this year, I might not be able to stay in my job back in Monterey."

Sylvie sat back in her chair. "Well, we have something in common, after all. My boss has handed me a similar ultimatum. Let's drink to our collective stoicism this year." She clinked her glass to Ade's beer bottle as the strings revived their melody. With Sylvie and Steph's attention on the musicians, Ade sank into the chair and traced Sylvie's picture-perfect cheekbones with her gaze. The candlelight trembled in the evening breeze, and a shadow danced across Sylvie's joyful face, while her chest inflated with every phrase of the music.

Ade sipped her beer, desperate to feel something other than a socially unpalatable urge to look, to memorize, to absorb every detail of her new colleague's appearance. This was new. This desire to hold onto the moment and fix Sylvie in her mind. Was it the strangeness of the city? Nothing would feel like home for a while. Maybe Sylvie would be someone safe to talk to when Steph left.

Steph crossed her legs, relaxed in the flow of the evening. Ade yearned for that kind of repose. To take something in so naturally, instead of analyzing every interaction as if she were performing an autopsy.

Steph would be gone tomorrow, but for the first time since they'd left home, hope rooted in Ade's heart and her pulse steadied. Could she stay in this moment, anchored by Sylvie's candlelit profile? That might not be so bad.

Chapter Five

THE CONFUSING SMELL FILLED Sylvie's nostrils. Salt? She touched the ends of her hair, already frizzing out of control. By the time she was done here, she'd look like a scarecrow. Sylvie squinted up at the strange building. The marine center squatted in the sunshine, short and functional, unlike her usual base in the stylish arts complex.

The receptionist seemed to study Sylvie's block heels and chinos while others filed past in cargo pants and tennis shoes. Sylvie shrugged. Of course she looked out of place. She had no place being there, and she had no desire to blend in with the science crowd. She was a proud professor of the arts. Her average day was filled wondering whether history could be rewritten with all the missing stories of brilliant women, not cleaning out cloudy fish tanks.

With directions in hand, Sylvie made it to the classroom and hovered at the threshold. With her head bent in submission, Ade had already lost her students.

"Folks, could I just get your attention for one more thing on my list?" Ade clutched her phone just as she had at the candlelight concert that weekend.

Sylvie tsked under her breath at her technology habit. She was meant to be a role model to the students.

"So, number one." Ade fumbled. "Check your schedules for the semester."

"Mine is out of whack," one of the girls piped up from the side.

Ade continued to scroll through her phone, ignoring the interruption.

Another student leaned forward. "Hey, what do I do if my

schedule doesn't make sense?"

Ade took a long breath. "I'll get back to you."

"I don't have enough lab time. Do you have six hours a week?" The stocky boy turned to his bench partner.

"I have eight hours, Greg. Do you want to trade? More beach time for me."

The conversation crossed over with another table and voices blended into one another. Ade put her head in her hands.

Sensing her imminent panic and a faint, if inconvenient, sense of duty, Sylvie stepped into the room. "Okay, let's leave it there, this morning. Your schedule finessing can be done at the office back at the main campus. You can send them a message in your student portal." She dropped her bag on Ade's desk. "Thank you all. Until next time."

The kids filed out, murmuring their hellos and goodbyes to Sylvie on the way. "Are you okay?" Sylvie asked, once the last one had drawn the door closed.

"Sure." Ade rubbed her eyebrows and gathered her things, then headed for the door.

"You know, I came all the way out here for an induction session with you. It'd be a huge waste of my time to turn around and go back without at least a conversation."

Ade turned and stared blankly. "You want to see the animals?"

Sylvie smiled. There was something about Ade which baffled her. Maybe it was her androgynous, science-geek fashion sense, or the way she navigated a room like she was the only person there. She followed Ade to a cooler part of the building, regretting the click of her heels, which announced her presence. Maybe she'd do best to blend in with the lab coats after all.

They emerged into a cool blue light, with walls of tanks on two sides.

"I came early to feed and check on them."

Ade moved through the room with a confidence and purpose that Sylvie hadn't witnessed in their previous interactions.

"This is George. He's a seventy-six-year-old turtle that we rescued off the coast of Africa. He's my new buddy, aren't you?"

Ade had revealed more in the past three minutes than she had in the past week. Her voice was crisp and clear, and Sylvie inched closer to hear Ade's intonation. Gone was the shaky staccato of her scripted instructions to the students. She was clearly in her element here in the marine lab.

"Are turtles your favorites?" Sylvie asked, wanting to hear more of Ade's voice.

"I love them. I was raising penguin chicks mostly in Monterey." Ade neatened the work surface. "I named my last chick Gerry. She's a feisty little thing. She had a tricky hatching, and I had to get her a couple of foster parents to take care of her."

"Why?" Sylvie stood still, not wanting to break Ade's rhythm and force her back into a stilted silence.

"Her birth parents hadn't raised a chick, especially one who needed extra care and attention. I wanted Gerry to have the best possible chance, so I gave her to our most experienced couple."

"You just gave her away? Weren't her parents bereft?"

Ade frowned. "I guess it sounds strange to pluck a chick from their parents. But that's kind of a thing. In the wild, she would probably have died because she needed more warmth, food, attention, and understanding than they were able to give her. It's not their fault; they just wouldn't know how to."

Sylvie shook her head, unable to equate this lesson from the animal world to her understanding of human civilization.

"Animals and humans are different in some ways," Ade said.

Sylvie contemplated the simplicity of the sentence. She admired Ade's reading of the world, and her anticipation of the needs of her animals. It was such a basic attention to detail that was so often overlooked in the busyness of life. Ade continued to work beside the tanks, taking notes of feeding stations and temperatures, leaving Sylvie captivated by her movement. Its natural flow was so different from the stiffness of her body in the classroom.

"Do you bring the students in here?" Sylvie asked.

"Of course," Ade said, lifting her gaze again to meet Sylvie's.

"They must like it," Sylvie said, enjoying the eye contact a little too much.

Ade frowned. "Sorry, did you want me to confirm that they do like it?"

"I guess so." Sylvie laughed at her own embarrassment.

"Some do. Some are more about the theory." Ade traced the movement of an octopus with her finger, not quite touching the glaze separating them. Its tentacles reached out then shrank away, in a strange, slow-motion greeting. Ade took a long breath, as if embracing the welcome. "Some are just here for the European credits and to brush up on their French. It looks good on their resumé back home."

Sylvie nodded. She had students of her own who were going through the motions and would graduate with just as much insight into social issues as they started with. "I need to go through a few things with you about the job," Sylvie said, strangely reluctant to draw the conversation back to practical matters. "Can we sit and talk?"

Ade gestured toward a desk, and they took their places. Ade resumed her awkward pose in the chair, and Sylvie wished they'd kept moving around the tanks where she seemed so much more at home.

Eager to keep it brief, she stuck to the essentials and made it back to her car by lunchtime. She checked the weather forecast and her timetable. Two study periods gave her a perfect window to head to the beach for the afternoon and settle down with her latest edits. Her publisher's schedule was taped to the fridge and scorched onto the back of her eyes.

From the marine center, the beach was a short drive, and after a prix fixe lunch, Sylvie slipped on a pair of sliders, wrapped a sarong around her waist, and removed her tailored chinos. She gathered her beach gear, which had been a permanent feature in the trunk this summer, and headed for her favorite quiet spot beneath an umbrella.

She must've drifted, because she awoke to a breeze across her face and the tall, boyish frame of Ade casting a four o'clock shadow onto her towel.

"You almost lost your papers," she said, holding a binder.

Sylvie stirred, gathering the folds of sheer fabric around her thighs. She didn't miss Ade's attention on her bare legs and folded them beneath her as she sat up. "I fell asleep."

"You did look asleep, yes." Ade pulled a can of Pepsi from her pocket. "I bought you one, in case you needed to cool off. Figured you might need the caffeine too."

Sylvie smiled. She liked the rhythm of Ade's explanations. So obvious, yet so charming. "Thank you. Would you like to sit with me for a while?"

"How long is a while, do you think?" Ade asked.

"Well, maybe ten or fifteen minutes. Or however long you'd like to."

"I'm going swimming. That's why I'm here." Ade dropped her bag onto the sand next to Sylvie's towel and sat cross-legged in the full glare of the afternoon sun. "Lectures are over, and the students are all heading home, so I wanted to come to the beach again."

"I love it down here." Sylvie leaned back onto her elbows. "It's one of the reasons I've stayed."

"Stayed?"

"I'm from Paris, originally. I arrived in Montpellier last year."

"Do you like it?" Ade asked.

"I do like it, yes. It took me a while to get used to its pace and personality though. It's very southern, and *I* am very Parisian."

"What do you mean?" Ade tilted her head.

"Have you ever been to Paris?"

"We flew into Paris for a few days before coming here." Ade ran her hand through the sand. "I hadn't been overseas until that."

"Pity you couldn't have stayed longer in the capital. Paris has everything: style, culture, cuisine. I miss its passion and conversation. But it's not always that kind to its people. It can be fast and abrupt."

"Yeah, I didn't much enjoy the pace. It sure seemed like everyone had their shit together and not much patience to spare for..."

"For?"

"People like me," Ade said.

"True." Sylvie nodded. "The people are kinder here. The pace is slightly slower. The vowels are softer and rounder." When Ade frowned, Sylvie recognized her confusion. "There's an accent which you might not hear, because you're American. But it's similar in the States, no?"

"Sure. We have accents." Ade gulped her can and stood. "I'm going in now." She stripped to her tank top and shorts and strode toward the break of the waves.

Shielding the falling sun from her eyes, Sylvie admired the length of Ade's body and how her broad shoulders flexed as she moved across the sand. Her firm thighs led to endless calves. Sylvie shook the vision from her mind and picked up the dog-eared pages she'd been leaning on to save them from the warm breeze.

This book isn't going to get itself back to the editor.

But Ade's silhouette carved a shape in the distance as she leapt into the water with the grace of a dolphin. It was a contrast from her awkwardness on the sand. Sylvie wondered at the puzzle that Ade presented. She stumbled over her words and missed every social cue in the book, and yet she regained her confidence in the presence of her animals and was a force to be reckoned with in the deep blue of the Mediterranean.

It would be an interesting year trying to fathom which Ade would show up when, and which would win out. As her default coach and supervisor, could Sylvie bring out the best in her? Or should she leave Ade to find her way? There were plenty more things to do on her list.

Staring over the crumpled pages of her book, she watched as her protégée swam across the horizon. Ade dipped beneath the waves and rose again with a consistency that took her further and further out. Sylvie squinted at Ade's shrinking silhouette, worried that she'd swum too far from the shore. She refocused on the pages in front of her, but Ade's progress drew her attention before she reached the end of the next paragraph. She had a nagging feeling that Ade might be a distraction this year.

Chapter Six

ALONE. CHECK. HEART RATE. Not too bad. For the first time in a couple of weeks, Ade had bagged the evening shift at the lab, and the silence was a soothing balm. Other people were too chaotic and loud. She checked off the last of the feeding stations and prepared the water testing. At the unexpected click of the latch, she looked up.

Greg poked his head around the door. "Hi, Ade. I don't want to bother you, but I was wondering if... Could I help you tonight?"

She clenched her jaw, biting any sign of frustration which threatened to show itself. "Sure. Come on in." Ade shuffled over to the second stool and passed Greg the tablet. "You can record all the values in the columns. Keep up, because I don't want to have to repeat myself."

Of all the students in her care this year, Greg had impressed her back in Monterey. Despite her supervisors' protest, she'd avoided leading any seminars, not wanting to engage face to face with a room full of enquiring young minds, but Greg had sought out lab time with her and always pulled his weight.

"I was thinking of specializing in husbandry when we get home," he said, swiping the tablet to the next window. "Do you think I'd be any good?"

"Good at what?" She looked away from his searing eye contact to the syringe of water she'd drawn from the tank.

"Husbandry. You know, looking after the animals and all that stuff. You're pretty amazing at it. Do you think I have potential?"

Ade considered his question carefully, wanting to answer him truthfully but with the tact and nuance that her pops constantly reminded her about. She scanned though the back catalogue of Greg's successes, revealing gaps in her files. "I think you show great potential for looking after the animals, Greg. You've got an eye for detail and a sense of what they need." She turned to face him. "But I don't know you all that well. I mean, how much time have we spent together? Twenty-two hours at the most."

Greg frowned like he didn't grasp what she meant.

"I can't vouch for you on that basis. You need to build up your lab time, on the record, so you can prove it to someone back in Monterey."

"I could spend more time here this year. Maybe you could teach me some of the techniques?"

She ran through all the possible reasons not to agree to his suggestion. She preferred alone time with the animals rather than with an audience. But someone who was so eager to learn, like Greg seemed to be, shouldn't get in the way.

She thought of the time she'd shared with Sylvie in the lab at the beginning of the week. That had been a pleasure rather than a chore. She'd enjoyed Sylvie's straightforward pattern of conversation, and the way her English was stilted enough not to be camouflaged by floral language and misconstrued sentences. When she'd seen her at the beach a couple of days ago, she'd made a beeline for her, eager to extend their talk. The urge to pursue another's company, rather than retreat from it, was a break from her norm.

Maybe she should open herself up to more opportunities like that. She glanced sideways at Greg and followed a line of acne healing on his jawline. It might do her good to have a few people around her this year. Not that she was missing Steph and her dads. Out of sight, out of mind as her pops would say. But it might be nice not to spend the whole year alone. "I'll be here most days, Greg. Let me know what free periods you have, and we'll work something out." She forced a smile, knowing he'd be expecting one.

On the tram home, she adjusted her headphones, suppressing as much of the background noise as possible. Cocooned in a world of predictable melody, her thoughts drifted back to Sylvie's glowing skin and wide smile, the way her shirt had fallen open as she leaned back on her beach towel. She must be a few years older than her, but Ade found it hard to age people based on their looks.

But Sylvie's essence had stuck with her. Her presence had slowed the rhythm of her heartbeat, in a way no one had really done before. She was attracted to all sorts of folks, given the right conditions. Usually, alcohol and a dark room. And a lot of fumbling.

She fiddled with her spinning ring, pushing aside the memories of bad sex and awkward goodbyes.

By the time she opened the door to her studio, the single room was dark, and her worn-out brain welcomed the absence of light, noise, and clutter. Although the southern Mediterranean summer had held out as long as it could, autumn was settling, and with it came chilly nights and sudden sunsets.

Ade turned on the floor lamp with her heel. She hadn't decided whether it was too bright for her, but it was the only alternative to the glare of the spotlights in the ceiling.

Her phone buzzed. *Steph*. Right on time.

Time for a video call?

She pressed the camera icon and waited for the call to connect.

"Hey you." Steph's wild red hair escaped from the bun she'd pulled on top of her head.

"Hey, yourself. Where have you been?" Ade settled on the sofa bed in her living room.

"Barcelona. I'm about to hit a bar in the old town. It's gorgeous here; you'd love it."

"Would I?"

"Well, maybe not." Steph laughed. "It's brash, loud, and proud of itself. *I* love it."

Ade grinned. She realized how much she missed her twin sister now she was staring her right in the face. "Have you been to any

Gaudi stuff?"

"There's a ton of Gaudi shit in Barcelona. I've been everywhere, Ade. My feet are hurting so much from pounding these streets. The metro is unreal. The cars and bikes blast their horns every few seconds. But it's pretty incredible. The Sagrada Familia is a real beauty. I wish you were here with me. How are things there?"

"It's all good." Ade knew she should give her more. "I've settled in at the lab. The students are finding their way through their schedules without much fuss."

Steph beamed. "That sounds awesome. I'm really pleased for you, Ady-baby. Have you made any friends yet?"

Ade wriggled under her scrutiny. "I have a student called Greg who wants to come to the lab more often."

"Well, he sounds pretty dedicated." Steph sat on the edge of her bed. "How about anyone else? You seen any more of your boss? What was her name? Sylvia?"

"Sylvie." Ade couldn't help her lips from twitching into a smile.

"She seemed really friendly when we met."

"I saw her at work on Monday. We had a good conversation. She's easy to talk to."

Steph smiled broadly. "Fantastic. It's good to make friends."

"I saw her at the beach too," Ade said.

"Oh, you did? Well, maybe you should see if she wants to go out sometime, show you some more of the town?"

"Maybe." Ade's tummy fluttered at the thought.

"You know, I heard from Dad and Pops last night."

"No, I didn't know that," Ade said.

"Well, we talked about them coming over for Thanksgiving."

Ade couldn't really think that far ahead. She braced herself for the onslaught of information that Steph was about to throw her way. Eventually, as was her playbook in these situations, she'd ask for an email to remind her what was happening.

"They arrive the week before, and they've booked a hotel nearby. I'll come back so I can help prepare everything. They're really looking forward to seeing us. Pops is beside himself."

Ade pictured her pops and how his beard scratched against her cheek. "He messaged me earlier this week. Asked me what I was eating."

Steph laughed. "He worries."

"And Dad?"

"More worried about when I'm getting back to my internship."

Ade groaned. At least Steph had a trajectory for her nursing career. "Well, it gives him a break from talking about what a disappointment I'm turning out to be."

"He's never said that, Ade."

"He said 'you can't spend all your time hiding in the lab, Adelaide. You'll need a real job sooner or later.'"

Steph huffed. "He's just anxious for us to make something of our lives. Anyway, you've got him off your back for a whole year while you're in France. That's gotta be a good thing."

Ade screwed her nose up, noticing herself in the little video pane on her phone. *Does my forehead always crease that way?* "It's a long way to travel just to shut Dad up."

"True. But you'll love it. And I'll love it. It's the gap year of our dreams, sister." Steph got up and spun around the room. "Make the most of it. Push your comfort zone. Drop Sylvie a little message and ask her to show you some sights." She winked.

Ade bit her lip. Maybe she would.

"I'll give you a call this weekend. See you in a few weeks so we can get ready for Thanksgiving. Save me a big squeeze."

"Will do."

"Love you," Steph said.

"Sure." Ade coughed. "Love you too." She did love her sister. More than anyone else, really, if she admitted it. She'd spent her whole life basking in the confidence of her slightly older twin. In the sudden silence, she missed her voice already.

It would be a lonely year if she didn't fill it with something. Her animals gave her so much, but they weren't the same kind of company. She craved the easy, low-key sense of self she had when Steph was by her side.

Maybe she should give Sylvie a call? Isolation was simpler, and sitting at the edge of her comfort zone did not come easily, but the idea of a whole year overseas with nothing but her own thoughts left her cold. Sylvie had already proven herself a worthy conversation partner; she wasn't too chatty either, which was a real bonus. Ade typed a quick text and studied her cell for a count of ten, weighing the pros and cons of sending it.

At home, she'd stuff her hands in her pockets and put it off. Today, though, something in the air gave her a newfound confidence. She lifted her chest with an unknown boldness. Maybe Sylvie would be good for her.

Chapter Seven

SYLVIE SIPPED HER STEAMING black coffee and brushed away the flakes of her morning croissant. Sunday mornings were a real treat. Colette was one of a handful of café owners who prescribed pastries and caffeine to hungover revelers.

It worked. Every single week, the city's finest clubbers filed in for their carb load, while the church bells rang across the square. Sylvie shuffled the pages of her book and scanned the crowd of hedonistic twenty-somethings. All hair and fashion choices, clashing in color and confidence; they wouldn't look out of place in the university common room.

She glanced down at the denim jeans and classic cashmere she'd pulled on this morning, a hint of her Parisian roots. She wouldn't be caught dead in some of the outlandish choices of her students. She sat upright, pondering her maturity. Was she showing her age? With the drama of leaving Paris and seeking a new career in the south, her mid-thirties had snuck up on her. She liked to think it wasn't obvious, but in a room full of students brimming with youth, she couldn't be so sure.

"Can I get you anything else?" Colette asked, balancing a tray of empty coffee cups at shoulder height.

"Not for now, thank you." Sylvie smiled.

"Anytime, my darling." Colette peered over Sylvie's shoulder. "What're you working so hard on there? You've had your head down for more than an hour."

She sighed. "I'm treading water on my book edits. I don't know why I put so much pressure on myself. It's not like anyone will read it."

"What's it about?" Colette wrinkled her nose with what looked like genuine curiosity.

Sylvie tried to think of something fun and entertaining. *Nope.* The truth was she was writing something so academic even her professorial peers had stifled a yawn when she pitched it at last year's conference.

"Well?" Colette shifted the weight of her tray. "Is it a secret? Some dark erotic fantasy that you've been working on deep into the night?"

Sylvie's scoff attracted the attention of a neighboring table. "Not likely."

"I find that hard to believe." Colette winked and whooshed past a group of undergraduates jostling each other on a bench.

A motley crew of individuals, all sharing the same brash optimism and spark. Their expressions were wild and free, their body language fluid and bold. As she rested her gaze on each person, their unique collection of clothing struck her. Androgynous and effortlessly neutral, but exotic and attractive.

Her thoughts drifted to the chaperone in her charge. Just a couple of years senior to this troop, Ade had a similar look. Rough at the edges, as if no care had been taken at all. Yet she seemed to pull off a look that was put together and deliberately magnetic. Sexy, even. Sylvie had never been attracted to a person with no deliberate definition of their gender.

She shook her head, reminding herself that Ade was also at least a decade her junior. *And* a member of her staff team. Thinking anything like that would lead to trouble.

But once born, the thought stuck and twisted inside her mind as she twirled the last of the croissant on her side plate before dipping it into her cold espresso. And it was much more interesting denying her attraction than picking up her pages and highlighter pen.

Romantic dalliances hadn't come thick and fast. Since moving south, she'd kept herself to herself.

But in the year since she'd arrived here, she'd isolated herself more than ever. Her friendship circle had shrunk down to Isabelle, and she couldn't possibly consider Colette her friend. Including the café owner from next door really was clutching at straws.

She missed Elda and was looking forward to their annual get-together. She scribbled in her notepad to remind herself to finalize this year's details. The year marched on, and they still hadn't agreed whether she'd be traveling to England or vice versa.

Her phone buzzed. She opened messages and squinted at the username, not recognizing the avatar.

Sorry to bother you on a Sunday. Do you have any recommendations for things to do in the city? I'm at a 'loose end.'

Who is this?

Sorry. It's Ade Poole.

Sylvie chuckled. So Ade was sneaking into her DMs as well as her Sunday wonderings. The interruption wasn't entirely unwelcome. *I was just thinking about you.* She groaned. Why had she written that? Of all things. It had just slipped away from her and onto the screen.

I thought of you too. That's why I messaged.

Sylvie laughed. Of course Ade wouldn't read anything into it. Hesitating, she scrolled to her calendar. A blank Sunday afternoon stretched down the entire screen. She replied before she had any more time to doubt herself. *How about we go to the cinema? There's a film on I've been itching to see.* Three dots indicated that Ade was thinking about it. Had Sylvie overstepped?

Yes, please. Sounds good.

Meet me at Place Jean Jaurès. At three o'clock.

I will. See you then.

Sylvie second-guessed her invitation at least a dozen times before she wandered to the noisy square where she'd arranged their afternoon meet-up. Why she'd offered to socialize with one of her staff members, she couldn't fathom. But there was something about the simplicity of Ade's message which betrayed the confidence it took for her to reach out in the first place. Plus, she was merely a colleague. Sylvie and Isabelle met socially all the time. What difference did it make that she was, in theory, Ade's superior? She forced the doubt from her mind and focused on the kindness she was showing a fellow academic as they found their feet in a brand new city.

She'd shown the very same hospitality and welcome to Elda when she'd turned up as a disheveled and chaotic artist five years ago. In fact, there had been many folks since, who had drifted in and out of her university circle. She'd met them for coffee or a glass of wine, enjoyed a concert or open mic night. None had really stuck around and had moved elsewhere through promotion or marriage.

Making new friends is a good thing. She repeated the mantra over and over as she turned the corner to the familiar square.

Jean Jaurès was already bustling with a late afternoon crowd as Sylvie took a seat at one of the street tables and ordered a glass of red wine. She wasn't sure what Ade drank and didn't want to presume. So far, their interactions had proven that Ade couldn't be read that easily.

After a few moments, she spotted Ade and gave her a wave. "You made it," Sylvie said as Ade approached.

"It's not far. I walked down the Rue Foch, and it brought me out by the bakery. Do you know that one? They make the best pastries."

Sylvie smiled, pleased to see Ade's enthusiasm for her adopted city. "If you like pastries, I know a great place. I'll take you there next time we meet." She gestured to the seat next to her, facing the passersby. "Please, sit. We can watch people come and go for a while. The film starts in forty minutes or so."

Ade took the seat and drummed her fingers until a waiter came to take her order. "I'll have the same, please," she said, pointing at Sylvie's red wine. "Thanks for meeting up with me. Steph told me I needed to go out, and I don't really know anyone, except you and the students. I didn't want to go out with them."

"So I came a close second?"

Ade's eyes widened. "No. When I really thought about it, I wanted to go out with you. I really liked talking to you the other day in the lab."

Ade's straight talk was nothing short of endearing. The ability to say something without subtext and leave nothing unsaid was an undervalued attribute. Sylvie had been criticized badly for doing just that, burning the bridges of her friendships. She'd walked away from the scorched embers perplexed, as if the other party's reaction to her honesty was entirely unwarranted.

Perhaps Ade could be an addition to her honesty circle. She straightened a crease in her blouse and leaned in. "I thought we'd watch a British film together. I've been meaning to see it for a while, and it's on at the arthouse in its original version."

"You're not treating me to something local?"

"Is your French up to la nouvelle vague?"

"New Wave? I doubt it. But I'm improving all the time."

Sylvie raised her eyebrow, impressed at Ade's knowledge of the term. "Perhaps next time. This film is in the same vein. It's a story told in the woman's perspective of the male gaze." Sylvie almost saw the cogs whirring inside her brain when Ade frowned.

"Tell me more about what you teach at the university. I feel like I've talked a lot about marine life, but I don't really know anything about you."

"That's true. I know more about penguins than I did two weeks ago." Sylvie warmed beneath Ade's curiosity. "So, I'm a professor of European feminism. I lecture four times a week and run five or six seminars, depending on how big the year group is."

"Sure." Ade fiddled with her thumb ring. "But tell me why you do it."

"That's a more complicated answer." Sylvie brushed a hair from her eye. "Part of me is passionate about the unheard stories of history. Part of me is half way up the ladder of academic success, and I can't imagine not reaching the top, so I'm digging in and taking one rung at a time."

"You don't like it?"

"I love it." Sylvie sipped her wine, giving herself some time to find the words to explain to a virtual stranger the depth of her ambition and the barriers that had stood in her way over the last five years. "I'm writing a book comparing the feminist theory of Virginia Woolf, a British author, and Simone de Beauvoir, a famous French philosopher."

"Wow. That sounds..." Ade looked like she was searching for the right word.

"Boring?" Sylvie asked, anticipating what a scientist would make of her arts and culture major.

"Impressive." Ade drank her wine. "I'm in awe of people who can read meaning into the world through stories. I don't have that skill."

"How do you see the world, if not as a culmination of everything that came before?"

"I see it now. As it is. Take the animals: you think they've survived by feasting on a diet of history? No way. They're all about what's in front of them, here in the present moment. Fight or die. Fed or famished."

"Nicely put." Sylvie leaned into Ade's space, intrigued by her take on the world.

"It's not like I don't respect your field of expertise. I'm genuinely envious of the curiosity it takes to keep studying something that's recorded in books and doesn't have a physical presence in the real world. I mean, I love the theory of marine science and all, but take me to a tank, even better, the ocean, and I'm in my happy place."

"But feminist literature isn't just books."

"It isn't?"

"Look around you." Sylvie nodded toward someone scribbling in their notebook at a nearby table. "I've seen that person perform her poetry at an open mic night near the cathedral. She's published several novels and is about to go on a European tour with her publisher."

Ade tilted her head, as if she needed more of an explanation.

"That mural up there is by a female graffiti artist based in Lyon. Her work is famous across the south." Sylvie paused. "That boutique in the corner, just off the square," she pointed, drawing Ade's gaze toward an elegant shop front, "is owned by a Parisian designer who has opened in all the fashionable French cities."

"Okay. What's this got to do with our conversation? I've lost our thread."

"Feminist literature is all around us. Its values, beliefs, and victories won these women a place in art and culture. Without the social commentary of the likes of Woolf and de Beauvoir, women would still be relegated to second place, second class. Maybe even silence."

"A part of me struggles to identify with all that. Women's rights are so tied up with binary gender. Isn't it much more complex? I feel like my right to be, in this moment, is because of who I am, not what's in my pants."

Sylvie shrugged. Ade had a point, not that she was going to roll over and accept it too easily. But the gender studies of the past were fast becoming literally stuck in the past. Was her work even relevant anymore?

She drained her glass and signaled to pay their bill. "Let's go watch the film, and we can continue our debate." She enjoyed nothing more than an interesting tussle of ideas, but Ade's ability to cut through her rhetoric had touched a nerve. She pictured the textbooks piled high on her desk back home and the matching stack in her office. Was she merely a collector of artifacts, of stale ideas gone to die inside the pages of a dusty hardback? She'd spent her whole career trying to leave a legacy of something worthwhile, to say something that no one had ever said before.

Was Ade right? Did it all just belong in a museum? The career ladder that she was intent on climbing stretched further out of view.

What did it mean for her future if all she focused on was the past?

Chapter Eight

THE BEAMED CEILING HUNG low across the bed. Ade blinked. Had it moved? She ran through the reels in her photographic memory to check everything was in its place.

The realtor had described the space as "versatile," but that really only meant the sofa bed could be put up and down to suit the needs of its occupant.

Aside from Steph, Ade hadn't invited anyone into her domain in the seventeen days she'd been in Montpellier and saw no immediate reason to. She'd only just unpacked completely and found the perfect home for her clothes and accessories in the bones of the apartment.

She'd warmed to the place. A couple of weeks in, she could now see beyond its scratched walls and faded drapes to a charming French pied-à-terre. Steph had worked hard to clean its surfaces and soften its edges, and while Ade hadn't appreciated her efforts at the time, she'd made a difference.

The city was beginning to feel a little less alien, which was mostly due to the role she'd gladly taken on at the lab and the friendship she'd struck with her supervisor, Sylvie. Plus she'd mapped out her commutes, memorized her tram timetable, and picked a favorite quiet space on campus to escape to.

The lab was a home away from home. Much smaller than what she was used to in Monterey, the downsize was welcome. The boss of the marine center had spotted her proficiency from day one, so on her shifts, she was left pretty much to her own devices, which was just the way she liked it.

As for Sylvie, she was providing ample induction on and off

campus. Ade drifted to the dark cinema on Sunday night. The velvet of the seats had itched where it had met her skin, so she'd shuffled and brushed against Sylvie, her bare arm warm to the touch. She'd tried to focus on the movie, and despite it being an English language title, much of it had passed her by. She grasped at snippets of the story but couldn't fathom why the female main character had stuck around when she was so obviously downtrodden by her male antagonist.

As they'd wandered back to their old town apartments, Sylvie had chattered about the deeper meaning behind the cinematography. She'd seen more in the pauses between the dialogue and the raise of an eyebrow. Ade had been baffled by its subtlety, wishing they'd gone for an action movie where she could follow a car chase without her head hurting.

She rubbed at her face, waking herself up. She hoped that her frustration hadn't been too evident at the theater. The last thing she wanted to do was accidentally offend Sylvie or her interests. She smiled, remembering how passionately Sylvie had spoken of her work. She'd opened up to Ade in an unexpected way. It made her feel good.

She glanced at the clock and counted the minutes she had left in the bed before she had to start her morning routine. A little yoga was on today's schedule, followed by her usual tasks of shower, dress, breakfast, and teeth-brushing. She'd hung her clothes out on the back of her door and put her packed bag by the main entrance.

Without Steph by her side, Ade left nothing to chance. She'd learned to overprepare rather than risk a meltdown during the day. Her pops had helped her adapt to new routines over the years by keeping as much as possible the same. Now, her morning routine was one of those things that, if done right, she could fly through with minimum brain tax.

By the time she got to campus, it was turning nine o'clock, just as she'd predicted. The tram had been a couple of minutes late, and it had been crowded. She could have gotten off and walked the last part, but that would have put her back by more than thirty minutes.

She had a full day of chaperone duties, and some students had signed up for one-on-one counselling sessions. But first, she was due to hold a group discussion about some of the social activities that could be planned through the semester. Ade gulped down the apprehension rising in her throat. Both scenarios were way out of her comfort zone. She'd gotten to know some of the students since they'd arrived, but they were still virtual strangers, and she didn't cope well with new relationships.

Sylvie popped into her mind again. She was fast becoming an exception to the rule. Ade didn't mind her company, however novel it was.

In the classroom she'd been assigned for the day, she set up the chairs in a circle, intending for everyone to have an equal voice in the group. She stood back and surveyed her positioning. She moved a white board forward so everyone would be able to see it and scrawled *Rules of Engagement* as neatly as she could across the top.

She rubbed it out with an eraser then wrote *Ground Rules*.

That wasn't right either. Desperate to convey a sense of belonging but floundering to find the words, she wrote *SAFE SPACE.*

When she turned around, she had an audience of three at the door: Greg, Madison, and Kelly. "Oh, hello. Take a seat," Ade said, avoiding eye contact. "Is anyone else planning to join us?"

"I doubt it." Madison twirled her long blond hair around her manicured finger. "They all think this is lame."

"But you don't." Ade sat in the circle among them.

"I heard there was a budget for socials," Kelly said.

Greg leaned forward. "We'd like to help you organize things, Ade, if that's useful."

Greg meant well. The others could be trouble. Before Ade

could make any further judgment, another two undergrads filed through the open door. Scott and Lisa pushed at each other's shoulders and giggled before throwing themselves into the vacant chairs.

"Sorry we're late," Lisa said, tossing her bag onto the floor and spilling half the contents of her pencil case in the process.

"You're not late." Ade looked at the clock to confirm her sense of the time. "We were just about to get started." She'd practiced her speech until late last night, worrying that her delayed bedtime would knock her routine out of whack. In groups like this, she had to be super clear about what she had to say, otherwise nerves would get the better of her and oftentimes, she'd fall silent. The emotional scars of stage fright, selective mutism, or whatever else her teachers and doctors had called it, had never quite healed.

Now older and wiser, she'd become aware enough to know what helped and hindered. Preparation was key. "As part of our year together, one of my roles is to arrange a social gathering of some sort at least once per semester." She scanned the tops of their heads, hoping that would pass for eye contact. "This session today is for us to gather some ideas about what that looks like and how we can organize ourselves. I don't expect to have all the answers, but we can start to form a plan." *Too robotic?* She looked up at Greg for some reassurance. With his nod, she continued. "As this is one of our first times as a cohort outside of the classroom or lab, I want to remind you that when we're together, it's a safe space to ask questions, put forward ideas, and maybe challenge each other, respectfully."

"Yeah, right." Scott, the one with the broad shoulders and big attitude, threw a pencil at Lisa.

Ade froze, running through all the ways she could handle the situation. "Guys, let's think about that respect from the start."

"Sorry." Scott grunted, sinking into his football shoulders.

Ade stared at her whiteboard, considering the crème-de-la-crème of the California state marine biology department. Maybe they saved their brains for lab time.

"Do we have any money for this stuff?" Lisa asked, filing her nail into a strange point.

"Sure." Ade scribbled on her board. "Three thousand for the whole year."

"Make a great frat party, huh, Greg?" Scott's belly laugh rumbled between them.

"I was thinking of maybe a sea excursion. Kind of fits with our studies." Greg said, his kind eyes seeking Ade's approval.

She wrote it on the board, ignoring Scott's suggestion.

"Beach barbecue?" Kelly unfolded her arms. "There's a great spot down at Palavas. We could head down there after a marine lab session one afternoon."

"In the winter, dumb ass?" Scott sniggered.

Ade took a breath. "Remember the respect we're showing one another?"

"Actually, we could plan it for the summer term. We're here a whole year. You're the dumb ass." Kelly turned away.

"Well at least I'm here on my own merit, rather than my daddy's donation." Scott's lips curled further.

"You know nothing about me. You barely scraped the grades to get onto this program, so don't act like you're some big shot. Everyone knows you're here to take the boats out and tinker with the engines rather than anything too scientific."

Two chairs scraped back as Greg and Madison broke from the circle of respect, leaving the others to continue their spat.

"That's insulting, Kelly. You've barely spoken to us this entire course, and now you're throwing out the trash talk as if we're your besties?" Lisa turned away.

"It's not that, Lisa. It's true," Kelly said.

The volume rose again as they began to talk over each other. Ade put her fingertips to her temples, rubbing away the noise and confusion. She blinked, desperately trying to think of what to say which would dissolve the conflict, which had burst from nowhere.

"Settle down." Sylvie strode into the middle of the room.

Everyone fell silent and shuffled in their seats.

"What is this chaos? I heard you from my classroom."

Ade looked up and realized Sylvie's question was directed at her. "Oh, jeez, I'm sorry. We were just having a little discussion about the possibilities for our social opportunities this year to complement our studies." Ade paused, rubbing her thumb ring. "It got a little heated."

Sylvie raised her eyebrow and turned her attention to the group. "My proficiency in English is arguably as good, if not better, than some of yours. So it's safe to assume I can understand what was being said." She stood taller, if that was possible, making herself so present in the room, there was an intake of breath. "Your attendance here is a privilege. Don't forget that." Sylvie put her hands to her hips. "And Ms. Poole?"

"Yes?"

"Take control of your classroom."

Ade nodded. It was all she could do. The spark of conflict had ripped through her rules of respect. Her own anger threatened to make itself known, but what good would that do? She was disappointed in herself for allowing it to happen. She should've had more control of the conversation. The feeling of inadequacy washed over her, not for the first time. This was the reason she hid away in the lab for hours on end. This was why she was better at taking care of animals than humans.

"Let's leave it there, everyone," she said. Deflated, she wiped the board of its meager record of their conversation.

Sylvie's disappointment replayed over in her mind. Ade could deal with letting herself down. She could even handle the criticisms of her bosses back home. But there was something about Sylvie's displeasure that persisted, and the discomfort of it hung heavy across her chest.

Why was Sylvie's opinion so important to her? She packed away the question at the back of her mind while she stacked the last of the chairs against the classroom wall. She'd leave the space neat and tidy, even if everything else was scattered.

Chapter Nine

SYLVIE CHECKED HER WATCH and scanned her class of nineteenth century literature enthusiasts. "Do you have something for us, Michèle?"

"Of course, you had to be rich to be a writer in those times. How on earth could anyone of any other class even conceive of the idea?" Michèle made her point with a flourish of her pen.

"That was Virginia Woolf's central premise: give someone a room of their own, and they might have the time, space, and enough silence to actually hear themselves think. And they might even get to write." Simone raised her hands, daring anyone to argue. "And who has a room of their own? Rich boys. And if you're lucky, a rich girl."

Rising from her seat, Sylvie smiled. She loved it when her students argued the points. "Okay, everyone. We're finished for today. Don't forget that next week is reading week. No seminars, just time to get through your texts for the coming term. I suggest you use it wisely. No excuses."

"No seminars. No excuses. Got it," Michèle said, generating a hum of laughter and grunting from her classmates.

Sylvie ushered them out of the classroom and gathered herself. She had an hour before she'd arranged to meet Ade for the recital. It wasn't long enough to go home for a shower, so she redid her light makeup and brushed her hair.

Sylvie had stewed all week on the way she'd spoken to Ade. She had been harsh and unnecessary. It'd been no different to the way she'd handled hundreds of unruly classrooms: put the students in their place and give the lecturer a cold stare and the hard truth.

But Ade wasn't just any lecturer. She was a fresh, junior academic with virtually no experience of handling difficult students. Her group were fast proving themselves to be the worst kind: arrogant, pushy, and with zero filter. Sylvie hadn't seen any redeeming features so far, except for those in their leader, Ade, who'd shown herself to be nervous but much more nuanced.

To make amends, she'd invited Ade to a recital in the music hall, where she loved to spend time listening to the post-graduates perfecting their classical scores.

On the short walk to the hall, she peeled off her cardigan. The temperature had bounced back up, and the campus was bathed in a glorious late afternoon glow. Squinting into the sun, she could just make out a backlit Ade, her tailored trousers draping exquisitely off her hips.

"Hey." Ade tilted her head for a brief moment before she dropped her gaze to the pavement.

"I'm glad you came." Sylvie stepped into her space and wondered what was appropriate for a greeting between colleagues.

"You invited me."

"Of course." Sylvie couldn't help but smile.

"What? Did I do something wrong?" Ade asked.

"Not at all." Sylvie went to touch her sleeve, then pulled her hand back. "I just love your ability to state the obvious in such a charming way. It's very French, actually."

"Huh." Ade scuffed her shoe against the concrete. "So this is the place?"

"That's right. Are you ready to go inside?"

Ade nodded, and they ventured in, Sylvie taking the lead.

Inside, Ade stalled at the front row, holding up a line of people behind them as she scanned the birch-paneled ceiling of the auditorium. "I like it in here. It's beautiful."

Sylvie gently touched her arm and coaxed her forward. "Me too. I guess the design is for the acoustics, but I just like the look of it, all clean lines and bare wood." Sylvie took the end two seats of a back row, not wishing to be trapped between people.

Once they were seated, the lights dimmed around them, casting a brief shadow onto the plain white walls before the audience was immersed in darkness. The orchestra took their places on the spotlit stage and after a brief, humble introduction, the music commenced.

Ade stilled her bouncing knee, and a calm seemed to wash over her body. Braving a further look, Sylvie studied the cut of her white shirt, and the way it clung to her slim waist before disappearing into the v of her firm chest.

Turning back to the musicians, she tried to focus on the tune, her heart stuttering with nerves.

Sitting in repose and admiring the music, Ade demonstrated the maturity that set her apart from her younger students. She was no longer their peer. And yet Sylvie couldn't quite place what kept Ade from being *her* equal. Was it the age difference? Was it her senior position?

She considered the gender queerness that Ade presented to the world. Tonight, she sported a pair of vintage slacks, almost mid-century, with a tucked-in shirt that gathered around the slight curve of her breast but otherwise cut a masculine silhouette for the world to admire. For Sylvie to admire.

She stopped herself from spiraling beyond style tips. Tonight was about resetting their professional relationship and letting Ade know that Sylvie welcomed her to the team. She wasn't the cold bitch who'd cut her dead in her own classroom on Monday.

Sylvie stole another glance. Ade's eyes were closed. Was she asleep?

"I'm enjoying the music," she whispered, as if feeling Sylvie's stare.

Sylvie smirked and refocused on the stage. The billing had drawn a typical Friday night audience of the city's intellectuals and their university pals. The front rows were completely full, and there were just a few seats here and there until the very back where Ade and Sylvie had two rows almost to themselves.

Sylvie often came to the recitals on Fridays to decompress after a long week of teaching or grading papers. The beat of the bass instruments and the harmonies of the strings transported her to a different place, away from the strain of campus life.

She was brought back into the room by the roll of the bass drum, indicating the score's shift in gear and a heavier tone for the piece.

"What's happening?" Ade asked.

Sylvie edged closer to speak gently into her ear. "This piece is about the fear of the unknown. I think the lower notes and bass instruments denote a trepidation of something looming in the future."

Ade turned her attention back to the stage, her eyes wide with curiosity. She hunched ever so slightly forward, affording Sylvie a view of her profile. She looked beautifully handsome, transfixed in the glow of the illuminated stage. Her face flushed with the emotion of the music, as if every scrape of the cellist's bow carved another tear in her heart.

As the melody came to its crescendo, Sylvie gripped the arms of her seat to avoid taking Ade's hand. As the piece steadied, she met Ade's smile, knowing she'd witnessed a first-time experience. "Have you ever heard something like that before?" Sylvie asked.

"Never. Not in real life. I mean, I've heard classical music. But not like that." Ade lifted the cuff of her sleeve to show the goosebumps on her skin.

The urge to stroke them away almost overcame Sylvie. She sat further back in her seat, staring directly at the conductor in an attempt to focus on anything but the temptation to touch Ade.

At the end of the show, Sylvie accepted Ade's offer of drinks and ventured outside to cool off. The evening sun had dropped further into the slumber of the sky as she took a table for two on the terrace.

On nights like these, she could almost forget this was her

workplace. The students had snaked back into the city to be tempted by its nightlife. She enjoyed the relative peace of the campus, the talent of its best musicians, the chatter of the city's literati, and the grown-up company of a colleague.

As Ade set two glasses of red wine on the table, Sylvie adjusted her posture, opening herself up for more of the contented conversation that they'd enjoyed together so far.

"I'm glad I came tonight. Thanks for inviting me," Ade said.

"You're really welcome. I wanted to make amends for being a little abrupt with you in your group session on Monday. It wasn't my place."

Ade dipped her head. "I was glad of your interference."

Sylvie laughed. "But that's what it was. Interference."

Ade looked pained. "That's not what I meant. I'm glad you saved me from anything worse, to be honest. They're a great bunch, but they can be energetic." She put her elbow on the table and rested her chin on her hand. "How do you do it?"

"Handle students?" Sylvie asked, and Ade nodded. "I speak clearly and set out my expectations.."

"Don't take any nonsense? Probably where I'm going wrong. Clarity isn't my strong point. I'm not often sure what I want from a situation. It's one of the reasons I've always steered clear of the teaching roles."

"Then why are you here? Why put yourself in this position for the whole year?"

Ade shrugged and looked away. "Everyone was looking at me to do something with my life. My bosses pretty much said that my PhD was untenable unless I took on some teaching hours." She sighed. "My dad said if I passed up this rotation, I should probably start thinking about getting a regular job."

Sylvie held the silence between them, sensing there was more to say.

"My sister, Steph, said Dad wouldn't follow through, but I got the sense that he'd cut me off just to make me stand on my own two feet."

Sylvie sat back. Despite their growing commonalities, here was a glaring difference between them: no one was bankrolling Sylvie's academic career. She was the solo funder of her ambition. Hearing Ade talk about her dad pulling his funding reminded her of the decade between them. She sipped her wine. "We should finish up here."

"Absolutely. This was a really lovely evening. Thank you."

"No need to thank me, Ade. It's what colleagues do." She raised her glass. "Well done for making it through the first half of the semester. Here's to a well-earned reading week." They clinked their glasses together.

Ade brushed her hand over her short hair. "I'm so glad of a week without any face time. You'll find me locked in the lab if you need me."

"I'm heading to my parents' house for the week to catch up on some marking. So sadly, I won't be here to distract you."

Disappointment flickered on Ade's face. "That's too bad. I would've put down my tools for you."

Sylvie bit her tongue, avoiding the temptation to flirt.

"Where do your parents live?" Ade asked.

"Not too far. About an hour in the car. They moved from Paris a while ago to be nearer to my mother's family along the coast. They live in a little town called Sète. It's beautiful in its own way." Sylvie slid her finger around the rim of her glass. "How about you? Do your parents live in California?"

"That's right. Monterey born and raised. My dad and pops met in San Francisco, but they moved out of the city when they were pregnant with us." Ade's brow furrowed. "I mean, when my birth mom was pregnant. Obviously."

Sylvie hesitated. "Do you and Steph know your birth mom?" She didn't want to pry, but Ade had brought it up, and she was always curious about same-sex families and how they came to be.

"Yeah, we know her. We're not all that close, but she's in our circle, if you know what I mean." Ade nodded to her cell on the table as if her mom's details were in its memory. "Our dads were pretty open about where we came from, and they encouraged us to have a relationship with our surrogate mom. When we were young, we saw her at birthdays. But in the end we drifted, because she has her own life. We were always a gift to our dads, and they're our parents, for sure."

"It's good that they didn't hide anything or keep you from seeing her though. I've seen plenty of kids troubled by family secrets."

"It's a pretty hard question to dodge when you have two dads," Ade said. "The first thing you become aware of is that everyone has a mom. People would ask where our mom was if Steph and I were alone in a room or at the park."

Sylvie imagined the strength it must take a little person to defend their family make-up, over and over.

"I guess Dad and Pops wanted to head it off by never making an issue of it." Ade sighed as if the conversation had drained her energy. "We keep in touch, and we know we can reach out if we needed her for anything. Like medical background checks and stuff like that."

The tapestry of Ade's life was revealing itself to Sylvie slowly. Every time they talked, she unfurled another image of the slightly awkward Californian who preferred animals to humans. Tonight she'd learned that musical notes, in the right arrangement, spoke to Ade's heart. The more she discovered, the more she wanted to know. Then she remembered how much younger Ade was, and how dependent she still was on her parents' wealth. She was barely out of grad school and needed a coach and mentor, not a friend.

Sylvie had to focus on proving her worth to Paul and the faculty powers-that-be. That would take all her energy for the rest of the term. She had no time for distractions. Even the most handsome ones.

Chapter Ten

ADE SANK A SATISFYING line into the large tank she was working on. She'd arrived just before dawn to get a head start before any of the staff came in. She scanned the sandy tank bed for old food and poop and vacuumed it up through the clear tube. Then she flossed through the old whale bone, which provided a habitat for her two elephant fish.

The rhythm soothed her racing thoughts, and she relaxed in the darkened room. Like her fish that lived in the deep, she couldn't handle the harsh lights.

Standing back from the tank, she admired the two specimens that had found their home at the marine center. They stretched out like a foot-long sub, and their smooth bodies were swirled like marble. They were the only fish to breathe through their nostrils, and Ade had always found them fascinating creatures.

She poured a heady mix of clam, shrimp, squid, and mussels into the tank and watched as they inhaled it, piece by piece.

Hypnotized by their natural movement through the water, Ade sat still and relished the moment of sensory silence. No noise, no people, and zero expectations except to clean and feed the animals. It was a joy like no other.

The creak of the door disturbed her peace.

"I wasn't quite sure whether to believe your resumé or throw it in the trash." Fernando Auster, the director of the marine center, approached the tank and folded his arms. "But you're the real deal, aren't you?"

Ade's mind was still on her animals. She hadn't shifted gears to handle the expectations of human interaction and in the inertia, she stared for a moment too long. "Sorry, I'm not sure what you mean."

He chuckled and dismissed her concern with a wave of his giant hand. "I mean that your resumé is outstanding. And I thought most of it was made up. But seeing you here in the lab with the animals, it's clear you've had the kind of hands-on experience with marine life that most post-grads would give their right arm for."

She decided not to question why they'd want to struggle without an arm. She'd heard that phrase before and found it very confusing. "I started volunteering at the aquarium when I was twelve."

"I read that. That aquarium is one of the best in the world. What a place to cut your teeth." He held a thumb up. "And the hours you've put in, even in your short time here, shows real dedication."

She smiled, enjoying the recognition for her hard work. "Thank you. I enjoy lab time more than most other things."

"There's a maternity leave position coming up in the new year."

Ade swallowed, remembering the last time she'd messed up an interaction that involved congratulating a colleague who'd turned out *not* to be pregnant. "That's nice." Sometimes, she wished people would get to the point quicker. Conversations like this were like walking through molasses, and they left her brain and body exhausted.

"You could apply for the job, and I'd sponsor your working visa, if you wanted."

"But I'm doing this job." She signaled to her tablet. The measurements weren't going to track themselves, and all this guy wanted to do was talk about his team. A label on her lab coat began to scratch her neck. She'd have to cut that out as soon as he stopped talking.

"I know you've got your role at the faculty. But this would be dedicated to the center. It might suit you better, that's all." Fernando floated toward the door. "Plenty of boat time when the spring comes too. I know you're going to love that."

He disappeared, and Ade breathed a long sigh of relief.

She'd been holding herself together, not wanting to betray any inadequacy through her body language or tone. She reflected on what he'd said: a job that was more hands-on with the animals and less about looking after the students did appeal. The first half of this semester had shone a giant spotlight on her lack of people skills. So far, she'd successfully taken a couple of rolls but almost caused a fist fight about social activities.

Sure, there had been a whole lot of marine care. She'd overseen all the students' time on the feeding stations, taking the water temperature, adding chemicals, and cleaning. But that was just going through the motions. When Greg had turned up for another of his shadowing sessions, she'd gritted her teeth the whole time, wishing she could have the space to herself.

She turned back to the tanks she'd been working on. A sablefish needed feeding, and she'd been a little lethargic these past few days. Ade worried there was something wrong. She made a note of the fish's current behavior and weighed out the feed. Despite concentrating on what was in front of her, her mind drifted back to the job opportunity. Securing a real job would sure get her dad off her back about her prospects. It might buy her some time to figure everything else out too.

Her gaze settled on her cell half-buried on the cluttered desk. If only Sylvie was around this week to talk it through. She would have a better idea of what Fernando was talking about. Even in English, Ade couldn't make much sense of his clichés.

Ade wondered what Sylvie was doing in the countryside with her parents. She hadn't had the chance to travel outside of the city boundaries. The furthest she'd been on the tram had been the university campus and beyond that, the beach. It struck her as pretty unusual to be thinking about Sylvie so much. Oftentimes, the folks in her life had to be physically in the same room for Ade to feel much of anything for them. She loved her dads and her sister, but she didn't pine for them in their absence.

So her reaction to Sylvie's absence was something of a surprise.

It would be great if she wandered into the lab right now, leaned her hip against the doorframe and raised her eyebrow, which Ade had learned was a sure sign of her unspoken curiosity.

Ade spun her pen around in her hand, perfecting the vision of Sylvie she'd conjured in her mind. She wore her trademark boots with a mini skirt, revealing as much of her taut, muscular legs as was appropriate for their educational establishment. A humble navy T-shirt would cling in all the right places, highlighting Sylvie's perfect upper body: the daintiness of her shoulders, her ample breasts, and the smooth, kissable skin of her arms. Her hair fell in its usual place, caressing her jawline and escaping, begging to be stroked back behind her ear.

Whoa. Ade steadied her breath. She had *not* expected to be swept up in a fantasy about her supervisor. Sylvie had shown her a warm welcome but had been nothing but professional in her conduct. Still, it'd been a super long time since someone had made such an impression on Ade. The spark of desire was a rare thing. When it did happen, it was ill-timed, ill-judged, and unrequited. There was nothing to suggest this time would be any different.

Ade put her fantasy Sylvie back in her box. The last thing she needed was to jeopardize her relationship with the only person in this foreign city who'd taken the time to make Ade feel welcome. Her students were immature, and she had nothing in common with them except a loosely similar undergrad curriculum.

With Sylvie, she was learning something new about the city, its arts and culture. The last three weeks had given her more new experiences than she'd had in the last three years back home. But Sylvie was better off in the friend zone, so that Ade couldn't frighten her off. She banished the mini-skirted vision from her mind and replaced it with the pissed and crotchety Sylvie in her crowded classroom.

That was better.

Ade tracked her elephant fish one more time. They trapped their mate during sex with antlers on their head and genitals.

Fascinating but hardly romantic. Ade needed to think more about animals and less about humans. That had always kept her safe and well. So far, so good. Right?

Chapter Eleven

SYLVIE PINNED BACK THE shutters to her parents' stone-walled cottage. Shards of autumnal sunshine flooded the bedroom, catching the dust as it fell to the oak boards. She skipped the wooden stairs two at a time, her feet landing perfectly on the flagstones at the bottom. Her parents' modest place in the country had been a sanctuary from her busy life in Paris since she'd been a teenager.

"Good morning, Mama." She kissed her mother twice on the cheek. They kept their Parisian greeting, despite moving south permanently when they retired.

"Bonjour, ma chérie. Papa is in the kitchen making breakfast."

Glowing, her mom wrapped her in the warmest hug. She'd missed the embrace of her family. Her two older brothers were scattered abroad and rarely had time for holidays.

The scent of rich, Colombian coffee and fresh bread tempted her into the rustic kitchen. Her father emerged red-faced from the stove, with a loaf tin between his oversized oven gloves. "You're awake! Just in time, darling. Sit and eat with us."

Sylvie glanced at the clock. *Merde. Is that the time?*

"The downtime is obviously doing you the world of good, my dear. Now, drink your coffee and relax." Her mom placed a perfectly sized ceramic cup in her hand.

Sylvie admired its uneven glaze, imagining the potter's hands creating the dimples around its body. "It is lovely having a week without classes." She yawned, releasing the remains of her fatigue. "It's a shame I have a pile of mid-terms to mark, otherwise I could really put my feet up."

"It won't be too long until Christmas break." Her mom passed a jar of homemade jam to her dad. "Can you open this, sweetheart?"

He effortlessly released the sealed lid. "You loosened it for me." His chuckle filled the kitchen with a joyful easiness. "Your mother and I are visiting Sebastien in Strasbourg for the holidays. Would you spend a week or so here to look after the dog?"

Right on cue, their elderly black lab, Henri, lumbered across the kitchen floor, sniffing for any breakfast scraps.

"He's really too old for the journey now, and we'll end up stopping every half an hour for bathroom breaks," her mum said, shooing him toward the hearth. "In your bed, Henri."

Sylvie smiled. The old boy had joined her parents' empty nest after she'd moved from their Parisian home, but their family had never been without a canine companion of one breed or another. "What do you think, Henri? Will you keep this old girl company over Christmas?"

Her mom's face fell. "Oh, darling, don't say it like that. Why don't you come to your brother's with us?"

"Don't be silly, I'm just joking. I look forward to the peace and quiet." Sylvie shrugged. "And there's no way I'm driving all the way north just to drive all the way back here for the start of term."

"Well, invite some friends to stay, won't you?" Her mom looked toward her dad. "It's gorgeous here over the winter, you know that. Who might come with you?"

Sylvie stirred her coffee more than it needed. There was no long list of names to reel off. The truth was, she'd become more and more isolated since her move from Paris. Old colleagues, once friends, had simply faded from her favorites. Acquaintances were just that. There weren't that many people she enjoyed the company of so much that she'd invite them to stay. Especially for a holiday as intense as Christmas. "I could invite Elda and Charlie and the boys?"

Her mom clapped. "Of course, that would be perfect. The boys will love the garden, and you can take them to the beach."

Sylvie's dad took a deep breath and unfolded a towel to dry his hands. "There's no one more local you could bring along?"

An image of Ade exploded in Sylvie's mind. "No," she said. "Plus, Elda and I are overdue a meet-up. We still haven't pinned down the detail, so this will be perfect."

"It's a long way for her and Charlie to come with the little ones, no?" he asked.

"Well, they're both adults; they can decide for themselves, can't they?" Sylvie's shoulders stiffened as her defenses rose. Why was her dad questioning her on this? Because he worried about her. He worried that she was lonely. Despite living closer to them, she hadn't made time this year to visit as much as she'd said she would. Maybe he was right. Her life wasn't brimming with friends and social engagements. It had become a routine of work, eat, and sleep.

"I'm going to take my breakfast in the garden." Sylvie gathered a selection of bread and meats and opened the French doors to the terrace. The humble cottage sat in oversized grounds, and Sylvie chose an old bistro table in the sun on the east side. The leaves on the small olive tree had faded, and the stack of bamboo canes leaning against the wall were sun-bleached from a whole season outdoors. The summer crops had been harvested from the raised beds, leaving the autumn stalwarts room to grow another inch or so before they were plucked from the ground too.

Autumn often brought a fresh start, the chance to buy a new pencil case and polish her shoes for the term. Sylvie closed her eyes. The reality was she was coasting as much as she was last year, as much as she had been in Paris.

The fast-track promotion she was promised hadn't come through yet. She was hanging on the expectation that she could just do a little more... A little more work, more supervision, more hours.

She wasn't sure she had much more to give. Nearer to forty than thirty, she'd expected to be settled in a flat, a steady relationship, and maybe even a family of her own.

Why was she thinking about this now? She looked around the ample garden her parents had had the foresight to invest in so many years ago. They'd had a plan. They'd had their life in the city, raised their children in one of the best places in the world, and then retired to their second home to enjoy their twilight years.

It was the perfect place for children to run around. She could picture Elijah and Arlo having sword fights on the lawn. She took a selfie and sent it to Elda, along with an invitation for Christmas. It was something to look forward to in the absence of any firm plans of her own.

Henri padded across the terrace and slumped at her feet, bringing her instant comfort. "Hey, boy." She tickled his head and as he raised his chin to her, she took another photo.

Hey, I have a friend this week. You'd like him.

Three dots showed that Ade was writing a reply.

He's pretty gorgeous. Just my type.

Sylvie laughed. *You can't run off with my dog. I'd be jealous.*

Of me or the dog?

For someone who wasn't that confident, Ade had a lot of text game. Sylvie hesitated. This was just the kind of text transcript she'd seen in tribunal cases where the junior staff had accused a middle-aged professor of inappropriate conduct.

How's your week going?

Not too bad. Lots of lab time which is good for me. Not much reading.

Don't take reading week too literally.

The three dots appeared. Sylvie held her breath and waited for Ade to finish her message. She wanted her reply. Was she missing Ade's company?

It's kind of quiet without the students around and no one to talk to.

Yeah. I know what you mean. It's quiet here too. I'm being well fed and watered by my parents. Looking forward to getting back at the weekend. Did she mean that? Sylvie hadn't ever missed her

Montpellier life before. Was it the city vibe that was lacking out here in the country?

Her train of thought was cut short by her mom striding through the garden with her spade and fork. Her dad followed with his arms full of old cardboard.

"You know, Sylvie, your father and I are worried about you." Her mom speared the ground with her spade.

"Why?"

"Because you've lost your spark. You left Paris for the south and all your plans for a promotion. Now you seem a little lost."

Sometimes Sylvie wished her mother was a little less direct. "Maybe I am. Maybe I'm not." She drew her knees to her chest. "I'm on track with work. This year I'll get my supervision badge, and the powers that be will find a senior professorship slot for me." She wasn't sure of it but couldn't let her confidence waver.

"And the next book?" her dad asked, raising his head above his cardboard shield.

"Coming along." She shot him a look. They shared the same impatience with the world. "Do you give the boys this much grief when they visit?"

"You all get the same grief, don't you worry about that." Her dad laughed, relieving the pressure from the conversation.

"Time to dig over the beds. I'm going to let these rest over winter." Her mom gestured toward a grid of vegetable plots.

Sylvie nodded. As a city girl at heart, she had little idea of what her mom was talking about, but she'd appreciate the harvest all the same. One day, if she was lucky, she'd have her own plot of land to tinker with. She might even find the right person to do it with.

Chapter Twelve

ADE PACED THE PERIMETER of her apartment for the sixty-seventh time. She couldn't settle. Her thoughts whirled, creating a tornado of confusion in her mind. She counted the days on her calendar until she got to a big circle with Steph's name inside. The time had marched on very quickly, but as Steph's return approached, Ade had to admit, she was looking forward to their brief reunion. She'd also missed the guiding hand of Sylvie. This week had been a kind of lonely Ade had never known.

She popped open her laptop. Fifty-four unread emails. That should keep her mind busy. She wriggled her fingers and opened the first one. *Boring.* She skipped to Sylvie's last mail, which was advance notice of their next catch-up, at which she was expecting a program for the next semester. Ade smiled at Sylvie's professional tone, knowing the unique blend of sharp wit and softness that lay beyond it.

Next, she opened a message from Greg, her faithful, if wet behind the ears, assistant. She squinted at the screen and re read the words. It was sent to the whole Monterey cohort inviting them to a club night at Bleu in the city. Ade was sure she'd ventured up that way last time Steph was in town, and if she trusted her memory, it was a cool part of town, if a little loud.

The university's messenger app pinged, and she instantly regretted showing her online status. The last thing she needed was an influx of demands over the weekend.

Hey there, Ade. Are you heading out with us tonight?

How did Greg pop up wherever she was? *Do you have a tracking device on me?*

What?

Nothing. You're just always around.

The messages stopped. Maybe he'd gotten bored with the conversation.

We're meeting up in half an hour for a drink before the club. Come along... It'd be really good for the whole group to get together.

Ade stared at the four walls that had contained her since Monday. Aside from a couple of lab shifts and a trip to the mini market, she'd had no contact with the outside.

Okay. But I can't stay for too long.

Within an hour of joining them, Ade had finished her beer, attempting to dull the onslaught of voices, beats, and scraping furniture around her. It worked. The alcohol found its path to her brain, subduing the noise.

After another liter and several vodka shots, it was like wearing a diving mask, with the piercing voices of the others muffled to an acceptable level. Greg's incessant attempts to strike up a conversation became almost bearable.

"We're heading to Bleu after these," he said, grinning with the reckless abandon afforded by an evening of cheap beer. "You coming?"

A tiny whisper inside Ade's head said, *No, thank you. I'll be heading home where it's safe and peaceful.* But the mix of liquor delivered an emphatic yes, and then she was arm in arm with Madison, trotting down toward La Place de la Comédie.

She'd been in the dark, dingy nightclub less than ten minutes, when her nervous system overruled her. She shielded her eyes from the blinding spotlights and dodged the swirling beams of the lasers. The heaviness of the bass beating against her chest was so oppressive, she doubted her own breath, worried it wouldn't make it far enough inside her lungs to provide the oxygen she craved. The stench of sweat and sugary drinks overwhelmed her nostrils, making her nauseous. She sought an exit for a breath of fresh air to cleanse her body.

When she awoke, she couldn't remember getting home. The dawn light streamed through the shutters she hadn't closed the night before. Her fuzzy mouth and weak stomach reminded her of the consumption of heavy liquor. Thank god it was the weekend, and she didn't have to drag her sorry ass to campus.

As she rolled over, another wave of sickness threatened, and the fierce buzz of the intercom disturbed the silence. She dragged herself from the creased sheets and hit the two-way mic, putting her best French accent on the word "hello."

The barrage of words that came back at her was indecipherable. She caught the words "air filter" and "rocks" but couldn't work out the meaning.

"Just come up," she said, beaten into verbal submission. Maybe the agency had sent a maintenance guy. Eventually, the heavy footsteps reached the fifth floor and a tall guy in overalls flashed her a smile, repeating some of the same words she couldn't understand over the intercom. Her hungover brain stalled, simultaneously translating and processing his meaning. She stared, her nostrils twitching at his smell. *Is that tobacco?* She glanced at his hands, seeking proof that he smoked so she could close that tab in her brain.

He gestured that he needed to come inside, and Ade showed him in. He scanned the room and headed for the bathroom. Inside, he pointed to the extractor fan and said something about cleaning it.

"Sure, go for it." She sighed. Anything to hurry him along so she could get back to her bed to relieve her exhaustion.

A few minutes later, the guy came out with a handful of stones. "This bad," he said, acting out taking them out of the filter.

"If you say so. I don't mean to be rude," she said, "but I really need to be horizontal right now."

He pursed his lips and nodded. "You live alone here? No one to help with stones?"

"No, no one to help get stones out of an appliance I've never noticed. Now, if you'll excuse me." She ushered him to the door. "Thank you."

"Thank agency," he said and disappeared down the stone spiral staircase.

Ade sank against the closed door, grateful that the contents of her stomach hadn't reappeared, at least for the duration of his visit.

Raised voices came from the fourth floor, but Ade couldn't make out what they were saying. She cracked open the door. It was the same guy she'd just let out of her studio.

By the time she'd reached her neighbor's hallway, he was gone.

"Are you okay?" her neighbor asked. "That guy was a conman."

"What?" Ade froze. What had just happened?

"He said he was some maintenance man sent by the building manager, but he looked like a rogue. Come in for a minute." The neighbor ushered Ade inside. "I'm Marcella. Sorry we haven't met before, but welcome to the building. I wish it was a warmer welcome."

"Thanks." Ade willed herself to say more, but the idea of a fraudster inside her apartment freaked her out.

"You look terrible." Marcella's kind eyes creased when she smiled. "Would you like a coffee?"

Actually, she'd love Marcella to look elsewhere while her brain melted with anxiety. Ade nodded.

"Did that guy frighten you?"

Ade closed her eyes, pulling down the shutters on the world to work out the chaos in her head. "Sorry, I'm having trouble processing what just happened. So that person wasn't employed by the realtor? He was just a random guy?"

"It happens. They bluff their way into people's apartments to see if you have anything worth stealing." Marcella poured freshly brewed espresso into a tiny cup. "Did he take anything?"

"No." Ade tracked back over his movements. "He came straight into the bathroom and took some stones out of my air filter."

Marcella scoffed. "Yeah, he told me he was visiting all the apartments for the same reason but made a quick exit when I challenged him for some identification."

"Shit." Ade's heart sank. "I didn't even think to ask for ID."

"Don't beat yourself up." Marcella shrugged. "He probably saw your name on the intercom."

"My name? You think he targeted me personally?"

"No, no. It's just you have a foreign name. Fraudsters love international students, because they're less likely to question what's happening or have a support network around them."

Ade hadn't questioned it, and she didn't have anyone around. If Steph had been there, she would never have let him inside. Ade had proven, once again, that she could be trusted to misjudge *any* situation. "What should I do?"

Marcella did that French thing, where she sort of blew her cheeks out as if that would eliminate the problem. "I wouldn't give it a second thought. I've sent him on his way. I just wanted to make sure you're okay."

"Well, thanks," Ade said, as if she'd borrowed some sugar, but reeling inside. "I feel a bit sick."

"You look it. Have you been enjoying the city nightlife a little too much?"

"Something like that. I should trust my instincts to stay home."

"Enjoy yourself while you can," said Marcella. "Before you know it, you'll be paying too many bills and won't be able to go out partying."

Ade looked around Marcella's apartment. It had twice the square footage of her own and even had doors leading off the main room, presumably to multiple bedrooms. Marcella was a real grown up. "Have you lived here a long time?"

"A few years now. It's a great city." She nodded out of the balconied window toward the impressive skyline. "Are you here for just a year? People come and go from the apartment upstairs."

Ade swallowed. Why were they suddenly discussing her

circumstances as if nothing had happened? She was freaking out right now. "Yeah, that's right. I'm a chaperone with a bunch of students from California."

"Nice. I've never been to the US."

"It's very different." Ade gulped down the short espresso and shuffled from one foot to another, wanting to leave without being rude. "I should go."

"Of course."

She paused short of the threshold, remembering her manners. *What would Steph do?* "I appreciate you taking the time to explain things to me. And thank you for the coffee."

"Anytime." Marcella squinted. "You have a kind face. Don't let people take advantage of it."

"Okay. Bye." Back in her own studio, Ade flopped onto her creased sheets and pulled the cotton over her head, creating a den of sensory deprivation. The raging hangover hindered her processing speed, so her brain's gears were grinding even more than usual. This is what happened when she was left to her own devices for more than a few days. Drama sprang up from nowhere when she least expected it. She couldn't read the same social cues as other people seemed to, and she got herself into scrapes.

Ade rolled over onto her side and rested her eyes. She didn't trust her mind or her body to do anything sensible until she'd slept off her hangover. Maybe then she'd pass for an adult capable of running their own life. She could hope.

Chapter Thirteen

SYLVIE HOOKED HER ARM through Isa's as she stepped off the tram. They'd made it to the very end of the tracks, where Sylvie had been promised a treasure trove of antiques.

The Sunday morning sunshine delivered, and she was glad to be back in the city after her séjour at her parents' place. She'd made it through the first weeks of the year without losing too many students to alcohol poisoning, spiraling debt, or homesickness. It was time to prepare for the coming winter months and hunker down until the spring.

"How was your reading week?" Isa asked.

"About a hundred and fifty papers deep and five seminar plans wide. How about you?"

"Same. With extra wine."

"Of course. I was waited on hand and foot by my doting parents, who seem to have a new lease on life now they're retired. It's all home-grown veggies and afternoon strolls."

"So it should be." Isa sidestepped a hurried trader. "That's what I aspire to once I've finished topping up my pension pot here."

Sylvie frowned. "Don't you think you're a bit young to be thinking about your pension?"

"I am very serious about retirement planning." Isa looked like she was trying to keep her face serious. "That is, will I have enough to buy a vineyard in my fifties?"

"I'll go Dutch with you on the vineyard. Tuscany? Or Provence?"

"I don't think we'll ever afford Provence on our teaching salaries, my angel. Let's set our sights a little lower. Perhaps a small plot in Bulgaria?" Isa's coarse laughter rang out across the rows of stalls.

"Speak for yourself! I intend to make my millions from touring a one-woman show with my unique commentary on European feminism."

"I'll buy a ticket."

"I'm not sure anyone else will." Sylvie groaned, stepping over the carpet of a stallholder laying out his secondhand wares. "I need to finish the book before I can go on tour."

"How's it going?"

"Let me think. If I was to compare my progress to say, the harvest of a vineyard, the roots are strong, but this season has yet to produce the yield we were expecting."

Isa chuckled. "The fruit has not yet sprung?"

"Oh, it has sprung. There are words aplenty: too many words, according to my editor. They've yet to ripen. To mature into their full-bodied potential."

"This analogy is making me thirsty."

Sylvie looked over the tram car park hosting the oversized yard sale. "Does this happen every weekend?"

"Yep."

"People just come down here and walk around people's junk."

"It's not all junk, sweetie."

Sylvie raised her eyebrow. Much of it looked like the rejects of a thrift store. It was hardly the Parisian flea market she used to meander on her free weekends.

Isa flicked her gaze beyond the stalls. "Shall we find a bar?"

"I thought you'd never ask." Sylvie rubbed her hands together. "Did you bring your chess set?"

"I don't travel without it. You never know when you might meet someone who's up for a quick game." Isa winked. "Talking of which, that woman behind us can't keep her eyes off you. You should chat. Maybe invite her to join us."

Sylvie snuck a look behind her at the figure in question. Tall, attractive, and looking straight at her. She cricked her neck to face forward, hushing Isa's gleeful excitement. "That's enough. She'll know we're talking about her."

"Well, don't talk about her, talk *to* her." Isa shoved her toward the next stall, right into the path of the stranger.

Sylvie smiled politely, raising an object to inspect it.

"Nice ashtray," the woman said, her voice like velvet.

"Isn't it?" Sylvie gulped.

"You don't see many of that type anymore. It could be mid-century. Perhaps even pre-war."

On any other day, Sylvie would've enjoyed a conversation about the weight of the marble. It may have even led to a drink or two at a bar. But today, she shut down and strolled to the next table. She had enough going on in her life without spending energy nurturing another connection that would cost her time and emotion.

She glanced at Isa, grateful for her company. As she moved along the stalls, she noticed a postcard of a Francois Truffaut film, its familiar New Wave artistry standing out among a table full of trash. "How much is this?" she asked the stallholder.

He mumbled something and pointed to the sticker on the back. A single euro. She remembered the night she'd shared with Ade a few weeks ago: the peaks and troughs of Ade's passion and ambivalence for the film. *What would Ade make of this little card?*

"You brushed her off?" Isa nudged Sylvie.

"The stranger? There was nothing to brush off. We were simply stood together at a table full of questionable antiques."

Isa pursed her lips. "I've told you before, Sylvie: your dream woman is not going to fall at your feet, however beautiful your shoes are."

"That may be. But she wasn't the one." Sylvie shrugged. "And I came to spend time with you, not some stranger."

Isa huffed. "Shall we go?"

"Let me just buy this card." Sylvie passed over a euro in exchange for the tatty postcard. A thread of connection was weaving its way between her and Ade. She couldn't describe it in words, but the anticipation filling her chest when she safely pocketed her postcard was undeniable.

***

"So you went out with them all to a bar?" Sylvie shook her head, horrified that Ade would hit the town with her students.

"You don't approve?" Ade asked.

"It's never wise to mix with the..." Sylvie hesitated. Who was she to dictate who Ade should socialize with? "Students."

"Hey, I'd prefer a hard and fast rule around it all. I like a firm boundary. But in this case I'm getting paid to see them through this year, and part of that involves organizing a social once per semester. It's kind of a gray area, don't you think?" Ade licked the remnants of her sticky pastry from her fingers, sending a flutter of interest through Sylvie's ribcage.

"You're somewhat of an anomaly when it comes to student and staff relations, yes."

Ade didn't fit in any of the boxes, and that wasn't helping Sylvie stick to her own ethics when it came to thinking about her.

Colette approached with a hand towel thrown over her shoulder. "Do you need any more coffee over here?"

Sylvie raised her eyebrow in Ade's direction, allowing her to take the lead.

"I'd like another one. How about you?"

Sylvie relaxed a little further under Ade's watchful gaze. The afternoon light was falling, and Colette's low lamps illuminated Ade's handsome features.

"Sylvie?" Colette said.

"Oh, yes, please." She giggled, caught out in her daydream. "Thank you, Colette. You look extra busy this afternoon."

"It's been steady all week. I'm grateful for the business, to be honest." She strode to the counter to ring up their drinks.

Sylvie turned to Ade, and the crowded room almost disappeared from view. Ade leaned her chin against the palm of her hand, and the hint of a smile played at her lips.

"What's funny?" Sylvie asked, a shyness prompting her to cover her cheeks with her palms. However much she indulged her enjoyment of Ade as a spectacle, the prospect of Ade staring back was too much.

"Nothing. I like seeing you in this space, that's all." Ade reclined. "You look so comfortable and relaxed."

"And I usually look like I have a stick up my ass, as you Americans might say?" Sylvie frowned with mock indignation.

"No. You're a little different on campus is all. Professor Boucher is revered and respected." Ade scratched her ear. "Sylvie is humble and loved by her neighbors."

It had been such a long time since anyone had seen past Sylvie's work wardrobe and persona that she was taken aback by Ade's insights. It revealed a deeper understanding than she'd given Ade credit for. Sylvie drew her cardigan closed in a moment of vulnerability. Not wishing to shut Ade down completely, she met her eye contact and mirrored her softened gaze across the table.

Colette returned. "Two more coffees. Enjoy."

"Thank you," Sylvie said. "Oh, I almost forgot. I have a something for you." She pulled out the postcard from her bag and passed it to Ade.

"Really?" Ade's eyes widened, and a faint blush crept up her neck. "*La Nouvelle Vague*." She traced the bright block of color with her finger, outlining the monochrome image of the short-haired woman smoking a cigarette. "She's beautiful."

"Is she?" Sylvie touched the tattered card, strangely a little embarrassed by the gift.

"She has stunning eyelashes and lips," Ade said, pointing at the card.

"I like how you see that." Sylvie looked into Ade's eyes. "This genre of film was about playing with the male gaze and how beauty was depicted."

"Why was it always from a man's perspective? It's annoying."

"It was just what happened at the time. Men were earning the money to make and consume films, so they made what they wanted to. Thankfully, it fueled a whole world of research into what makes a woman when she's portrayed through her own eyes or the eyes of another woman." Sylvie took a breath. "Women see other women completely differently."

Ade bit her lip in a way that made Sylvie want to reach out and run her finger along her cheek.

"I just prefer the natural world, where there's an equilibrium of roles." Ade straightened in her seat, as if she was aware of Sylvie's lingering gaze. "Everything has its purpose, and one sex isn't more important than another." She stared at the image for a moment longer and stiffened. "Thank you."

Sylvie drew back. *What had happened?* Ade seemed closed off, and her cheeks reddened with embarrassment.

"I have to go," Ade said, pulling a handful of euros from her pocket.

"It's okay; I'll get these," Sylvie said, a little confused by Ade's sudden exit.

"I really appreciate the postcard," Ade said.

And then she was gone.

Sylvie sipped at her own drink and replayed the last minute. *Did we just have a moment?* It was like they'd connected on a deeper level, only for the wires to cross. Maybe she'd misread Ade's signals again. She was hardly the easiest person to have a conversation with. Sylvie rubbed her temple. She'd been enjoying a wonderful sense of ease, only to be jolted in her seat by Ade's mood swing. Maybe that hadn't been the connection she thought it was. Perhaps she could trust neither her reading of Ade, nor her own emotions. Which was a shame, because the more time they spent together, the more Sylvie wished for more.

Chapter Fourteen

ADE PULLED THE COOL morning air into her lungs and wiped the dew from the painted windowsill with a cloth. She opened the dormer window to welcome in the blue sky. It was Halloween. Back home, the town's porches and lawns would've come to life with tricks and treats, and she'd spend the night avoiding the jump scares. Halloween brought strange noises and a change in routine, neither of which she relished. Here, the city's nightlife played up the occasion. She'd seen more posters of orange and green cocktails in the last week than she had in her lifetime.

Leaning against the makeshift window seat that she'd fashioned from a spare cushion, she contemplated the day ahead. She'd made it to Thursday with minimal drama. The classes had been fairly calm. Her lab time had been golden. Greg had come and gone for his shift, requiring the briefest of small talk, which suited her. She'd bumped into Sylvie in the faculty staff room, and they'd met for coffee. Ade glanced over at the wall where she'd stuck the postcard Sylvie had given her. It brightened up the blank space.

She cringed, going over the awkward way she'd reacted to the gift. She'd botched her thanks and came off as aloof. Maybe even rude. She hadn't meant to, but she'd been spooked by the gesture and couldn't think fast enough.

Sylvie graciously smoothed the whole thing over, of course. But it wasn't enough for Ade not to rethink it over and over. Re-rehearsing what she would have said, given a second chance, she jumped at the noise at the door. She froze, hoping she'd imagined it, but feared with every fiber of her body that someone was behind that door.

Holding her breath, she strained to hear any movement.

The lock. The lock began to turn. Someone was turning it from the outside.

Ade swallowed. All moisture had evaporated from her mouth, and she almost gagged from the dry air. *Focus.* She closed her eyes to drown out the extraneous information in her head, allowing her to zero in on what she could do next, and she calculated all the possibilities in a fraction of a second. Her brain wasn't slow; it was overflowing.

She grabbed a metal ladle from the work surface and smashed it against the door. "Get out!" She sucked in a breath. "I'm in here and if you try to get in, I'll call the police."

The footsteps retreated. They got quieter until she heard the slam of a door at the bottom of the staircase. Shaking, she sank to the floor. Someone had tried to get into her apartment. If she hadn't been here, they would have. All at once, the tabs in her brain reopened, flooding her with every thought she'd had that week. Top of the pile was the imminent danger she'd just faced and the overwhelming fear it had prompted.

She needed to call someone. Steph was too far away, and she'd only worry. Her dads were still asleep and ditto. What could they possibly do from California except drive themselves insane with "what ifs." She thought of Marcella downstairs. She'd been so wonderful last week when that fraudster had turned up. Was it that same guy? A circuit in her mind fired up, and she flicked through a picture book of the fraudster who'd been in her apartment. She zoomed into the detail of his uniform, the ruffled collar, the texture of his hair. Then panned back out to the apartment door, imagining him behind it.

Her hands trembling, Ade touched the door lock. Had he really gone? She hesitated. Maybe she should just stay safe in here for the next few hours. But then it would get dark, and she'd be stuck.

She pulled out her phone. There was only one person who might come, only one person she wanted.

An hour later, the intercom buzzed, ringing in the silence and Ade jumped out of her skin once more. She put her ear to the entrance, listening for the familiar footsteps, and once she was sure, she opened the door. "Thanks for coming," she said.

"It's nothing. I wanted to make sure you're okay." Sylvie strode in with two coffees. "Those stairs are a killer. Next time, find a lower apartment, second floor at most. Worse views but no heart attack."

Ade laughed, her heart rate dropping for a moment.

"Now." Sylvie looked her square in the face. "Tell me."

Ade relayed the morning's events and also filled her in on the air filter scam from the week before.

"We need to go to the police. You've obviously been watched by them."

"What?" Ade paced the floor of her tiny studio, relieved to have Sylvie as company but wanting to crawl out of her skin with worry.

"I wouldn't joke about such a thing." Sylvie pursed her lips and rolled up her sleeves. "They prey on foreigners. They assume you have an apartment full of gadgets, cash, and booze. He probably thought you'd left for the day."

"I usually would have, but I had a free period."

"Exactly." Sylvie stroked Ade's arm. "That's why we need to go and report it."

Ade couldn't move. The rhythm of the touch soothed and overstimulated her all at once. But she couldn't move out of Sylvie's reach.

"Ade?"

Sylvie's soft words pulled her from the trance. "Sure," Ade said, finally accepting that she couldn't stay frozen in her apartment forever.

By the time they'd walked across town, the fresh air and motion had helped to stabilize her nerves. Ade wore her earbuds to block out the crowds, and they took the quieter streets, away from the crowded, noisy squares. Outside the station, Ade looked to Sylvie for desperate reassurance. She had no idea what to do.

"I've got you." Sylvie smiled and handled the whole painful interaction.

Ade couldn't make out much of the spoken communication, but there was a lot of shrugging and blowing out of cheeks from the police officer at the front desk. She kept her focus on the lines between the floor tiles, looking for anomalies in the grout. They were everywhere. Thin lines and thicker lines in no particular order. It calmed her down, and she zoned out, grateful to have Sylvie by her side.

"Ade?" Sylvie gently nudged her arm.

"Huh?" As requested, she contributed a few details and a signature on a triplicate form before they were dismissed.

"They said there's a gang going around pulling similar stunts with other students," said Sylvie. "They look for the apartments which have been let to internationals and play their silly games."

Ade nodded.

"You have classes this afternoon?" Sylvie asked.

"Yeah. I've already missed two counselling sessions."

"Let's get to campus." Sylvie drew alongside as they walked to the tram stop, her shoulder nudging against Ade's. "Don't feel too awful. This sort of thing happens, especially in the city."

Ade couldn't shake the fear hardening inside her chest when she worried that someone might intrude on her space. It dawned on her that she'd never lived alone. Steph and her dads had always been around. The last few weeks had been a novelty, and she'd enjoyed the quiet freedom to do her own thing without really processing it.

The rest of the day passed with the minor troubles of her students. Madison was in tears over a lost credit card, and Scott was grumpier than usual due to a failed assignment. Ade tried her best to help them navigate their challenges, while pushing her own worries to the very back of her mind.

By around six, the skies had grayed, and exhaustion weighed on her body, while the fear of walking home alone took up residence in her thoughts. She looked up from her notes over the rows of empty desks after the last of her students had left for the day.

"Knock, knock." Sylvie leaned against the open door frame. "I imagined you might be hanging around."

"Why?"

She tilted her head and stepped into the room. "You don't want to rush home, do you?"

Ade dropped her gaze, drumming her fingers on the underside of the desk. "It's ridiculous to say this, but no. I feel kinda weird about it."

"It would be weird if you didn't." Sylvie pulled up a chair and sat next to her. "You stopped someone from coming inside your apartment earlier. That's a big deal."

"That's not helping," said Ade.

Sylvie smiled, and everything lightened for a moment.

"I'm sorry," she said. "Would you like me to come home with you and check everything's okay?"

"Yes. Definitely." Ade stood to collect her things, relief washing over her. She might have stayed at her desk all night if Sylvie hadn't come back for her.

They strolled from the campus building and took the next tram back into the city. By the time they reached the old town, night had fallen, and they walked the familiar streets by lamp light until they reached Ade's building.

"Halloween revelers are in full swing." Sylvie nodded toward the open window, through which the screeches of passersby on their way home from the bars floated up. "I'm glad we're safe in here. Students and their cocktails can be a terrible combination." She frowned in Ade's direction. "You do feel safe up here now, don't you?"

Ade pondered the question. "I do. But you're here with me."

"You'd be fine without me."

"I'm not so sure I would be. I've never really been left to my own devices much." A sense of shame washed over her. Was that really something to be worried about admitting? She was only twenty-four, and she was well on her way to getting a doctorate. Just because she hadn't left home at eighteen for the bright lights and hedonism of San Francisco didn't mean she was any less of an adult. But she didn't want Sylvie to think she was different. She didn't want to scare her off. "Sometimes, I think I'm a little out of the ordinary."

"You are." Sylvie looked her dead in the eye. "What do you want me to say?"

Ade stiffened. "No one's ever agreed with me before." She gripped the arm of the sofa bed, steadying herself. *It's happening.* Every time she met a new friend, they drifted away with a throwaway comment like this. Eventually, they'd discover that she wasn't like everyone else. She orbited social circles, but she wasn't part of them. She was never going to be anyone's sun.

"You *are* out of the ordinary. You see the world differently to most people." Sylvie touched her sleeve. "That doesn't make you inferior to anyone else."

"You think I'm different, in a good way?"

"Absolutely." Sylvie said. "You're you."

"I feel inadequate. Especially today," Ade said. "You had to escort me to the police station and come home with me because I couldn't put my lights on by myself."

"Nonsense." Sylvie huffed. "I wanted to help translate the whole baffling situation. You'd still be at the station with your phrase book if I hadn't been there."

"And tonight?" Ade wasn't sure what she wanted from the question.

"Tonight, I'm simply enjoying a glass of wine with a colleague—a colleague whose company I have grown to appreciate." She nodded with a finality which drew a line under the subject. "Another glass?"

"No, not for me. Alcohol isn't my friend." Ade ran through all the times she'd choked back a shot of liquor just to get through the next conversation. "It gets me through parties, and nights out, and awkward moments. But I feel worse afterward, without fail."

"I get it. Alcohol is a wonderful lubricant for social situations."

"I find I don't need it so much...with you." Ade froze. Had she said too much?

Sylvie glanced at her watch. "I should be heading home."

Ade held her breath. Her palms grew clammy, and every nerve stood on end.

Sylvie hesitated. "I could stay for a little longer, if you'd like?"

She'd seen. The panic that Ade struggled to keep inside was clearly visible to Sylvie. And rather than flee the scene, she rested her hand on Ade's shoulder.

"Will you stay the night?" Ade asked. The words were out before she had the chance to reflect on the question. What must Sylvie think of her?

"I'll stay for a while longer, and then we'll see how you feel. How about that?"

It was all she could ask for. They barely knew each other, but she'd embroiled Sylvie in a whole day and night of drama. *Don't leave now.* She looked so right in Ade's space. No one had ever looked so at home.

Ade struggled to peel away from Sylvie's hand. How could she withdraw from such warmth? Such tenderness? Her fingertips hadn't tingled like that for a long time. She couldn't remember an attraction so magnetic that she actually wanted to stay in someone's company rather than withdraw from it, in need of a break from the conversation or the intensity of the contact. Was it the fear of being alone that rooted her to the spot? Or was it the comforting tone of Sylvie's voice? Her authority? Or the fact that she was so in control of her speech and movement, as well as the actions of everyone else around her?

She was a force to be reckoned with. But in her presence, everything seemed a little easier on Ade's soul.

It was peace that Ade realized she'd been craving, giving her the chance to turn off her mind and relax inside her own body. She rested further into Sylvie's space, and when she wasn't rejected, her heart stuttered. Was this real friendship? Was this why people had best friends?

Chapter Fifteen

SYLVIE RUBBED THE SLEEP from her eyes and squinted at the strange ceiling above. At some point the previous evening, she'd refilled her wine glass and abandoned all intentions of going home, not wanting to leave Ade to face her fears alone. She turned, knowing full well Ade would be stretched out, fully dressed, beside her. Sylvie closed her eyes, unwilling to accept the line she'd crossed by staying over last night. Her judgment had been way off, and she couldn't blame the wine.

Ade stirred. *Damn.* She should've left already. She should be out on the street and far away from Ade's slumbering body, however clothed they both were. The cadence of Ade's breath faltered, and Sylvie looked away, cringing inside.

"Hey," Ade whispered.

Her beautiful, sleepy voice cut through Sylvie's doubt. What was it about that voice, that face, which was so magnetic?

"Good morning." Sylvie sat up, meaning to gather herself. "I should get going."

"It's Friday. We have our regular catch-up scheduled." Ade yawned, her bare arms popping from her sleeves. "I look forward to it."

Sylvie averted her gaze, her head spinning more and more with every inch of Ade's body uncovered from the duvet. When had they decided to make up the bed? She shook her head, not wishing to replay the events too vividly. She'd really tried to keep her distance yesterday, but Ade had been so vulnerable that all her instincts kicked in to protect her.

"You want to get coffee and talk here?" Ade asked.

Sylvie shouldn't stay any longer. She'd hurdled all kinds of professional boundaries. But Ade scratched at her hair and rubbed her eyes, looking more gorgeous than ever.

"Why not?" The answer slipped from Sylvie's lips.

"What do you mean?" Ade's brow furrowed.

"I mean, yes, I'd love to get coffee and talk here." Sylvie smiled, losing herself in the depth of Ade's wide pupils. "Do you want to grab them from the bakery while I have a quick shower?" It was presumptive, but Sylvie couldn't stay without cleaning herself up.

Ade jumped out of the bed and pulled on her shoes. "I'll go now. Help yourself to whatever you need." She threw open her closet, revealing a line of identical black T-shirts. "If you need clothes, they're in here."

Sylvie drew the line at wearing Ade's clothes. "And towels?"

"On the bathroom shelf. If they're folded, they're clean. That's the Poole household golden rule." Ade seemed to come to life with excitement.

As she practically skipped out of the front door, Sylvie breathed a sigh of relief. She'd gotten through the night, and she could come back from this. She'd done what any responsible adult would have done: she'd helped a friend in need. A younger friend, who was away from home and on her own.

Under the shower, she washed away the questions reverberating between her ears: why couldn't she leave, really? What had her fixed to the spot last night, sipping her drink and gazing into Ade's eyes while the conversation flowed between them?

"I'm back." Ade clattered something around behind the flimsy bathroom door.

Merde. She'd hoped to be dry and dressed. The only thing between her naked body and Ade was a six-foot length of plywood and a towel. She peered into the steamed mirror and groaned at her tangled wet hair. *Nothing says professional like stepping out of a fresh shower.*

Sylvie hopped up and down in the petite bathroom, pulling on last night's clothes over her damp skin. She inspected her makeup free face and screwed her nose up at the creases around her eyes. Ade had no signs of her age. Her skin was smooth and without a single blemish. Without a face of armor, Sylvie shrank from the situation and snuck back into the kitchen area, not wanting to be noticed.

"There you are," Ade said, without a hint of self-consciousness.

"Listen, maybe I should head off," Sylvie said, ducking her head.

"But why?" Ade's face fell with disappointment. "I have the coffee, and you said we could have our meeting here."

"I know I did." She took a cup and perched on the edge of the sofa bed, eager to get it over with. "Let's do this. How are things going with your group?"

Ade took a deep breath and sat down opposite. "I think I'm making progress, then something happens, and I realize I'm terrible with people."

Well, that cut to the chase. "You are terrible with people. Sometimes."

Ade glared at her. "That's not helpful."

"You're right. I'm here to be helpful." Sylvie smiled. "But the truth is, I've seen you at your best. You're full of empathy. You're attuned. You're in sync with what's around you."

"What?"

"When you're with your marine animals—*not* with your students," said Sylvie.

Ade crossed her arms, as if she was processing the scale of the insult, then she cracked a smile, and her laughter filled the room. "You're so right."

"So don't beat yourself up about it. Focus on what you're good at. What you're pretty great at."

"Sometimes I don't feel good at very much," said Ade. "I don't feel like I fit in the world."

Sylvie sat back into the sofa, which had been re-made, and tucked her bare feet under her, just like she was at home. "Have you always felt that way?" She really wanted to get inside Ade's head for a minute, fascinated by Ade's complexity and the depth beneath her fragile surface.

"I guess so. It's been my narrative since I was born, really."

Sylvie blinked. "Tell me more."

"When Steph was born, she came out screaming apparently. All legs and lungs." Ade bit her lip. "I've struggled with everything my whole life. I was the 'weaker twin.'" She raised her hands for emphasis. "According to my dads, I came out after a long-ass labor, and I had to go into the neo-natal unit for three weeks. My dads said I was always the one who needed the most care and attention. Steph practically looked after herself."

"I doubt that." Sylvie raised her eyebrow. "You think your birth story sets the tone for the rest of your life?"

"No, I'm not that naive. But it *has* been the family way of describing us both. Steph can manage things. She's independent and ambitious." Ade shrugged. "I need help with everything."

"You're here, aren't you?" Sylvie asked.

"Yeah, but only because my sister brought me over, helped me find an apartment, and settled me in before she left." Ade tightened her arms across her chest. "I couldn't even make it through yesterday without you."

Sylvie sat up. "Hey, not many people would have brushed yesterday off without a little help from friends. Don't beat yourself up about that."

"You think so?"

"I know so." Sylvie desperately wanted to slip her arm around Ade's shoulders and draw her into an embrace. She looked so in need of comfort. Instead, Sylvie flashed her biggest smile. "When do you feel at your most confident?"

"I think you already know the answer to that."

Sylvie's stomach skipped. Did Ade mean to say when they were together?

Ade blew across her coffee cup. "When I'm with the animals in the lab. Or when I'm out in the water."

"Right. Yes." Sylvie nodded. Of course Ade wasn't thinking of them together. They were just colleagues. There was no "together."

"Why is that, do you think?"

Ade chewed at her nail. "They don't judge me, I guess. I get a lot of judgment from people sometimes."

"You do? In what way?"

"Trust me, I'm self-aware enough to know I miss a ton of cues. You know, the way people look at each other and their tone. But there are some that are way too obvious to miss. I see the way people frown at me if I say something wrong." Ade dropped her head. "I see way more frowns than anything else some days."

Sadness washed over Sylvie. "And animals don't frown?"

"Right."

"Perhaps that frown isn't always disapproval or judgment. Sometimes, people might be trying to work out what you mean. Or what they should say."

"Yeah, I guess." Ade nodded. "Hard to decipher which is which though."

Sylvie sighed. She hated the thought of Ade feeling so alone. "I'm sorry if I've ever made you feel sad."

Ade perked up, meeting her gaze. "You don't make me feel sad, Sylvie. You're one of the only people I've ever met that speaks in a way that I kind of get, most of the time. And your face—"

"What?" Sylvie recoiled and touched her face.

"I'm sorry, I don't know why I'm suddenly talking about your face."

"Tell me. What's wrong with my face?"

"Nothing. Not like that." Ade laughed. "I just mean that your face is so clear. I know what you mean by looking at you. It's not the same with other people."

A contentment flowed deep inside Sylvie. No one had ever told her that her facial expressions were readable. It was a weird compliment. But from Ade, it meant the world. She loved that she could relieve some of the agony of her failed communication, and that she made it a little easier to be understood.

In the silence, the room's air grew closer, and Sylvie's cheeks burned with the intensity of the moment. The electricity buzzed between them and Sylvie found a little something of herself, a meaning she didn't know she was craving until that very second. Her ears popped with the pressure when she swallowed. "I'm glad for you." They weren't the words she'd intended. They fell flat, in a patronizing way she hadn't meant. What she'd wanted to say was something like "me too." But the right formation of sounds and letters eluded her.

She searched Ade's face for signs of recognition or understanding, but Ade was clearly no mind reader. She'd just admitted she could barely read people's tone and body language, what hope did she have of interpreting what was left so devastatingly unsaid?

Sylvie rubbed her eyes until all the colors of the rainbow collided inside her brain. "I'm sorry. I don't think I've slept all that well, and the words aren't really coming to me right now."

"I get it," Ade said, with a finality that drew their sweet moment of connection to a close.

Sylvie had wasted the opportunity to mirror Ade's emotions. She'd shut the door on her openness and honesty. Her regret flooded the room, and she stood, her legs twitching with anxiety, wanting to escape more than ever. "Let's reconvene when we're both refreshed and back on campus. We can go over the schedules and milestones for the next semester."

"Absolutely." Ade nodded, her shoulders dropped as they moved to the door. "Sylvie?"

"Yeah?"

"Thank you."

Guilt crept through Sylvie's chest. "What for?"

"For staying with me last night. For helping me at the police station."

"No problem." Sylvie left and wound her way down to street level. Troubled by the last twenty-four hours, she weaved through the morning rush, sidestepping both the commuters and her feelings about Ade. Why was she so conflicted? Their friendship was barely beyond the workplace, but there was a hint of so much more. Was it a threat? Is that why she'd recoiled when Ade had shown so much of herself. The real question was: what was at risk? Her career or her heart?

Chapter Sixteen

ADE STEADIED HERSELF, ADJUSTING to the swell of the docked boat beneath her feet. Closing her eyes behind her sunglasses, she lifted her chin toward the brightness of the sky and enjoyed the warmth on her cheeks.

She counted her students on to the boat and awaited further instruction from the skipper that the center had hired for their day trip. Grateful for a moment to herself, her thoughts drifted again to Friday morning and waking up next to Sylvie.

It'd been a dream, laying shoulder to shoulder with the woman she'd developed a growing fascination with over the last six weeks. She'd focused every one of her muscles on making the right movements and acting as naturally as possible, so that Sylvie would stay just a little longer. Their conversation had flowed well into the early hours, and Ade had revealed more of herself than ever before.

The weekend had passed without any further drama, and her uneasiness about being in the apartment alone had faded slightly. Either way, she could hardly beg Sylvie to stay longer. She'd already overstepped some sort of unwritten line between professionalism and friendship.

"When are we expecting your colleague?"

Startled from her daydream, Ade looked blankly into the expectant face of the skipper, George. "My colleague?"

"Yes. You need a ratio of one member of staff to four students," George said.

Ade ran through the safety documentation she'd meticulously poured over the week before. "But we do have two members of staff: you and me."

George grimaced. "I can't be counted, I'm afraid."

Ade's heart sank. How could she have missed this?

The students giggled at something in the water, obviously excited to be on their first marine trip venturing out on the Mediterranean. She couldn't bear to let them down now, not with their life vests zipped and smiles on all their faces. She'd never seen them look so happy in each other's company. She grabbed her cell and fired off a quick message to Sylvie, the only person who could get her out of this. *I don't suppose you want a trip on the ocean?* There was a long pause. The three, blinking dots teasing.

Morning. This is a surprise. When are you thinking?

Err... no time like now?

Her phone rang, and Sylvie's name glared at her from the dark screen like she was already shouting.

"I'm sorry," Ade said. "I've messed up the staff ratio on this sea trip, and I need an extra person."

Sylvie sighed. "The trip you've been planning? Today? What time are you due to leave?"

Ade contemplated which of Sylvie's questions to answer first. "What?"

"When do you need me?"

Ade cleared her throat. "The skipper is waiting."

"Jesus, Ade, you know how to press my buttons." Sylvie snorted. "I'm at the campus filing some paperwork. I can be with you in fifteen minutes. Message me the dock location, and I'll drive straight there."

Ade ended the call. The students screeched and tousled at the other end of the boat. Suddenly the sea breeze had lost its meditative power, and she pressed her ears to ground herself.

"Ade, when are we heading off? The others are getting a bit restless." Greg held a stack of clipboards in his hand. "Should I give these out to keep them busy?"

"Great idea." She put her head in her hands, struggling to come up with a plan until Sylvie arrived.

"You okay there?" Greg asked.

"We're just going to be a bit late getting started. Professor Boucher is on her way." She stared at Greg's eager, innocent face. He was much more of a help than a hindrance. "I got a bit mixed up with the safety guidelines."

"I'd be happy to keep everyone entertained while we wait," Greg said. "We can go over the safety procedures and take a quick quiz on the parts of the boat."

Ade drummed her fingers on the boat's fiberglass hull. She hated herself for screwing up the plans.

Within fifteen minutes, Sylvie arrived.

She pulled on a life vest and folded her silk blouse beneath its zipper. "I'm hardly dressed for this excursion." She nodded to the group of students huddled on deck. "Can we talk somewhere privately?"

"Head below deck if you need to," George said, flashing Ade a concerned look. "I'll steer us out. It might be a bit bumpy to start with, so hold onto the rails."

Ade followed Sylvie down the short stairs. "Before you say anything, I know I've fucked up here."

"That's correct." Sylvie's eyes flared.

"I'm really sorry." Ade swallowed.

"But you're not appearing to learn any lessons from your mistakes."

Ade tried to work out whether Sylvie was asking something but came up empty. Silence seemed the best option.

Sylvie ran her hand through her hair, already windswept from boarding the boat. "Aren't you going to say anything?"

Ade clenched her fists. This was going badly wrong. She'd called Sylvie because she might know what to do, and she didn't have anyone else to turn to at work. "I'm sorry. I didn't realize you were asking me to respond." *And we're late. We really should've been out on the water by now.* She shuffled from one foot to the other, fanning her hands to expel some of her nervous energy. "I tried to get my head around the paperwork for this trip, and I really thought I'd nailed it. But when George said he wasn't included in the numbers, I didn't know who else to call." Ade bit her lip. "I don't have anyone else to call here."

It was too much, dumping her problems on Sylvie. That she'd stayed with her on Thursday night had been a wonderful surprise, but it had obviously pushed Sylvie to her limit of helping Ade out.

Sylvie's shoulders dropped, and her face softened into the hint of a smile. Was it pity?

"I'm sorry." Sylvie touched Ade's sleeve. "You should be able to reach out to me when you need to. I'm your supervisor; it's what I'm here for."

Ade scratched her head, confused by the unraveling situation. "So, it's okay that I called you?"

"Yes. I'm just flustered by having to drop everything and come over here. Now I'm on a boat trip instead of marking test papers." Sylvie laughed.

"That's a good thing?" Ade craved clarification and needed to repair the tiny tear in their rapport.

"I guess it is. Who wouldn't want to go out onto the water first thing on a Monday?" Sylvie pointed to the ceiling. "Talking of which, we'd better go and keep an eye on our fledglings."

They wandered onto the boat's deck, where the students had gathered at the stern with their clipboards, ready for observation. For a group that could make a lot of noise and trouble, they were on their best behavior this morning.

"Let's go up to the bow and watch from there," Ade said, gaining her sea legs now they'd made it out into the water.

At the front of the boat, the horizon stretched out before them, a wide expanse of nothing but blue sky resting on top of an indigo blue sea. Ade breathed in. She beckoned Sylvie, craving her closeness, but conscious of the audience of George and the students beyond the helm.

"Is this not too loud for you, Ade?" Sylvie asked, raising her voice above the engine noise.

Ade nodded. "A little. But I grew up out on the Pacific. I guess I'm used to the rumble of a boat. It can be quite therapeutic."

"I see," Sylvie said. "Are you feeling better after Thursday night?"

Ade paused. She was feeling a little better. In fact, now that she was on the water with Sylvie by her side, she was feeling pretty good. "Yes, I am."

Sylvie smiled. "Good. How has it been over the weekend?"

"I didn't really enjoy being there alone."

Sylvie frowned and looked out into the wide expanse of the sea. "You could've called me."

"I know. But I didn't want to bother you again." Ade smiled, content that Sylvie wouldn't have minded the interruption. She cupped her hands around her mouth and inched nearer to Sylvie's ear to make herself heard. "We're heading for a cove up the coast a little. It's a great place for bird sightings, and it's really quiet. I checked it out with Fernando at the lab."

Sylvie smiled. "You picked a beautiful day." She put her hands on her hips. "I wish I had dressed for the occasion. But I'm happy to be here."

"You mean, you've stopped being angry with me?"

"I'm not angry with you, silly." Sylvie tilted her head and frowned.

Ade pondered Sylvie's frown. Its angle wasn't as sharp as her dad's, and her eyes looked like they were sparkling. She went to rub the frown away with her fingers and drew back suddenly, realizing the inappropriateness of the touch.

Scott's deep voice carried across the deck, and Madison howled.

Sylvie snuck a look to check on them. "They're fine."

"All accounted for?" Ade asked.

"For now." Sylvie grinned. "You know when you messaged, I thought you were inviting me out on the water."

"I was," Ade said.

"I mean...just the two of us."

Ade replayed Sylvie's words and her heart skipped. Was this really happening? Or was she misreading Sylvie's signals? She couldn't really be trusted to interpret this kind of conversation. "What would you have said?"

"Exactly what I did say. When and where?"

The boat sliced through the water. The rhythm calmed Ade's heartbeat, and she raised her eyes to meet Sylvie's.

Sylvie stepped into her space. "What I mean is, wouldn't it be more fun if we didn't have to babysit these teenagers?"

"Sure." Ade gave a deliberate, slow nod, which bought her some time to work out what was happening. "I'd love to take you out on the water sometime."

"It's a date." Sylvie flashed her the widest grin. "Now, we should check their clipboards."

They rejoined the group, and Ade busied herself with a checklist of things she needed the class to do before the trip was over. Glad of the distraction, she dissected the last few moments. She'd been caught out by the boiling point of Sylvie's irritation, but it had simmered to something confusing. Was Sylvie flirting? Did she want to go out with Ade romantically?

A sea bird flew overhead, too far away to work out the breed. Ade craned her neck up to the sky, shielding her eyes, hoping for answers to the questions that baffled her. Sylvie's presence was both calming and exhilarating. She was like an addiction to nicotine: an anchor and a rush. But she wasn't bad for Ade, was she? So far, she'd been nothing but good. She'd been Ade's safe space and a helpful friend.

Maybe Ade was reading too much into this morning's conversation. She wasn't sure of anything except the sway of the boat and the flight of the birds above her. Everything else was temporary, moveable, shakable.

She stole a glance at Sylvie, sitting on deck with her face to the breeze and away from the glare of the sun. Her cheeks were flushed, her hair bouncing in the wake. The smile that twitched at her lips was barely there, but Ade stood fixed to the spot, entranced by the joy that Sylvie brought with her, wherever she went.

Ade could never have predicted meeting Sylvie. She couldn't imagine a person who would make her feel safe enough to relax and trust herself. If they could be friends this year, it would transform the whole experience from just about bearable to pretty damn wonderful. Anything else would be a bonus.

Chapter Seventeen

"No one gets banned from the library, Madison." Sylvie quickened her pace down the long corridor, eager to escape the clutches of the American student.

"But, ma'am, they said I had a three month ban because I hadn't returned a weeklong loan. I mean, how was I supposed to know it was a short loan? The whole thing was written in French."

Sylvie stifled a groan. "You're here studying in France, my dear. A prerequisite is a working knowledge of French."

"Well, yeah, but it's so much harder here. There are just so many more words. Back home, I understand French."

Sylvie turned on her heel, intrigued. "Who taught you French?"

"Mr. Clarkson."

"Et voilà, ma chérie. You've learned French from a non-native, what do you expect?" Sylvie held a stack of textbooks to her chest. "No one is going to slow down for you just because you're American." She entered her office, assuming the young student would take the hint and rejoin her friends, but her footsteps followed her all the way to the desk.

"Ma'am, I really need to complete that assignment for next week, and I can't get it done without my library access."

Sylvie found a space on her cluttered desk for the heavy pile of books and collapsed into her chair. She was lurching from one problem to another, troubleshooting for everyone else except herself. This particular drama was Ade's to solve, but she'd been off campus since their boat trip on Monday. "Why isn't Ade helping you with this?"

"I tried to message her, but Scott said she has a lab shift today, and she'll have her phone on silent, so she doesn't disturb the animals."

Sylvie nodded. Always putting the animals first.

"Could you like, put a call in to someone, or write me a pass?" Madison flicked her long blond hair away from her shoulder, as if she had better things to do than hang out in Sylvie's office begging for access to the library.

"Trust me, Madison, I have more pressing items on my list today." She bit her cheek. But the quickest way to get rid of this particular nuisance was simply to deal with it, so she fired off an email to the head of libraries and printed Madison a copy. "Take this to the front desk. Tell them I have given you special dispensation. But no repeat offences. Do you understand?"

"Absolutely. Thank you, I really am so grateful." Madison stuffed the paper in her bag and ran for the door.

"And hit that deadline."

"Will do."

Sylvie took a long breath. She had a mountain of work to do before the day was out. There was a disturbance outside her classroom, and Madison called out another apology.

"Knock, knock. May I come in?" Paul came in without waiting for an invitation. "I didn't realize you had student hours today?"

"I don't. That's one of the internationals with another rescue mission."

Paul frowned. How could he understand? He was so far away from the day-to-day running of the faculty, he had no idea about the reality of juggling a teaching post with the demands of academia. He also hardly ever came looking for her. If she wanted to talk about something, usually the prospect of her unlikely promotion, she had to hunt him down. "What's going on, stranger?"

"Well, I'm glad you brought it up." Paul nodded.

"I didn't," she said.

He chuckled at the joke she hadn't made. "Come on, Sylvie. You've been a little aloof with me since the start of the year." He pulled a chair to her desk and sat. "I had a call from your editor on Monday. She's been trying to get hold of you."

Sylvie stiffened in her seat, her mind racing with the reasons she'd been avoiding this conversation with both Paul and her editor. "Yeah, Monday took an unexpected turn."

"Of what kind?"

She didn't want to drop Ade in it. But Paul's stern look wasn't going to soften anytime soon without a decent reason. "If you must know, I was called to supervise the California group with a marine expedition."

Paul laced his fingers together, resting his elbows on the desk. "Let me just get this straight. My up-and-coming professor of European Feminism missed a career-defining deadline to go on a sea safari?"

Sylvie laughed, despite the growing tension between them. "Number one, it was all work and no play, I promise. Second, I had to attend otherwise they'd have been short for their ratios, and it would've been called off. And third, Paul, you insisted I supervise this group, so it's down to you if I have to juggle this role and the book." She sat back, bubbling with her defense. "Another thing: that deadline wasn't 'career-defining.' I don't get the sense that anything I could do would propel me anywhere other than sideways at the moment. I'm like a pinball in a rigged machine."

Paul regarded her, his bushy eyebrows coming together in a wistful judgment. "You're wrong. You're on the rise, Professor Boucher. But only if you keep going, and you're the only driver in your car."

"Your complicated analogies aren't helpful." She folded her arms. She needed more support than this from her own manager. "What do you want me to do? I have a full timetable, a bunch of teenagers with a calamitous pastoral supervisor, and a book to edit. Something's got to give."

"We all have to make dynamic choices. Particularly in leadership roles."

"You think the stuffy old guard are making dynamic choices? They're topping up their gold-plated pensions while rereading dusty philosophy and sipping cognac." She rose from her chair, energy pulsing through her calves. "I'm doing more than my fair share in this department. I'm probably doing more hours than they're all doing put together. It's a shame they don't clock in and out, otherwise you'd see for yourself."

Paul's lips twitched in a grin.

"You find this funny?" Rage churned in the acid of her stomach.

"Calm down, Sylvie. You're right. But the old guys are on their way out of this place. You're on your way in and up. All the way to the top if you're able to focus." He crossed his legs casually, as if the strain of their conversation had no effect on him whatsoever. "I want to help you. What do you need to make this work?"

Sylvie looked to the ceiling tiles for answers. As if there'd be a list of helpful things she could ask her boss for pasted up there. "I'd like to reduce my teaching timetable. Slightly." She couldn't push it too far. "Then I can dedicate some regular hours to edits and fulfill the leadership task you set me in September."

"Wonderful. I'll talk to Elaine and see what we can do to cover your hours. Shall we say three hours a week?"

Sylvie blinked, surprised by how easy it had been to secure Paul's support. "I could probably make that work."

"Very good. Have a good rest of the day." And he was gone.

Sylvie sank back into her chair. Freeing up her time was one thing, but she had to get the head space to make this work. She'd given her book no time at all since the start of term, since Ade had turned up with her gaggle of students.

By the end of the day, Sylvie dragged her tired, aching bones home. In the dusky commute, she wandered across Place Jean Jaurès as the street lamps glowed orange in the falling light. At the far end of the square, she noticed a familiar silhouette, headphones in, hunched over a book, lost in her own world, and blocking out the overwhelm of the city's sounds and sights.

Sylvie approached the front of the table and waved, so she didn't startle Ade.

"Hi." Ade pulled on her ear buds, her face lighting up when she recognized Sylvie.

"Hey, you. Don't you have a home to go to?"

Ade's smile faltered. "I'll get there eventually. I just wanted a warm drink." She gestured to the empty chair beside her. "Will you join me?"

Home beckoned Sylvie. But the fatigue that had weighed so heavily on her shoulders as she walked up to the square had lessened. "Why not? It's Wednesday. We've made it through half the week." She raised her hand to the waiter and ordered a glass of wine. "You got me into some trouble earlier."

Ade's eyes widened in shock. "Me? Why?"

Sylvie grinned. "Nothing to be worried about. I'm just teasing. I had a visit from my boss asking me how I'd been spending my time recently. I had to confess to being a little distracted." There it was. That flutter in the pit of her stomach whenever she spent time with Ade, such an enigma of a person. "You look different today," she said, looking at Ade's asymmetrical jacket, a much more feminine look than Sylvie had ever seen her in before.

"Do I?" Ade looked down at herself.

"You do." Sylvie stayed in the pool of Ade's gaze for a moment longer, unwilling to tear herself away.

"What did you mean about being distracted?" Ade asked.

Sylvie blinked slowly, not yet willing to admit to the depth of disruption that Ade was causing to her usual focus. "I had to cancel a few plans on Monday to take the boat out with you."

"Right." Ade nodded, guilt written on her face.

"Paul was fine with it." Sylvie waved away any further awkwardness. "He was worried about me not meeting book deadlines. But to be honest, it all worked in my favor. Now I have some free periods from next week to get my head down."

Ade mirrored her relief. "That sounds like a decent outcome."

"How was your day?" Sylvie asked, as if it was the most natural thing in the world for them to download their days to one another. It was as if their friendship wasn't in its infancy, and their souls had known each other far longer than each of them was able to articulate.

"One of the best. Checklists at the marine center. And I almost had the place to myself." Ade's eyes shone with satisfaction. "Greg turned up right at the end, but he's no trouble."

"Sounds pretty perfect." Sylvie raised her glass. "Here's to making it to Wednesday."

The mid-week hump didn't seem like such a hill with Ade sitting by her side. Her company buoyed Sylvie's mood, and a contentment settled somewhere inside her stomach.

It was a strange situation in which to find herself, developing a connection with the American PhD student. But she couldn't deny the strength of it. She'd been drawn across the square by a magnetic desire to hear Ade's voice, to observe her static movement, and sit with Ade in her repose.

The force of Sylvie's feelings scared her, but she couldn't do anything about it except dwell in it and watch the evening pass by. She turned the key in her mind to lock away the doubt and rested in the contentment she'd found with Ade. Her worries would keep for another day.

Chapter Eighteen

ADE PULLED AT A thread on her sweater. She'd have to cut it with scissors otherwise the whole thing was going to unravel beneath her busy fingers. Like anything when she got to work, she'd pull and pick until she destroyed it. Steph had bought this sweater for her a few Christmases ago, and she loved it. Its fleece inner was soft enough not to irritate her skin and she'd cut out the tags. She'd air dried it, so it hadn't shrunk an inch, and it hung loose around her waist and armpits.

It wasn't just the sweater that bothered her. She couldn't stop going over the last week. Every time she'd seen Sylvie, her thoughts had jumbled up like she'd been through a washer. Had she said too much the last time they met? Had she been too needy asking her to stay that night? She'd been second-guessing herself for days now, unable to settle at work, restless at home.

She wandered along the beach at a safe distance from the waves breaking against the shoreline. The sun warmed her back, but the breeze was enough to whip up foam at the water's edge. November was gently easing in the autumn air, and she was thankful that the bitterness of the European winter hadn't yet delivered on its promise.

Her phone buzzed, and she removed it from her pocket. "Steph."

"Hi, you. How's it going?"

Ade sat crossed-legged on the sand, hoping she and her sister could talk for a while. "Not too bad. Just enjoying the beach."

"Me too, little sis. I'm back in Barcelona, enjoying the sights and sounds." A fit of giggles interrupted her. "Sorry, that's a new friend."

"A new hook-up?"

"Something like that. Give me one sec." Steph spoke away from the phone. "Okay, now we can talk. That was Emeline. Smokin' hot, God damn. We met in Sitges on the naked beach. It was full of men, except for the two of us."

Ade closed her eyes, wishing she *couldn't* picture things. "I don't need the details."

"But, Ade, you'd love it here."

"I very much doubt that." She wrote the letter "S" in the sand with her finger.

"Anyway, I can't wait to see you. I've missed your bony shoulders to hug." Steph laughed. "I'm heading to you in about a week. We're coming via Perpignan."

"We?"

"Me and Emeline. I just told you about her."

"But you only met a few days ago." Ade sat taller. She'd only just gotten used to the space herself; she didn't want it invaded by some stranger.

"She's gorgeous and yada, yada. Fill in the gaps, honey. We're having amazing, hot sex all over Europe, and she's never been to the South of France, so I said she could come and crash."

"In my studio apartment? We barely had room for the two of us when you were here last time." *No, no, no. No way.*

"We'll work it out. We always do."

The sound of a car horn sounded on the line.

"How're you doing, anyhow? Any more break-in drama?"

Ade took a deep breath of salty air. "No more break-in drama. Work is going fine. I'm—"

"What is it?" Steph's tone grew serious. "Are you worried about something? Tell me. I can help."

"It's nothing. We can talk next week, when you're here. I have to get to work now." She didn't have time for Steph's chaos.

"Okay. Can't wait to see your face." Steph blew a kiss.

By the time Ade reached the marine center, she'd wound herself as tight as a coiled spring about having to share her apartment with Steph and her random new girlfriend. It was just like her twin not to realize what an imposition that would be. Not to mention there was literally no space in the studio. With the two of them sharing the sofa bed, Ade would be relegated to some makeshift cot. What if Emeline, or whatever-her-name-was, was too loud, or too messy?

Swiping her pass at the door, she nodded at the security guard. They hadn't ever talked, but over the past weeks his frown had softened and sometimes he even waved her through. Voices came from the lab, and Ade hesitated. She'd been expecting a shift on her own and didn't have the energy to face anyone else today.

"Don't make a mess; she won't like it." Greg's silhouette appeared in the door frame.

She sighed. There was no going back now. He needed supervising, and her name was on the roster, so she'd be on the hook if anything went wrong with the animals. Plus, she'd been looking forward to seeing the fish all day.

"Hey, Greg." Ade forced a smile. "And Madison. I wasn't expecting so much company."

"I hope you don't mind, but I asked her to join me. She needs extra credit to pass the semester." Greg bit his cheek, looking sheepish.

"Will you sign my paper to say I was here?" Madison asked.

Ade pinched the bridge of her nose, already regretting not turning back. "What paper are you talking about?"

"You know, the little slips of paper the teachers sign to say you've been turning up to stuff. I can't remember what they're called." Madison yawned.

"Attestations," Greg said, butchering the French pronunciation.

"Sure. I can sign you off on this lab time. How long are you two planning to stick around for?"

"As long as you have jobs to do." Greg clapped his hands together, while Madison's shoulders dropped an inch.

"Then let's get to work." Ade pulled up the day's task list and handed them the tablet. "Work together on this. Greg knows the drill, so follow his lead but come and ask me if you're not sure. It's best to double check than risk harming the sea life."

Greg beamed with pride at being given a position of relative seniority in the lab, so Ade left them to it. "Just going to check on my sand dollars." Ade pulled on her gloves, pursing her lips as the latex pulled against every pore on her skin. In all the years she'd been in the labs, she'd never gotten used to the sensation.

Adjusting the dial on the microscope, her cheeks stretched into a huge smile as the six white circles came into focus. "Wow. There you are, you little beauties."

"What's that?" Madison hovered at her shoulder.

Ade took a deep breath. She'd hoped for the solitude to be able to record the progress of the breeding program, but she couldn't pass on the opportunity to teach these kids a little about culturing. "These are sand dollar cultures. You know the skeletons you sometimes find on the beach? All flat and round?" Ade moved so Madison could see for herself. "Take a look inside. They're wrinkly, which means they're doing really well."

"But what is it?"

"A kind of sea urchin. In about eight weeks, it'll have eight arms. Then, for a couple of weeks, they'll all live in the water, and once they receive a signal from an adult, they'll settle on the sand. It's unbelievable, really. They wait for their cue, and then they settle down, usually all together in one big group."

"And we're breeding them here? But they're minuscule. How do you know what you're doing?"

Ade chuckled. "It's not the easiest of marine life to work with, that's for sure. There's a lot of staring into a microscope. Plus, it's almost impossible to tell the males from the females unless they're spawning. They're a real lesson in how gender is socially fabricated."

"Huh." Madison stared into the microscope for a few moments, apparently lost in the tiny specimen of life.

"Are you interested in the breeding program? There's always work to do if you want to get involved?" Ade surprised herself with the invitation. But there was something about Madison's demeanor that reminded her of herself a few years ago: not quite knowing where she fit but finding a peace in the lab.

"I'd like that." Madison looked up above the scope. "Truth is, I'm flunking all the minor subjects I was given."

"You are?" Ade kicked herself for canceling the last student counseling session. She should have known about this already. "What's been going on?"

"I can't keep up with the French language lessons. It's all too fast for me." Her head dropped, and she sniffed. "I missed a rent payment too."

Ade blew her cheeks out. "That sounds like a tough time. What's going on with the rent? Are you having money trouble?"

"No, I just got all confused." Madison wiped her eyes. "It's paid off now. I don't know, it's just too much to handle sometimes."

"Hey, I totally get that. There's a lot to manage when you're somewhere new by yourself." Ade bit her lip, grasping for ideas. What would Steph say? What would Sylvie say? "But you're not alone with it, you know? We're here together."

Madison looked up, her eyes filled with emotion, and smiled.

"How about you and I look over your schedule this afternoon and work out whether anything could be changed with your modules. This year is about enjoying the experience, not wasting your time on credits that won't benefit you in the future."

"I'd like that."

Ade wondered whether she'd said the right thing. She had no real idea what she was doing. She just said what she thought Madison needed in the moment. She snuck a look back at her: long hair tied up in a ponytail, pristine clothes underneath an ill-fitting lab coat. Ade had really overestimated her confidence. Madison was certainly not what she presented to the rest of the world.

Ade chewed her lip. Her head ached from trying to second-guess everyone's feelings and meanings, but this made it ten times worse. Was everyone just presenting their best side all the time? How could she trust her own interpretation when the whole world massaged their appearance to fit in? She had no chance of finding her own place when the rules of the game kept shifting. Would she remain trapped in the bubble of her own making forever? It could be a little lonely in there sometimes.

Chapter Nineteen

SYLVIE STEADIED HER BREATH and rushed into the meeting room. Juggling everything was doing her punctuality no favors. Every seat was already taken, so she pulled a chair from the back and forced her way between a smirking Isa and a sullen Professor Laurier.

Paul opened with a state-of-the-nation style monologue, and Sylvie switched off, tuning in for the rousing finale where he told everyone to work hard and enjoy themselves. She scanned the next items on the agenda: a call for papers for the annual conference, a trip to Paris, and staff well-being.

"Let's move onto the next item. The call for papers," Paul said. "And volunteers to attend the Paris convention."

Sylvie held her hand at shoulder height, aiming for somewhere north of confident but south of desperate.

"Sylvie?" Paul looked in her direction. "Would you be happy to represent the faculty in Paris this year?"

"Absolutely." Her heart raced. A decent speaking opportunity was just what she needed to raise her academic profile.

"Excellent. You'll need to work up a paper in the next couple of weeks."

"No problem at all. I'll have something with you in the next few days." Sylvie sat back, satisfied with the outcome of that item.

Paul scanned the room. "We usually send two people. Any other takers?"

Sylvie poked Isa's thigh sharply. She didn't want one of the elder professors volunteering.

"I'll go with Sylvie," Isa said, rubbing her leg before she glared at Sylvie.

"That settles it. Thank you both. Let's move on. I'm looking for a volunteer to take the lead on the university's well-being program for new staff. The chancellor's team is all over it, and they need a rep from each faculty. Any offers?"

Every tweed jacket in the room visibly shrank into their chairs.

"It wouldn't be too much work for anyone to take on. A couple of corporate meetings and a few follow-up actions, I'm sure." Paul searched for eye contact around the table and landed on an aging lecturer to his left. "Professor Gaultier?"

The slumbering giant made no attempt to reply.

"Antoine?" Paul asked, tapping his enamel pen.

The professor lifted his lidded eyes, his frown creasing further with the disturbance. "I cannot possibly take on any additional duties, Paul. My timetable is creaking with obligations."

Sylvie tsked under her breath. *Something's creaking, but it's not your timetable.* Most of these over-the-hill professors hadn't taught a full week of lectures in their academic lives.

"Sylvie? How about you?" Paul raised his eyebrows. "It would complement the work you're doing with the internationals really nicely."

She counted the male colleagues around the table. Not one of them had been forced to take on additional duties this term. They leaned back into their seats, enjoying the privilege of their position without further expectation or burden.

"Paul, I just took on the Paris convention, and we agreed that my priority should be publishing," she said with as much finality as she could muster, given the audience. Most of her colleagues were past their best, in her opinion, but she was still their junior. She didn't want to attract any criticism or skepticism that she wasn't worthy of her position in the department, and despite the smoke that Paul had blown up her ass last week, there was still a whole crew of the old guard who would rather not have her type around the table.

Paul scratched his receding hairline, clearly clutching at straws and desperate to move onto the next agenda item. "Of course. We did." He braved one more look around the table, with every single pair of eyes averted. Everyone clearly had very important papers to read. "Isabelle, perhaps you and I can discuss your timetable commitments when we next meet? I don't want us to be the only faculty who cannot field anyone. It wouldn't look good."

"Who for?" Isa added, sitting up a little straighter.

"Let's move on," Paul said, his whole demeanor sinking beneath the threat of the encounter.

The remaining items passed while Sylvie and Isa seethed between them. When the last call for business came and went, they stomped to Isa's office for a debrief.

"What a dick." Isa threw her hands into the air. "I despair of this place. If you and I weren't here, they'd get nothing done."

"I can't believe Paul asked me to take even more on when we'd explicitly talked about reducing my timetable. It's like we'd never had that conversation." Sylvie folded her arms in defiance. "I should've told him to go fuck himself."

"You did. Kind of." Isa giggled. "It was pretty clear that you weren't going to roll over."

"What makes me so mad is that those stuffy old guys sit daydreaming, waiting to put their feet up and light cigars." Sylvie stamped her foot. "I'm so sick of us making the only intelligent contribution in those meetings and them taking the credit."

"You know old Gaultier is in a bit of trouble this year," Isa said.

"What do you mean?" Sylvie hadn't heard a sniff of any gossip, but she liked to stay out of the rumor mill.

"His new assistant has made a complaint. Inappropriate behavior." Isa rolled her makeup-heavy eyes. "So predictable. If you give an aging professor a pretty, youthful assistant, of course he's going to leer all over her." She made a vomiting gesture.

Sylvie's stomach churned.

"And you know, they can't ignore stuff like that anymore. It's a major power play."

Sylvie's eyes darted across Isa's face, searching for more meaning than what she'd been given. "I don't get it."

"He's in a major position of power as her de facto supervisor. The woman is saying she had no choice but to go along with it. He invited her to drinks, and she couldn't say no. He asked her to stay late, and she felt obliged. You know the drill."

"I do." A clamminess came over Sylvie. Could Isa see the sweat beading on her top lip? The kernel of dread grew inside her mind, sprouting leaves of worry until they bloomed into a fully articulated spiky thought. Had she put Ade in a similar position? Did Ade feel pressured to spend time with her? Sylvie ran through the list of their encounters, most of them social, or at least extra-curricular. *Merde.* Could she be accused of something inappropriate just like Professor Gaultier?

"Are you okay? You look like you've swallowed an ashtray." Isa lifted the lid to her laptop.

Sylvie shook her head. There was no way that she could confide in Isa about her concerns; she was disgusted enough about Gaultier. "What do you think constitutes a power differential in a relationship?" she asked, dreading the answer but desperate to rationalize her actions.

"Gaultier and his assistant aren't in a relationship. He pulled rank, and she thought she'd lose her position over it."

"Yeah, I get that. But from a feminist theory perspective, I think this is kind of an interesting topic area." Sylvie fudged. "What is it about power? Is it an age gap? Is it a gender thing? I'm intrigued, academically."

Isa took the bait, turning in her swivel chair. "Okay, Professor Girl Power, you want my view? I think age and gender are, without doubt, differentials. But there are plenty of healthy, consensual relationships with that at play. The red flags are when there's one party in control of all the cards. They have a senior position at the workplace, for example. Or they hold some influence."

That didn't make Sylvie feel any better.

"What's going on here? Are you trying to defend Gaultier?"

Sylvie strained every muscle in her face trying to create an impression of ambivalence. "I don't care one way or another what happens to Gaultier or any of the other relics of misogyny still cluttering up the payroll of this institution."

"I completely agree. It's the assistant I feel for. Maybe I should've taken that well-being role and given corporate my honest take on it. We need to advocate for each other."

Relieved to have put Isa off the scent, Sylvie's inner turmoil simmered. She was losing her mind for no reason. Gaultier must have thirty-five years on his young assistant. There was just ten years or so between her and Ade. Plus, she hadn't done anything inappropriate. Bumping into someone and having drinks was hardly a crime. Okay, the optics of staying overnight at Ade's studio weren't great. But Ade was scared and had no one else to turn to. Maybe Sylvie should've reported the incident to Paul, or to someone. "I need to tell you something."

"This better be good, because I'm late for a date," Isa said, retouching her lipstick in the black screen of her phone.

Sylvie doubted herself. "A couple of weeks ago, Ade called me in a bit of a crisis. There'd been an attempted break-in at her apartment. I took her to the police to report it."

"Jesus, I hope she's okay. Sounds scary, poor thing."

Sylvie rubbed her clammy palms on her slacks. "It was unsettling, and she didn't feel comfortable, so she called me."

Isa plucked a glob of clotted mascara from her eyelid. "So you helped translate with the police?"

Sylvie swallowed. "I ended up staying the night."

Isa's freshly painted lashes widened. "I wasn't expecting that, Sylvie."

"I mean. I didn't *stay* the night. Nothing happened. But after what you said about Gaultier, I wanted to tell you. I don't want it to come out later and look like something untoward might have been happening."

Isa laughed. "And you're certain nothing 'untoward' happened?"

"No." Sylvie raised her hands in defense. "She couldn't settle on her own, and I stayed. Before I knew it, the sun was rising. We were both fully clothed."

Isa smirked. "Were you disappointed?"

"Are you serious? We've literally just been talking about the creepy age gap between Gaultier and his assistant. I'm worried that it might look weird that I've been for a couple of drinks with Ade."

"And stayed in her bed." Isa nudged her in the ribs.

"Don't. I already feel bad enough."

"You're hardly three times her age though. And she's not some frail wallflower. I get the impression if Ade didn't want to keep company with you, you'd already know about it."

Sylvie frowned. Was she comparing Gaultier's apples with her pears? Nothing had actually happened between them.

"I'm more intrigued than ever though." Isa tilted her head, glowing with curiosity. "I didn't see this little friendship blossoming between you."

"It's not like that at all. She's a colleague who doesn't know anyone in town." The urge to defend Ade's personality rose as hard as the heat to Sylvie's cheeks. "And she's pretty talkative, when she's relaxed."

Isa laughed. "So you've spent some time together then? Other than the sleepover?"

"You're making fun of me." Sylvie slapped her lightly on the arm. "We've had a couple of drinks, that's all. We don't live that far apart, so we've bumped into each other. Plus, I have to see her for supervision and things."

"Ah, yeah. Because you're her 'supervisor.'" Isa chuckled. "Is that why you've been acting like you've got ants crawling in your pants since I mentioned Gaultier's investigation?"

Sylvie looked at her shoes. "Maybe. I'm overthinking it."

"You sure are. For someone who has simply been welcoming

an international colleague. There are no rules around socializing with colleagues. Look at us: we've become the best of friends this past year."

"I know. I guess I'm worried that someone might look at our circumstances and jump to conclusions."

"Not if there aren't any conclusions to jump to." Isa raised her eyebrow. "Unless you've been jumping in her panties."

"You're terrible." Sylvie stood. "Aren't you late for a date?"

"This is much more fun."

"I doubt that." Sylvie closed the door behind her, shutting out Isa's cackling laughter. She smiled, despite the uneasiness about the situation. Maybe she needed to give Ade some space for a few days. Their paths wouldn't cross unless she made an effort to see her. And why would she do that if they were just colleagues? Because that's all they were. That's all they'd ever be.

Chapter Twenty

"Am I glad to see your face." Steph jumped from the train and pulled her oversized backpack onto her shoulders.

"We have the same face. You see it every morning," Ade said and smiled.

"Not the same thing, honey. Yours comes with that biting sense of humor that I've missed so much." She landed two sloppy kisses on Ade's cheeks. "Miss me?"

"Not really. But I'm glad you're here." Ade looked behind Steph, then turned on her heel. "Where's your friend? What was her name?"

"Emeline? We parted ways in Barcelona." Steph wrinkled her nose. "It's for the best. She was clingy. It became awkward, you know? Plus, you reminded me that the sleeping arrangements would be less than ideal. Best to cut and run while I could."

"You broke up with her because you didn't want to pay for a hotel?"

"When you put it like that, it sounds more like something you would do." Steph swiped playfully at Ade's head. "It wasn't a long-term thing, and we were both well aware of that. I knew you wouldn't really be that cool with an extra house guest."

They strolled up the main street toward the city's Place de la Comédie.

"Let's stop for a coffee here and watch people come and go for a while." Steph set her bag down with a groan. "I've been desperate for a good coffee since dawn."

Ade navigated to her favorite spot on the square away from the bustle of the crowds but with a view of the opera house and the statue of the three angels. She shielded the sun from her eyes, as its rays bounced off the gleaming white marble slab. She caught the waiter making his rounds, ordered for the both of them, and rested her back against the wicker chair.

"Good spot, Ady-baby." Steph observed from behind her oversized sunglasses. "You seem all settled in here. Is it starting to feel like home?"

Why would somewhere she'd been for a mere eight weeks feel like the house in which she'd lived since birth? "Not at all."

"I mean. Do you feel happy here?"

"Yes, of course," Ade said.

"Tell me why, then. I want to hear more." Steph said, crossing her long legs.

"The university campus is clean and easy to navigate once I got used to it. My students are all quite capable and haven't needed too much counseling, which is a relief. Greg is the most enthusiastic, and I even kind of enjoy his company in the lab." Ade drummed her fingers on the table. "The lab shifts are flexible, so I can get as much time as I like in there, and the manager seems to admire my work."

"That's fantastic."

"And then there's Sylvie," said Ade.

Steph raised her eyebrows and grinned. "Sylvie? Tell me about her."

"She's my supervisor. You met at the concert by the church a few weeks ago." Ade's mind rewound to that moment, and a vision of Sylvie's profile in the candlelight filled her vision.

"Of course," Steph said. "I'd forgotten about that."

"She's become a friend. Sort of. She helped me when I had the attempted break-in. She's good to talk to and great to listen to. I've really missed her this week."

"What do you mean?" Steph asked.

"We haven't seen each other. It's unusual. We'd usually bump into each other or catch up on a supervision." Ade folded her arms.

"She sounds like someone you've really connected to."

Ade sat with her sister's assumption and rolled it around her mind. They *had* connected. She didn't want to get into it with Steph: it was her secret for now. Her heart rate spiked at the memory of Sylvie walking across Place Jean Jaurès.

She avoided Steph's glare as their coffee arrived. "Did you like Emeline?" Ade asked.

"Yeah, she was fun to hang out with." Steph tore at a packet of sugar and dumped it into her foam-topped café crème, leaving a dusting of granules in its wake.

"Why did you leave her in Barcelona then?"

Steph rested her head in her palm. "What's all this about? You never ask me about my hook-ups."

"I just wondered whether you'd connected with her, that's all. What it might have been like."

"Okay, precious, let me tell you. I did feel something with Emeline, but it was purely physical. We chatted, for sure, but about nothing in particular. Nothing too deep." Steph shrugged. "I guess that's a connection of its own kind."

"Did you feel comfortable with her? Like you could be yourself?" Ade asked, desperate to understand more about the kind of relationship her slightly older and much wiser sister had known.

Steph frowned, as if she was working out the hidden meaning of the question.

"It's not a trick question." Ade smiled. She'd been told the same so many times.

"I just want to give you an honest answer." Steph sighed. "We didn't know each other for all that long, but I guess I wasn't always myself. I was flirty and hilarious. I was upbeat and chatty. When I was out of sorts or lonely, I didn't tell Emeline because I didn't want to bring the mood down."

Ade had shown Sylvie her most vulnerable self. As the Halloween revelers had paraded around the city in costumes, she'd unmasked, allowing her new friend to see all her fears without a filter. "Do you think Dad and Pops bonded emotionally before they got together?"

"What is this? Some sort of relationship 101 you haven't warned me about?" Steph's brow creased with confusion. "What's going on with you?"

"I just wondered, that's all."

"You don't wonder, Adelaide. You hypothesize and interrogate, and you find the answers. All this meandering around a topic is unnerving me."

Steph was right. Her patterns were way out of character. But she couldn't level with her sister, because she hadn't worked out what was going on inside her head.

"Okay, if we're done on that, let's make a plan for the day." Steph said. "Thanksgiving isn't going to organize itself."

***

Ade pushed a cart into the warehouse-style grocery store, keeping her shades on to avoid the glare of the overhead light. "I already picked up all the basics: butter, eggs, flour, sugar, oil, red wine vinegar." She tapped her earbud back into place to block out the unbearable noise.

"So we should pick up a turkey and herbs a little later in the week, but we could get the dry and canned goods." Steph scanned the overhead signs for clues. "Do they have bake-at-home rolls?"

"They have bakeries on every corner." Ade rolled her eyes. "Who needs to bake at home?"

"Good point. Do you think we'll be able to get canned pumpkin?" Steph asked.

Ade shrugged. "Honestly, it's been really hard to get anything that tastes like it's from home. Even the cheese tastes different over here."

"Different, as in better?"

"Not really." Ade shivered. "It's not what I'm used to."

"What have you been surviving on?" Steph plucked a jar of cinnamon from the shelf.

"Pastries and chicken tenders."

"Jesus, kid. You're impossible sometimes." Steph shook her head and darted down the next aisle.

"It's not my fault that stuff tastes weird." Ade organized their cart like a game of Tetris. "This isn't going to be easy. There's no sign of condensed milk. What are we going to do?" Her shoulders sank. She wanted everything to go to plan.

"We'll just have to tell Dad and Pops that things might feel a little different this year." Steph rubbed her shoulder. "They're coming to see us, not for a perfect Thanksgiving meal."

"I know that. I just wanted things to be the same."

"Ade, we're making a meal for four in your living room-cum-bedroom. Nothing is the same." Steph handed her a jar of cranberries and held her hand. "But we'll all be together, and that's the main thing."

They wandered through the market until the glare of the lights forced Ade to call it a day. Steph packed up the last of the groceries while Ade waited outside on a bench, staring at a patch of cobblestones and counting the number of shoes that stepped across it.

Back at the apartment, she laid on the bed while Steph made them something to eat. She hadn't lied earlier when she'd said she hadn't missed her twin. But now Steph was around, moving in and out of the small kitchenette, it was like an empty part of her had filled in.

"Whatcha thinking about there?" Steph wafted a cloud of steam rising above a boiling pot. "You're miles away."

"I'm right here, thinking about how it's nice to have you around."

"I love that." Steph's face lit up. "You know, you're kind of different."

"What do you mean?" Ade asked.

"You're softer around your edges. Fuzzier. Almost glowing."

Ade wriggled under Steph's gaze. She wasn't aware of being any of those things.

The buzz of an incoming call disturbed them, and Steph dived at her own cell. "Hello?" She nodded excitedly at Ade and fumbled with the speaker button.

"Hey, girls." The crackly voice of Pops filled the studio.

"Pops! Are you here?" Steph beamed.

"We just got to London and checked into our hotel. Your dad and I are pretty wiped."

"Hey, you two. I hope you're behaving yourselves over there. We'll be with you in a few days. Make your beds and polish your shoes." Their dad's deep laughter rang out between them. "Ade, are you there, or has Steph tired you out already?"

"I'm here, Dad. Hey, Pops." Ade scooted closer to the phone, leaning on Steph's shoulder, a warmth radiating around her heart. She'd forgotten how it felt to be surrounded by the people she loved, by the people who loved her so much, no matter what.

"When will you be here?" Steph asked.

Ade tutted. "It's on the calendar." She'd been marking it off until Thanksgiving, looking forward to the reunion of her little family.

"We're going to do a bit of sightseeing here for a couple of days, and we'll be with you on Wednesday. We're flying down south. Your dad didn't want to spend that many hours on the train."

"We just don't know what they're like, Sam," their dad said. "You never know about the quality of the transportation."

Steph laughed. "The trains are pretty good over here, Dad. You don't need to worry."

"Your father does nothing but worry, you know that."

"Not true, Samuel. I worry about the important things in life and if I didn't worry, who knows where we'd all be. Anyhow, we just wanted to check in with you guys. You need us to bring anything with us for Thanksgiving? We managed to sneak a few treats in our luggage, but are you missing any essentials?"

"Actually, we have a whole list of things we can't get over here."

Ade peered at the shelf. "We had an agonizing trip to the market today, and I had to leave because I felt sick."

"Oh, honey, that sounds rough."

Ade imagined the crease of their pops' brow in concern.

"What d'you need out there?"

"We'll send a list. But don't worry too much because we're making do, aren't we, Ade?" Steph shot a stern look in her direction.

"Sure. It's just about us being together." Ade folded her hands.

"Okay, well, shoot over that list, and we'll see what we can do. See you both in a couple of days. Be good. Love you."

"Love you." Steph blew a kiss.

"Bye, Dad. Bye, Pops," they said in unison.

Steph went back to her boiling pot, and Ade relaxed against the comforter, the sound of their dads' voices echoing in her heart. She missed them now they were so close to arriving. The last eight weeks had been pretty lonely. She'd had to paper over a lot of cracks in her ability to build rapport with others.

There really had only been one person she'd clicked with on a meaningful level, someone who she could be herself around, like she was with Steph and her fathers: Sylvie. This week her absence had grown like a nagging doubt. She wasn't used to that. Everything about Sylvie was new and scary. Too scary to interrogate too deeply.

Chapter Twenty-One

SYLVIE SCRIBBLED MONDAY'S DATE on her board and readied herself for the day ahead. Paul still hadn't come through with her reduced timetable, so she faced another jam-packed week of lectures and seminars. It was for the best. Staying busy would keep her mind from wandering.

It had been a fairly easy task to avoid Ade for the week, once she stopped straying into their mutual locations. Just a lick of discipline and a little diary management was all she'd needed. She'd still procrastinated through her book edits for the whole week, but any progress was progress.

But even Isa's midweek excursion to a poetry reading hadn't totally rid her of the sense that her little world had grown quieter without her favorite Californian's commentary. She spent the whole night thinking of how Ade would've loved to have been at the poetry reading too.

Popping open her calendar, she scanned today's agenda. "What is this?"

Ade had requested some time with her this morning. She glanced at the clock. Three minutes to wriggle out of the tentative appointment, which was blinking away, slicing through her peace with its jagged edges. She could hardly say no. That would cause even more trouble, and she'd have to admit to herself that there was something she couldn't face. There was only one way to handle this: be the professional she should've been all along. Keep her distance and definitely no sleepovers.

"Hi there," Ade said softly, announcing her arrival as if she didn't want to disturb Sylvie's train of thought.

All at once, Ade's presence filled the room, flooding Sylvie's senses. Her clothes hung off her strong body with an effortless style, like she hadn't even noticed what she'd put on that morning. But it had all worked out perfectly. Her scent floated in ahead of her, a unique, natural aroma so far away from the synthetic perfumes that made Sylvie gag in the malls.

"You're early." Sylvie cleared her throat and wished she could be more commanding and authoritative.

Ade frowned and flicked the screen of her cell. "No, I don't think so."

"Come on in." Sylvie rubbed her palms. "Please take a seat." Rolling back to a time before they were familiar with each other was going to be much harder than she thought.

"Is everything okay? Maybe now isn't a good time. I saw that you hadn't accepted the invitation I sent."

"No." Sylvie met Ade's eye contact and froze in her gaze for a moment too long. She wasn't going to be able to brush her off like this. Ade was a good person, and she didn't deserve that. "Please, let's talk. I've missed you this past week."

"Me too." Ade fiddled with her cuff. "Steph arrived from Barcelona. We went shopping for Thanksgiving."

"Of course. Are you looking forward to it?"

"Sure. My dads arrive on Wednesday." Ade's expression lit up the room.

"It's wonderful that they're able to make the trip over here." Sylvie loved Ade's obvious excitement.

Ade's smile faded. "Part of me wishes I could've gone home for the holidays. It's not going to be the same here. But Steph keeps reminding me that it's more about us being together than being somewhere specific."

"You Americans are very enthusiastic about this holiday, aren't you?" Sylvie asked.

"It's bigger than Christmas in our house," Ade said. "My dads go crazy for all the traditions. Usually, the whole family joins us for a huge dinner. It's a big deal."

"Must be strange though, having to celebrate away from home. And it's not like we have the same holiday here in France. Most people don't even know about it."

"You mean, the United States' colonial victories aren't in your calendar?" Ade's eyes widened with a sparkle. "Sorry, I shouldn't joke about it. I love the holiday, but its origins are flawed."

"Trust me, we have our own ways of marking our country's questionable role in history." Sylvie chuckled. "I find it fascinating though, how the world continues to honor these historical events through the rose-tinted glasses of modern times, without making more of the unheard voices of history."

"It's all turkey. Hearing untold stories might bring the mood down."

"Exactly." Sylvie bit her lip. She could talk to Ade all day.

"So, you wouldn't want to join us for lunch? With my folks?"

"For Thanksgiving?" Sylvie asked.

"The day after. They'll be here for a few days, and they want to fill their time." Ade blushed and looked to the floor. "Forget I asked."

"I'd love to meet your parents." That sounded wrong. "I mean, it would be lovely to welcome them to the city."

Joy radiated from Ade's face. "That's fantastic. I'd love them to meet you."

"Why?"

"Because they'll see that I'm doing okay out here." Ade nodded.

Sylvie wondered why her presence would validate Ade's success. Sometimes she forgot how young she was. Ade sought the approval of her parents in a way that Sylvie no longer needed. It was another good reason to maintain the professional boundaries between them. So why had she just agreed to a family lunch? That suddenly seemed much more intimate than she'd thought it would be. Sylvie straightened in her chair. "Did you want to go over some work items?"

Ade retrieved her notebook from her bag. "Sure. I'm more or

less up to date with supervision meetings."

"All the students are on track?" Sylvie asked, poised to take any notes.

"As far as I'm aware." Ade fidgeted, as if she was being stretched out of her comfort zone.

"What do they all have planned for Thanksgiving?"

Ade frowned. "I'm not sure."

Sylvie raised her eyebrow. It wasn't that Ade was self-centered, but she could be so blind to the needs of others sometimes. "Might be worth checking in on people to make sure they're not missing their loved ones back home."

Ade studied her notebook. "I guess so. I'd hate to spend Thanksgiving alone."

"Right." Sylvie fought the urge to tip Ade's chin in her direction. "The whole group is away from home, and they might be struggling just like you would be if your sister and your dads hadn't made it here."

Ade withdrew into herself in the way that Sylvie had gotten used to over the past few weeks. She guessed it was Ade's way of digesting and making sense of the world.

"I'd better go. Thanks for your time," Ade said, gathering her things.

Ade took away some of the room's warmth when she left. Even though her impromptu meeting had interrupted Sylvie's morning, it had been a welcome distraction. Left alone, Sylvie busied herself with preparation for classes but continued to drift to the shape of Ade, her closeness, the rise and fall of her voice. Was she ever going to maintain the professional distance she needed to get through the year? Every time Ade was around she melted, drawn ever nearer to her heat. Ade lit a spark inside Sylvie that hadn't flickered in a long time. She enjoyed the warmth of her rekindled desire but feared its unknown depths. Allowing herself to think about Ade was sparking a fire that could rage out of control, its white heat scorching everything in its path.

Chapter Twenty-Two

STEPH BALANCED ON A rickety chair, stringing up the last of the fairy lights against the dormer window. "How about that?" She turned on the garland of bud-shaped bulbs, and it cast an incandescent glow in the hollowed-out frame.

Ade squinted at the lights blurring into one another. She loved the ambience they'd created in her tiny home. "I think it works."

The intercom buzzed from the street level, and Ade jumped. She hadn't yet shaken the fear that came from her uninvited houseguest. But this time, she knew exactly who was waiting at the foot of her stairwell.

"Come on up," Steph hollered down, hanging over the iron railing and stretching to catch a first glimpse of their fathers.

Their heavy footsteps made slow progress up the five stories and by the time they reached the top, they were panting.

"Come here, you two." Their pops set down his bags and grabbed Ade and Steph in his arms, lifting them slightly off the ground. "Have you grown? You seem taller."

It was an old joke, but Steph giggled like a small child, and Ade wriggled out of his reach to bask in his love from a distance. She hugged her dad and kissed him gently on the cheek.

"Hey, you. Missed your little face." He grinned and tapped her on the cheeks. "Now, let me in so I can catch my breath. I need a cardio exam after that stairwell."

"I warned you, Dad. These buildings don't have elevators," said Ade, leading them into her living space.

"I know, honey. But jeez, I had no idea they'd be so tall and skinny. It's like living on the top of Rapunzel's tower in here." Their dad moved toward the dormer to admire the starry sky and the backlit rooftops. "Pretty though, hey?"

"It sure is." Their pops put his strong arm around the shoulder of their dad.

Ade melted a little inside, reminded of the strength of their bond.

"I'm surprised a burglar made it all the way up to this floor." Their dad scrutinized the lock on the front door.

"I would've kicked him all the way back down if I'd been here." Pops' face hardened. "No troubles since though?"

"Nope," Ade said.

"Good thing too, otherwise I'd be bundling you into my suitcase and taking you all the way back to California with me." He poked her playfully in the ribs.

"Now, girls. We got the supplies you asked for, but it sure was tricky to find everything." Her dad placed a heavy bag on her small kitchenette table.

Ade twiddled the ring on her finger.

"Don't fret, honey. Your dad is being dramatic. We got your canned pumpkin." Her pops punched his husband lightly in the arm. "Don't wind her up, Nate. You know, we talked about this." A look passed between them.

Steph bounced on the spot. "So you can see we're working in a really tight kitchen here. But I've cooked the ham already, and I've made something with the green beans on the stove top." She gestured with a flourish that suggested a meal far grander than the one they'd actually managed to prepare.

"Ham? No turkey?" Her dad's lips downturned.

"No can do. It's just not in season here yet." Steph put her hands to her cheeks. "We didn't think you'd be able to fly with a turkey in your carry-on."

Laughter rippled between them.

"It's so good to see you both, truly. We've been rattling around like two old folks without you, haven't we, Nate?"

"Absolutely," their dad said. "Mrs. Steiner was asking about you both just last week."

"She was?" Steph sprinkled salt into a pot. "I miss our chats."

"Her daughter just moved to San Francisco for work. I think she's feeling pretty lonely too."

Ade closed her eyes and pictured Mrs. Steiner's house, just down from theirs. She imagined she was there right now, strolling along the coast and watching a paddle boarder out in the bay.

"What else has been going on?" Steph asked.

"Your dad has been playing more golf than is really necessary." Their pops laughed.

"Not entirely true, Samuel. And I didn't hear you complaining when you had time to finish that model railway of yours in the attic." They bumped shoulders. "Pops has finally completed the money pit of a hobby he started when you girls were three years old. If you're still interested in seeing steam trains rush through fictional villages, then you have a real treat waiting for you at home."

"I can't wait." Steph giggled. "Should we have a grand opening?"

"Oh sure, with a big fancy ribbon?" Pops asked.

"That would all be very well, Stephanie, if we had any idea when you were coming home from your little adventure over here." Dad pursed his lips.

"Don't start with that. I told you, I'll come home when I've finished my itinerary. I still have a few more places to check off."

"Care to share this itinerary?" Dad scratched his head. "From where I'm sitting it looks like you're making it up as you're going along."

"And what's wrong with that? I'm young, and I'm enjoying myself before I have to settle down to forty years of work." Steph said, rubbing flour from her forehead. "You want to help me with this, or just enjoy eating it?"

"Come, sit with me." Taking Ade's arm, Pops led the way to the sofa. "Tell me about what you've been up to here."

She embraced his bulky frame and let go of all the tension

holding her upright. "It's been a fast few weeks. I can't quite believe you're here already."

"It's crept along so slowly for us. The house is empty without you two filling it with your antics." He bopped her on the nose. "Have you made any friends?"

"She's made a special friend, haven't you Ady-baby?" Steph asked from her makeshift chef's station.

"Oh, yeah? Anyone we should hear about or something casual?" Dad asked.

"Ignore her. She's making a big deal is all." Ade stiffened in protest.

"Oh, sure. You've done nothing but talk about Sylvie since I arrived, and I'm the one making something of nothing."

"Sylvie, huh?" Pops nudged her gently in the ribs, his eyes creasing.

"She's a friend. A colleague, really. But she's become a friend." Ade wanted to say that she'd become the best friend she'd ever had. She yearned to describe the easiness they shared together, the fact that she didn't feel all zipped up and tense when she was around. She almost compared the feeling she had with Sylvie to the safety net that her parents provided: that she couldn't fall, however much she stumbled on life's ups and downs.

But that would have all been too much to tell them in the little room they were all cooped up in. Her body ached, and she flapped her hands to expel the awkwardness trapped inside.

"I'd like to meet your friend. Is she coming out to dinner while we're here?" Pops asked.

"Actually, she is. I already invited her."

"Wonderful. And anyone else we should meet?" asked Dad.

She shrugged. There wasn't anyone else special enough to introduce to her parents. "No one, really."

"How's the actual job going?" Dad took a seat opposite her.

Ade breathed deep into her lungs, steadying herself. "It was a little tricky to begin with, but I've been given free rein at the center, so it's all good."

"What center?"

"At the marine center. You know, lab time: shifts to take care of the animals."

"Nate, we talked about this." Pops' warning tone made Ade sit up straight.

"I know we talked, but I'm interested in the progress our daughter is making. We didn't send her all the way across the world to sit with more animals and not make something of this opportunity."

"Dad, do we really have to get into all this right now?" Steph poked her head above a steaming tray. "It's Thanksgiving. We could be thankful for what we have this year."

"I'm plenty thankful, Stephanie. I just want to make sure your sister is grateful for the chances she's getting. Most people would give their right arm to get a job at a university in Europe."

"I am thankful, Dad," Ade whispered, not certain how he needed her to demonstrate her gratitude.

"Sounds like you've slipped into the same routines as back home: plenty of solo lab time and no time to carve out a career."

"Actually, I've caught the eye of the center director, and he's been pretty impressed with me."

"That's great, honey," Pops said, squeezing her arm. "Tell us more." He glared at their dad.

"He said I was a natural, and there might be a job opening later in the year."

Their dad sat taller, raising his eyebrow. "Anything specific?"

Ade froze, familiar with his pattern of questioning: she'd fail to come up with the answer he wanted, and he'd get frustrated. Then Pops would get in the middle of them, and everyone would end up upset.

"Ade? Has the guy said what this opportunity might be?"

Steph stepped forward. "Dad—"

"Stephanie, I'm catching up with your sister. You don't need to get involved."

Steph pulled a face, and Ade stifled her laughter. "He said something about maternity cover. I don't know. I need to talk to him more about it."

"You need a plan, Adelaide. You can't keep floating around like this and expecting to get paid for staring at marine life. You want to work in a pet store, be my guest, but don't expect me to keep bank-rolling your PhD."

"Nate, that's enough." Pops stood in between them. "Your father's still jet lagged, honey."

"No, Sam. The girls need some home truths. We've already spent several thousand dollars on this gap year. Stephanie should be making her way home to start her nursing internship, and Adelaide should be a whole lot clearer than she is about what she's going to do when this year's out."

"Oh, now I'm involved?" Steph put her hands on her hips. "I'll make my way back home soon enough. That internship is open for me when I'm ready to take it."

Ade blew a big breath, thankful for Steph taking the heat of the interrogation.

"Let's change the subject," Pops said, running his hand over the table decorations they'd laid out earlier that day. "Did you make these, girls?"

"We did." Ade smiled, recalling the calming motion of folding the paper into shapes. "I'm glad you're here, Pops."

"Me too, baby." He wrapped his arms around her and kissed the top of her head, just like he'd done every day since she could remember.

Both her parents worried about her in different ways. Her dad fretted for her future and what she'd make of it. Her pops wanted her to be comfortable in her own skin, getting through the day with the least amount of friction with the world. He bumped along at her side through every awkward interaction. It had been that way forever.

With her fathers in the room, it was like Ade had the bumpers on at the bowling alley. Safe to err from the path, knowing they'd guide her back on track today, tomorrow and for the days to come.

She just hoped that one day she could be her own guide rails. That she could make her own way. Because right now, that wasn't certain. If this year abroad had already shown her one thing, it was that being alone wasn't all it was cracked up to be. But sitting in the closeness of her fathers and sister, she couldn't imagine a future where she didn't depend on them.

Chapter Twenty-Three

SYLVIE CHECKED HER LIPSTICK in the reflection of Isa's sunglasses. "I'm already running behind."

"Just drink your coffee." Isa pouted back. "You can be fashionably late. They're Americans, they'll just think you're being European or something."

"But I don't want to let Ade down."

"I don't know why you agreed to go along with the plans at all. The last time we talked, you were going to keep your distance and safeguard your reputation." Isa gave Sylvie a wide grin. "That didn't last too long," she whispered theatrically.

Sylvie had been over this in her own mind but had been unable to lock down her feelings for Ade. Putting her in a professional box had failed miserably. Sylvie deserved a little pleasure, and Ade's friendship brought just that, as well as a lightness to her day, a gladness in her heart. She couldn't explain it all to Isa, but she knew it deep down. Ade was a friend. Maybe even more than that.

Sylvie had stalled her response to Ade's invitation just long enough to witness the disappointment spread in Ade's face and body. Her shoulders sank, her lips turned down. Her gaze fell to her feet. Sylvie didn't want to be the person that made Ade sad. She wanted to be someone who lifted her spirits, made her confident in the world, spread happiness in her soul and body.

"Earth to Sylvie?" Isa nudged her in the ribs. "You're miles away."

"I'm sorry. I was just thinking."

"About Ade, no doubt."

There was no point in lying. "I was thinking about whether to take a gift. For her dads. Do you swap gifts on Thanksgiving?"

"Wow. Be careful, sister. You do not want to fall in deep with this one. She'll be gone by the end of the year."

"I don't know what you mean." Sylvie shrugged. "I was mulling over the social graces of the situation. It's a perfectly reasonable question."

"Then why are you blushing?" Isa asked, smirking.

"Because it's still unseasonably warm for November." Sylvie gathered her bag. "I'd better hurry. Will you settle the bill for us? My treat next time."

"Of course."

Sylvie kissed Isa's cheeks. Walking away, the second thoughts she'd been entertaining all week boomeranged between her ears. Why was she going to lunch with Ade and her folks? Was it going to be weird?

She twisted and turned through the city's old town maze of streets. Christmas trees had started to appear suspended high in the air from tall buildings and at crossroads. She admired the precision of the red ribbons, tied at the ends of the branches. She loved this time of year, the coziness of the warm fires and the generous season of gift-giving. Sylvie had never experienced Thanksgiving but, weaving her way to the restaurant she'd helped Ade pick out, she channeled her most festive feelings for the occasion.

As she approached, she could see that the Poole family had already taken their places at the table by the window. Stephanie and Ade sat together, strikingly indistinguishable, except for the length of their fiery hair. Sylvie observed the scene for a moment, as if it were a large tableau at a gallery. The father figures appeared strong and heavy-set, protective of their offspring like the alpha males of the herd. One of them gazed lovingly at Ade and pulled her into an embrace. Ade appeared to freeze for a second, then she melted into the hug. Steph threw her head back in a hearty laugh that Sylvie couldn't hear but that reverberated in the deep chambers of her fast-beating heart.

Ade's demeanor softened in the family portrait. She maintained bold eye contact for longer than Sylvie had ever seen before. Her chin lifted higher, and her hands moved around as she spoke.

Smiling, unwilling to tear herself away, Sylvie hesitated a moment too long; Ade looked out the window, and her eyes fixed on Sylvie as if she'd called to her. Ade gave her a beaming smile, and Sylvie smiled in response. Her stomach flipped at the simplicity of their mirrored exchange. Why did it feel anything but ordinary? Unable to delay any longer, Sylvie strode through the doors and left her coat with the waiter.

"Hey, you." Ade rose in her chair to deliver three kisses in a row. "Dad, Pops, this is my friend, Sylvie."

"I understand that's the accepted greeting in this part of France, Sylvie, but I hope you don't mind something as reserved as a handshake." The shorter man rose from the table first, extending his hand. "I'm Nate, Adelaide and Stephanie's father."

"Or as we like to call him, Dad." Steph pulled Sylvie into a hug. "Good to see you again. We met so briefly at that church thing."

"Nice to meet you, Sylvie. Ade's been telling us a little about you and the work you do at the university." The taller man smiled and opened his arms wide, every part of his being extending the warmest welcome around their family table. "I'm Sam, or as the girls call me, Pops."

"I'm so pleased to meet you all. Welcome to France." Sylvie took the only available space around the table and adjusted her cutlery. Nerves fluttered in her chest, and she sought out the wine waiter to fill her empty glass.

"We're very pleased to be here. We couldn't miss Thanksgiving with the girls," Nate said.

"So we decided to make a huge trip of it." Sam placed his hand over his husband's. "We flew into London and had a couple of days there. From here, we're going to Florence and Venice, and then we're planning to travel for six weeks until we meet the girls for their birthday in January."

"A grand tour?" Sylvie raised her glass. "What a wonderful idea."

"Yep," Sam said. "Plus, I have a big birthday coming up, and Nate always promised me a European vacation. We just never quite found the time before now. I'm even toying with the idea of finishing the trip somewhere warm and super indulgent. Maybe Morocco or somewhere." He winked at Sylvie. "Don't tell anyone."

"See, we've done you a favor, Dad." Steph tore off a piece of baguette. "Venice is on my list too. Any tips, Sylvie? Have you been?"

"I have, and it's a wonderful city. Don't go in the summer: too busy, and it stinks."

Sam gave a belly laugh. "What do you mean?"

"The canals. They smell terrible in the summer months. It's best avoided."

"You okay there, Ade?" Sam focused on his other daughter, his brow furrowing.

"Sure." Ade shifted in her seat.

She'd lost some of the ease that Sylvie had seen through the window. Sylvie touched Ade's arm.

"I'm just taking it all in," Ade said.

"So, tell me about your role at the university, Sylvie. Ade has given us scant details, but I want to hear more." Nate placed his elbows on the white linen and interlocked his fingers.

Sylvie could see the resemblance between him and Ade in the slight twist of his smile and the furrow of his brow. But his hard outer shell was nothing like his daughter's. She was soft and fragile, where he seemed bold and unbreakable.

"Well, I assume Ade's told you I'm a professor of feminism."

"She sure has. What an interesting area of research." Sam unfolded his napkin into his lap.

"Are you published?" Nate asked, ripping a piece of bread in two and maintaining intense eye contact.

Sylvie sipped her red wine. "I am. Several times. I came to

Montpellier to work on my fifth book."

That earned a nod from Nate and a high-five from Sam.

"Good job. Nate here is also an academic. I don't know if you could tell?" Sam poked his husband in the ribs. "He tends to take life pretty seriously."

"As you can see, Sylvie, my family keeps me pretty grounded." Nate smiled, a genuine warmth spread to his cheeks and eyes as he regarded the people around the table. "They don't tend to let me get above my station."

"What's your field, Professor Poole?" She guessed at his title.

"Oh, there's no need for formalities, please." He held his palms up. "And either way, I'm not a Poole. We gave the girls Sam's last name when they were born. I kept mine. It's Ashford."

"He's into psychology and social habits. Not that you'd know. He can't read a room that well." Steph made a face at her dad and giggled into her wine glass.

"My daughters haven't really ever paid attention when I explain what I do for a living. It's nice to be lunching with a fellow academic."

"Ade is working on her doctorate though." Sylvie attempted to draw Ade into the conversation. "You two must love a late-night chat about the contrasts between the human and animal societies?"

Ade blinked, leaving Sylvie to fill in the gaps.

"Adelaide is more of a thinker than a talker. But we love her for it." Nate leaned back as the entrées were brought to the table.

Sylvie had seen that part of Ade. But she'd also seen Ade light up with ideas about the world.

"She's always been our little angel, haven't you?" Sam cupped Ade's chin, and she wriggled away. "Steph came out screaming the house down, but Adelaide had us a little worried."

Sylvie had gathered the bare bones of this story from what Ade had already told her. But she was intrigued to hear it from her fathers' perspective. She glanced at Ade for a hint of permission.

Ade raised her eyebrow. "See, I told you."

"You must've been so worried," Sylvie said.

"Oh, we were beside ourselves. I mean, Professor Control Freak over there doesn't like to hand over the reins for many things at all." Sam gestured at Nate. "And there we were, watching the birth of our daughters with our tongues tied and our hands behind our backs. It was twenty-four years ago, but it feels like yesterday when I think about it."

"Me too." Nate huffed. "Most stressful night of my life."

"And you haven't had a good night's sleep since, hey, Dad?" Steph raised her glass in her own honor. "To me and Ady-baby."

Sylvie chuckled. "Ady-baby?"

"They call me that because I'm the baby of the family." Ade rolled her eyes. "I try to ignore them most of the time."

"There's no getting away from us." Steph flashed a grin at Sylvie.

The twin thing was rather disconcerting. Steph had the same face as Ade, but she was so different in every other way.

"We just like to look after our little one, that's all." Sam put his arm around Ade and squeezed her shoulder.

"Thanks, Pops. I'm doing okay over here though."

"What do you think, Sylvie? Is Ade doing well at the university?" Nate asked.

"Definitely. Her group of students is thriving, and she's carved out quite a reputation at the lab."

"Ah, yes. Always at the lab." Nate crossed his knife and fork over on his plate.

"Not everyone has an eye for detail and a natural way with the animals like Ade." Sylvie wanted to tell Nate that he should be proud of his daughter and that, despite every cell in her body telling her to flee, she remained and got the job done. Instead, she smiled, not wishing to cause a scene. Under the table, she shifted her thigh and made the slightest of contact with Ade's. The thrill raced through her entire body, making her cheeks flush with heat. "Nice wine."

"It's a lovely bottle," Sam said, nodding. "A real treat for a Thanksgiving week."

The slate November day looked like someone had switched the sun off. But inside, delighting in the warm and welcoming coziness of this little troop, doubt grew inside Sylvie. Why did being this close to Ade feel so good but so hopeless? Isa was right: within a few short months, she'd be bouncing back home across the Atlantic, back into the bosom of this wonderful family. And Sylvie would be left fighting fires in the corridors and clawing her way to some sort of promotion. She couldn't deny her friendship with Ade had been an unexpected delight this year. Just as Ade would say: she should stay in the moment and enjoy it. So why did the anticipatory grief for Ade's absence weigh so heavily? Sylvie had seen many friends come and go in the past. Ade would be no different. But she was different. Sylvie's fondness of Ade had taken root. When she pulled herself away at the end of the season, Ade would leave a gaping hole.

Chapter Twenty-Four

ADE STEPPED ONTO THE viewing platform with a tremor of vertigo threatening to eject the insides of her stomach.

Her pops slipped his arm around her shoulder. "Can you believe this view?"

Ade had never seen anything so ancient. A Roman viaduct stretched across the river and beyond. She and her pops teetered on the left bank, almost hidden in the evergreen trees and vegetation. Her dad and Steph had walked on ahead, eager to get their bearings at the historic spot and find a decent place for lunch.

Ade breathed in the cool air and crunched the bed of golden leaves with her boots. It was the first time she'd ventured out of the city since she'd gotten there. Her folks had insisted on seeing some sights, so she'd enlisted Sylvie's help to put together a shortlist. The Roman architecture of the neighboring city of Nîmes had peaked both her fathers' interest.

Ade had worked out that renting a car would be much less traumatic than navigating the train, bus, and God-knows-what-else. But even that had come with a sunrise alarm clock and then motion sickness for most of the journey. Only now, warmed by the low-hanging sun, had the nausea subsided, leaving in its wake a nervous anxiety that followed Ade into most unusual circumstances.

"You okay, baby?" Her pops nudged her shoulder gently.

"Sure."

"You know, I'm real proud of you for making this happen."

Ade was grateful that he continued to look out beyond the viaduct's tall arches. Eye contact would've tipped her over the edge. "What do you mean, Pops?"

"This whole thing can't be easy for you. Moving abroad on your own, settling into a new job, and taking care of the younger students. It's a big deal. Your dad and I know that."

She stayed silent because he hadn't requested any kind of response.

"Your dad..." Her pops kicked at the loose ground. "He worries about you. Sometimes it comes out less caring than it really is. You know he loves you though, don't you?"

"Of course." She'd never questioned her parents' love. "I don't know whether I'm ever going to live up to his expectations though. He has it all worked out, and I just don't feel that way most of the time."

Her pops nodded. "Dad likes things to be neat, tidy, and all dressed in a bow. When things are messy, he feels out of control. He's like you in so many ways." He blinked at sunshine. "You know, like when you feel worried about something, and it's like your body can't settle. Like you have ants crawling all over you."

"Something like that, yeah."

"Your dad gets unsettled sometimes, just like that. When you were little, he couldn't handle the chaos. Everything upside down in the house, routines all over the place, not knowing whether one or both of you would sleep through the night or cause another drama."

"That was then. Why is he so hellbent on controlling our lives now and having us both back home?"

"Well, he misses you desperately, for starters. And he prefers everything pinned down and buttoned-up. He needs to know you're safe, now and in the future."

"But the future doesn't matter much if we're not happy right now." Ade picked a browning leaf from a tree and crumbled it between her fingers.

Her pops chuckled. "I know, I know. You and I like to live here in the moment. But we can only do that because your dad has been looking out for us the whole time. He's had his eye on the what happens next, giving us a roof above our heads, a college fund, money for traveling the world. You think that would've all been possible if it weren't for him showing his love in the only way he knows how?"

Ade had never considered her father's love language in any detail. Pops was for hugs and kisses, while Dad was for permission and protocols. This shed a whole new light on her dad's parenting style.

"Let's go find them, honey." Her pops led the way out of the bracken, and they strolled along the river bank.

Ade contemplated what she might do after this year was up. She'd been forced into it, but in the last few weeks, she'd somehow broken free of the loop she'd been stuck in. She could imagine things beyond this year and maybe even think about that job at the marine center. Or about sticking around for a little while and enjoying the summer with Sylvie.

She stubbed her boot on a rock sticking up from the verge. "Ouch."

"Deep in your thoughts there, kiddo?" He tsked. "You hurt yourself?"

A nostalgic warmth filled her to the brim as a memory flooded every one of her senses: her pops kneeling at her feet, dusting off a graze when she'd fallen from her first bike. The smell of the grass from her scratched hands. His voice just as soft and tender now as it had been all those years ago. "I'm fine. Just a little distracted." Ade squinted into the distance for any signs of her sister and Dad. "Where are those two? They should've looped back toward us by now with a plan."

"You know them. Your dad will have found an interpretation board of Roman artifacts to memorize. He'll entertain us all afternoon and evening with his facts and figures." Her pops pointed at two figures leaning over the viaduct, waving enthusiastically. He cupped his hands around his mouth. "Hey, you two."

Ade's dad gave half a salute in the distance, while Steph waved like she was on a landing strip.

As Ade was pulled toward the other half of her family like the magnetic north, she couldn't help but wonder what Sylvie was up to. She would've loved for her to have joined them on their day trip, if only to fill in the gaps in both her local and historical knowledge.

But it was enough that she'd spared time for a family lunch. Once they'd gotten over her dad's interrogation of her academic credentials, both her parents had shown her a warm welcome, and Ade loved them for it. As for Sylvie, she'd been perfect. Sophisticated, unfazed, confident. Everything that Ade wasn't. Sylvie's ease with the world smoothed over Ade's flaws like a polishing cloth, and Ade was better for it. Sylvie celebrated her difference like it was a good thing, but it was hard to believe someone could see how she fit with the world, when she felt like a jigsaw piece in the wrong box most of the time.

***

Steph raised a glass. "Today was so much fun. But I'm glad that Dad and Pops went back to their hotel and left us to it. We haven't been able to hit the bars in forever."

"It hasn't been forever. It's been weeks." Ade crossed her arms.

"You know what I mean, know-it-all." Steph flashed her big grin.

Given the choice, Ade would've retreated back to her dads' hotel room for a cup of cocoa and an early night, but Steph had been verbally and physically persuasive, practically dragging Ade into the old town for early drinks. She could only hope that they wouldn't be going onto another bar.

"You had a good few days?" Steph asked, picking out the umbrella in her glass.

"I really did. It's been great to see Dad and Pops."

"I think so too." Steph circled the rim of her glass. "You and Dad seem to be getting on better this afternoon."

"What do you mean?"

Steph shrugged. "You just seemed less prickly with him is all."

Ade mirrored the gesture. "Pops told me he was just worried about us both."

"He needn't worry about me. I've got my job all wrapped up for me when I get back. I just need to wring a little more fun from this trip before I head home and start adulting for real."

"At least you have a job to go back to." Ade stirred her Diet Coke with a straw.

"Don't start. You're finishing your PhD when you get back. Dad wouldn't cut you off."

"And what if I wanted to stay?"

"What the fuck?" Steph coughed and held her chest. "Where'd that come from?"

"I don't know, really. I just keep going over that casual job offer at the center. I have people here now—"

"You have one person: Sylvie." Steph tipped her head back and laughed. "Is that what's got you all worked up?"

Ade closed her eyes, wanting to form the most accurate answer possible. "Maybe it is."

"Wow. I was not expecting that, little sister." Steph smiled like some kind of proud godmother. "Then you have to do what your heart wants. Is it your heart?"

Ade froze. She had no idea where the idea had come from. It had entered her head and slipped from her lips. But had it come via her heart? It seemed ridiculous to think that. "I'm confused now. All I know is that I feel more comfortable here with Sylvie, in the real world. I'm more myself than I ever felt back home. That's why I retreated to the lab most days: to avoid people and get away from the endless interactions."

Steph turned her around and gripped her shoulders. "I love Sylvie. She's fantastic and I'm really pleased you've found a friend in her. But it might be that you're growing in confidence all by yourself. Try talking to some other people. See how that makes you feel." Steph looked around the bar. "There's a couple of folks over there; let's go hang out."

Dread collected in Ade's gut. She didn't want to talk to strangers. She'd had enough interactions since she'd arrived in Montpellier to know that her entire personality hadn't morphed into something more neurotypical. It was Sylvie who brought out the most relaxed, unmasked version of herself. If Steph couldn't see that yet, then so be it. But she knew it, here in her heart.

Chapter Twenty-Five

THE COOL AIR RUSHED at Sylvie's cheeks as she disembarked the high-speed train at the Gare de Lyon. "Welcome to Paris." She grinned at Isa and took her duffel bag.

"Delighted to be here, especially with a local to show me the best sights and sounds." Isa made a jazz hand motion. She'd made it clear for the past three hours that dragging herself all the way north on the train was a chore. "Let's get this over with."

"It will be fun, I promise. I've managed to squeeze in some things to keep you entertained beyond the conference." Nerves fluttered in Sylvie's stomach. "But first, I need to get my speech over with."

"You have nothing to worry about. You know your subject inside out. And you're a natural public speaker; people follow your every word."

"That may be so. But it doesn't mean I love every moment." Sylvie had overprepared. She'd rewritten the paper so many times she'd lost count. And she'd practiced her opening in the mirror for two hours last night.

"Then why put yourself through it?" Isa asked.

Sylvie had churned over that question all night. Because she'd never get that promotion if the board didn't take her work seriously. "I need the kudos."

"But you do this kind of stuff in your sleep. What's really eating at you?" Isa asked as they made their way to the line of taxis.

Sylvie shrugged. "The pressure's getting to me. There was a time when I would turn up, give a talk on my latest topic of interest, and think nothing more of it. Now it feels like my very position depends on how many stars the audience gives me in their feedback."

"Damn those surveys." Isa groaned. "They should measure us by how many students keep coming to our lectures. We're outranking all the old fucks by three-fold this semester."

"True. And we cost a third as much, no doubt." Sylvie gazed out of the window as the streets of Paris sped by. Nothing had changed since her last visit almost a year ago. The same drab lines of shops suddenly burst into a fit of sophistication. Its people hurried along, draped in style and confidence. Even the sky's shade of steel dripped with class.

"Do you miss it?" Isa asked.

"A little." Sylvie's lips twitched. "Less these days."

"Well, that's a relief." Isa turned to face her in the back seat. "Anything to do with our recent addition at the faculty? A taste of the USA?"

Sylvie stared. "Must you tease me for the whole trip?"

"I can't help but be intrigued. Surely you don't hold that against me."

"I don't." Sylvie said.

"So how was it?" Isa wiggled her eyebrows.

"Lovely. Ade's family is a delight to be around. One of her fathers is a little intense, but he means well."

"I can't believe you've met the parents. Serious business."

"Don't make more of it than it is. If your parents were in town, I'd meet them too." Sylvie hoped the brush-off would work. Deep down, she'd loved hearing about Ade's roots and seeing a different part of her.

"You can kid yourself all you like. I know that look."

"We're here," Sylvie said, grateful for the chance to change the subject. "Let's check in before we head out somewhere for dinner."

"Of course."

***

"I bombed. You know it. I know it." Sylvie sank further into the pit of her self-pity with every step.

"You didn't bomb." Isa sped up to keep pace as they marched along the bank of the Seine.

Sylvie pulled her scarf tighter, annoyed that winter had started to show its face. Not that she'd admit it, but there was something to be said about the mild temperatures of the south.

"I witnessed the entire thing. You could hear a pin drop while you were speaking." Isa nudged her elbow.

"It wasn't the speech. It was the questions." Sylvie stomped her heel.

"You've got to admit; it was a fair question from the crowd. Feminism really has moved on since the days of Woolf and de Beauvoir."

"You think I don't know that? That's the entire premise of my book. I've spent my professional life explaining this." Sylvie put her head in her hands. "Let's get on the boat."

The water taxi approached the dock, and they joined the back of the queue.

"Thank God, there's a bar." It was a little early, but Sylvie needed to take the edge off her nerves. "I'll get the drinks while you get a seat. Don't venture outside: that's just for tourists."

Isa glanced at her watch. "Why not? I'll have a Kir."

Sylvie bought their drinks and returned from the bar. She stepped over several backpacks, taking care not to spill the filled glasses, and collapsed into a low seat.

"You know what I didn't grasp?" Isa asked. "Why that woman back at the conference was so angry."

Sylvie raised her eyebrow. "I think they'd prefer 'person' rather than 'woman.' That was the point. They felt that historical feminism didn't represent the whole story. It's too narrowly focused on the gender construct of 'being a woman.'" She sighed. "I get it. I do. So much of the old narrative is about protecting women against the prejudices of men. But it's much more nuanced than that. Now traditional theory is being weaponized by some groups to attack other queer people."

"Yeah, I guess."

"Not in my name," Sylvie said, squeezing her hands together with the frustration of not getting her point across well enough back at the conference. "You know, Ade would've totally gotten where that delegate was coming from. She's really opened up my eyes to the flawed binary."

"In what way? Is Ade non-binary?"

"She's whatever she wants to be." Sylvie swirled her drink, smiling to herself at Ade's unique, mysterious magnetism. "I like that in a way I never expected to."

"She's never mentioned it." Isa's brow furrowed.

"I guess it's easier to let these things go than address them head on. Ade doesn't like to attract conflict." Sylvie gulped her flavored wine.

"But why are people using old theory to create even more prejudice?" Isa asked. "I don't know why everyone just can't support each other, whatever their identity."

Sylvie closed her eyes, allowing the boat's rocking motion to calm her. "I don't know. Older women, many of them lesbian, fought long and hard for women's rights. I guess they see themselves and their hard-fought identity being diluted by a kaleidoscope of genders." She coughed. "I don't agree with it. I think it's flawed and wrong. But having digested a lot of feminist theory, I can see why people are pissed off sometimes. And misinformed."

"Are you feeling better?"

"About my speech? I suppose so. But it doesn't make me feel better about the world. What the fuck is wrong with people?"

"I don't think we're going to fix that this evening." Isa tilted her head. "But I'll allow you to escort me somewhere special so we can take our minds off it."

"Deal." Sylvie sank into the seat and watched the Parisian landmarks float by. "I'm sorry that I'm being such terrible company."

"It's no big deal. To be honest, you've been out of sorts for a while now. I thought it might be just work stuff, but you seem to be turning yourself inside out with this Ade business. What is it with you and her?"

Sylvie couldn't find the words to explain how she was feeling. She'd gotten far too close to her new colleague than she ever should have, and her heart ached.

"I really like her," Sylvie said, accepting that honesty might be the best option.

"My God, we've had a breakthrough." Isa's laugh rattled through the hull of the boat, attracting the attention of the passing tourists.

"Shh." Sylvie waved her hands, trying to temper her reaction. "What do you mean?"

"I mean, I'm glad we can finally have a proper conversation about it. It's been so painfully obvious to anyone who's been around you the past couple of months."

"It has?" Sylvie shrank. That stung. She'd been so convinced in her performance that even when she doubted herself, she never thought anyone else would see her true feelings. "Do you think Ade knows?"

"Unless she lives under a rock, it's pretty clear that you have a thing for her." Isa's brow furrowed. "Except, she is kind of oblivious to even the most basic of vibes."

"Oh God, yeah. She needs things completely spelled out. No doubt." Sylvie laughed, her body aching with a magical blend of pride, intrigue, fear, and lust for her new friend. "I think that gives me an edge."

"An edge on what? Are you trying to hide this from her?" Isa asked.

"Well, yeah, of course. It would be extremely awkward if it became a thing between us."

Isa looked baffled. "Would it?"

"Absolutely." Sylvie exhaled, growing impatient with Isa's questions.

"What makes you think it would be a negative thing?"

Sylvie fell silent. She didn't know. But it couldn't be anything, could it? She blinked away the remnants of last night's fantasy: the dream of holding Ade's hand, touching her cheek.

"Sylvie? Why would it be a disaster if something happened between you two?" Isa asked.

"It wouldn't work. I'm practically her boss while she's here. She's only in town for a year. It'll be over before it starts."

"You're writing you both off? Isn't that a little presumptuous given Ade hasn't had a say in this?" Isa shot her a challenging stare. "And don't give me all of that 'boss' and 'employee' bullshit. We both know that's not what this is."

Sylvie sighed. "We're almost at our stop."

"Have you ever had a proper relationship?" Isa asked.

The answer was a simple no. Sylvie had never invested herself in another person. She hadn't ever found anyone worth giving up her time, her energy, her brain power, and her heart for. "You know the answer to that." Sylvie stiffened, not wanting to rake over her failure to truly open up to another person. Ever.

"Indulge me."

Sylvie stood, ready to disembark. "No, I haven't ever had a proper relationship. You think that means something? You think that's the key to unlocking my heart?"

"I think that you admitting you've never unlocked your heart for someone is a step in the right direction," Isa said. "I was talking about your pants."

"Don't be crude." Sylvie laughed. "I'm scared that she doesn't feel the same way. It'll all fizzle out in the end. Or my heart will be broken when she goes back to California. It all takes up too much of my time when I have a book to write and classes to teach."

"That's real progress." Isa folded her arms with satisfaction.

Why did the burden of Sylvie's feelings continue to grow heavier? The noose of unexplained emotions tightened around her collar. She couldn't articulate this to herself, never mind Ade. The whole thing was becoming impossible and messy. Sylvie needed a simple life and time to focus on her work. Distractions of the heart were a waste of time and energy.

Chapter Twenty-Six

MOISTURE POOLED AT ADE'S armpits. This afternoon was sure to test all her new people skills. Her counseling sessions had been dwindling for the last few weeks while the students were getting their heads around assignments and deadlines. But as the end of term crept up on them all, a sense of panic had set in. Now she had a line of people waiting to see her.

"I don't know what to do," Madison said, rushing into the room.

"About what?" Ade rubbed at her hair and gripped her forehead, the glare from the strip lighting shining too bright for her brain to function.

"Everything. I just can't handle any of it."

Ade tracked back to their previous conversation, joining the dots in a beat. "We talked about lightening your timetable last week. Did you manage to discuss it with any of your tutors?"

Madison huffed and threw her bag on the floor. "I don't think we're on the same wavelength. When I suggested it after French Lit on Monday, he looked at me like I was crazy."

Ade suspected that the quality of Madison's French or her complete reluctance to speak the language might have played a part in her teacher's resistance.

"Ade, I don't think I'm going to be able to pass this semester." Madison's tone grew serious, and her lip trembled. "Will I be sent home?"

No crying. Ade could absolutely not deal with tears right now. The buzz of the overhead light grew louder. She glanced up at the restless line of people waiting at the door. "Listen, this semester is no big deal. Just make it up when you come back after the holidays."

"But the attentions or whatever the f–"

"The attestations?" Ade squinted at Madison. For some reason, every student had to have proof that they'd been attending seminars and lectures. "That's a simple signature. Just ask your tutors to autograph your slips next time you have class."

Madison's jaw dropped, and tears sprang to her eyes. "That's the thing. They won't know who I am. I haven't been attending many classes."

This was worse than Ade expected. Madison clearly hadn't been showing up for quite some time, and there was no way any teacher worth their salt would sign a declaration of attendance when there was no sign of willingness.

"What can I do?" Madison asked, clearly expecting all the answers.

"Hey, are you going to take the whole damn hour, Madison?" Scott called from the hallway.

"Yeah, some of us need some real help here," another student said.

A cluster of thoughts circled in Ade's busy mind, and she couldn't choose between them. She rubbed at her temple, desperate to slow down her racing heartbeat and settle on the right advice. "It's just a signature, Madison. It's not like anyone will even check back home. Jesus, I could sign it myself."

Madison's eyes flicked around, as if she was trying to work out some hidden meaning behind Ade's remark. "You mean, fake it?"

"No." Ade rolled her eyes. How did she get here? Advising a bunch of grad students when she was barely a few years older. "That's not what I said."

"Yeah. Got it, Teach." Madison winked, her tears drying up with a wild grin. "That's me figured out. I'll send Scott your way." She scooped up her bag and ran out the door.

Ade sighed, grateful to see the back of Madison but kicking herself for not having a firm grasp on the solutions her students needed. She looked up to the lumbering shape of Scott entering the room, wearing a sports vest. Whatever came next couldn't be as bad. She couldn't handle anymore ethical nightmares. On days like these, she really wondered why she was still here. To prove her bosses wrong back home? To convince her dad she could hold down a proper job? It sure was making her head hurt.

***

Montpellier's festivities were in full swing. Opposite the opera house sat a giant globe made of a thousand tiny bulbs. The tree-lined promenades twinkled, leading to where the tall Nordman Fir, surrounded by a hundred and one gifts, presided over the merriment.

Ade squinted up at the tree, blurring the bulbs like fireflies one by one until they bled into a single glow. She loved this time of year back home, but here, the chill had finally made itself known across the south, and where modern met ancient, the season trebled in significance.

Under the canopy of fairy lights, the unique shadow of Sylvie strolled up, right on cue. "Hey, stranger."

"It's been a while." Ade had counted the days they had spent apart.

"Miss me much?" Sylvie asked.

Ade's whole body lightened in her presence. "I don't usually miss people while they're not with me, but yeah. I've missed talking with you."

Sylvie broke into the widest smile Ade had ever seen. "Me too. Shall we walk?"

Ade offered Sylvie her arm. "How was it? Your trip?"

"Mixed. Wonderful to be in Paris again. Isa humored me by visiting most of my old haunts."

"And the speech?" Ade asked.

Sylvie's smile faltered. "Challenging, actually. I wish you'd been there to listen in."

Excitement and intrigue flowed through Ade's veins. She would've dropped everything to go to Paris with Sylvie. "Why? What do you mean?"

"I was exploring the same old themes in my previous books. I touched on the new stuff. But the audience was pretty provocative when it came to old feminist theory and new thinking. They really went at me about gender constructs and discrimination against trans people." Sylvie drew her closer. "It was a tough gig. It made me think about how I present my ideas in the new book. Maybe change it up a little and challenge some of the theory and language."

Silence extended between them as Ade waited for a specific question before she gave her feedback.

"Sorry, I don't want to go on about it. It wasn't that bad; it just wasn't a smooth ride." Sylvie's spark seemed to fade a little.

"Did you need my input on it? Or did you just need to say it out loud?"

Sylvie laughed, her beautiful jaw line extending above her scarf. "I love the way you clarify things so perfectly. Most people would just head right in there and say what they think." She stopped for a beat and turned into Ade, holding onto her arm. "I would like your views on this. I feel like you might have something to say."

"Gender is a complete construct and the discrimination against trans and non-binary people is completely fueled by old-fashioned misogyny and a hard core of trans-exclusionary radical feminists. But you know that." Ade nodded.

"I do know that. But it makes me think that I have spent my life's work defending theories which have fueled something divisive and hurtful."

"Those theories stand on their own merit. It's what people have done with them in a different context that can be divisive and hurtful, which is not on you or your work." Ade held her hands, and Sylvie's pulse beat in her thumb. "Don't take responsibility for someone else's errors or intentions."

"Thank you. I don't know why it got to me so much." Sylvie

bumped against Ade's shoulder. "Tell me about your day."

They walked in step with each other for a few beats. "Strange one. I had a line of students for an open counseling session."

"You did? That sounds like a headache."

"It sure was." Ade rattled off the story of Madison's faked attestations.

"You told her to fake her paperwork?" Sylvie's mouth gaped, and her eyes widened with horror.

"No. I told her not to do that."

"But you suggested it, and she went skipping off. You don't think that tells you something?"

Ade stuttered. This whole situation was getting away from her.

"Ade, can you really not read the room?" Sylvie's movement stalled. "It's infuriating sometimes."

Ade sank into her coat with shame. She hadn't meant to give Madison bad advice. "I panicked. But I did tell her *not* to do it."

"Do you know nothing about teenagers and young adults? Give them an out, and they will absolutely take it." Sylvie pressed her hands to her forehead. "We might need to do something about this before it gets out of hand."

"I think you're overreacting." Ade was fixed to the spot, her body unwilling to move until she'd figured a way out of this.

"Oh, you do? The professor with fourteen years teaching experience versus your—how many?" Sylvie shook her head. "That's right. You don't actually have any teaching experience, because you avoid the classroom and like to spend your time with more simple creatures."

"Marine life is anything but simple. They're some of the most complex and clever creations in the world," Ade whispered. She suspected that Sylvie's tirade was meant to hurt, but a numbness overcame her body like a shell, designed to protect her from the insults and injuries Sylvie's words intended. "I'm sorry. You're right."

Backlit by a storefront, Ade couldn't make out Sylvie's expression.

"No. I'm sorry." Sylvie's tone had softened, to almost a whisper. "You're right. You did tell her not to do it, and it's not your fault if anything untoward happens. I don't know what's wrong with me. It's like I could snap at any moment."

"I didn't mean to make you angry," Ade said.

"I know. It's not you. I mean, it is you. But it's not anger, not really." Sylvie looked into Ade's eyes.

"What?" Ade scanned her face for the meaning.

Sylvie smiled. "I'm very confused about how I feel about you."

"In a bad way?" Ade asked, silently begging Sylvie not to say yes.

"In a really good way."

Ade pieced together all the information she possibly could, trying to figure out how it had led them to this moment, but she still failed to grip Sylvie's meaning. "I'm going to need a bit more information."

"I like you," Sylvie whispered. "More than I should, all things considered. And I think you like me too."

She bit her lip in a way that made Ade want to kiss her on the exact spot. "Just to confirm your hypothesis: I do like you." Ade grinned. "More than I should, all things considered."

Sylvie blew out a puff of air, which they could both see in the cold. "I don't know what to do about it. I've been mulling it over since Paris." She studied the sidewalk. "I wondered if you could help me work it all out."

"Well, I'm pretty good at asking questions and getting to an answer."

"I know." Sylvie giggled.

"So what would you like to do?" Ade stepped into Sylvie's space, her lips hovering inches away.

Sylvie shivered. "Maybe kiss you?"

"Yeah. That could be arranged." Ade ignored the terror building inside. Was this happening? The thing she'd toyed with inside the guide rails of her fantasies. "Now?"

"Yes. Now—"

"Sylvie!" A male voice broke the trance they'd weaved.

"Paul." Sylvie took two steps backward, almost losing her footing. "How lovely to see you."

"You too." He smiled broadly. "What a wonderful evening. The Christmas markets are beautiful this year, aren't they?"

"Paul, you might not have met one of our pastoral care leads." Sylvie gestured to Ade. "This is Adelaide Poole from the science department's international cohort."

"Pleased to finally meet you. I've heard lots of good things about your group." Paul shook her hand. "It's really breaking down barriers bringing science and art into one team. It's a marriage made in heaven, isn't it?"

Stunned by the whiplash of having to pull back from almost kissing Sylvie, Ade forced a breath into her lungs. "Yes. Pleased to meet you."

"You must both join me and my family for drinks," Paul said, hooking his right thumb over his shoulder.

"No, please. We couldn't possibly intrude." Sylvie's voice strained with politeness.

"Nonsense, it's Christmas. My wife has a table in the square." He spread his arms wide, ushering them toward a bustling café.

Ade caught Sylvie's eye, and they shared a wild look. She replayed the near miss as she followed in the footsteps of the head of department and Sylvie. She squeezed her palms together, trying to ground herself from losing all control.

That had been amazing, until it had been wrenched from her reach. The hum of the crowds suddenly filled Ade's ears with unbearable noise, and it took all she had not to run off and find a quiet place. She wanted to stay with Sylvie. She yearned to finish that kiss. Nothing mattered more than discovering just how soft Sylvie's lips were, how they tasted. But the moment had slipped through their hands like a flurry of snow. Would she get a second chance at that kiss? Or would Sylvie have second thoughts?

Chapter Twenty-Seven

THEY HADN'T DISCUSSED THE not-kiss. Paul's timing had been awful, but it had given Sylvie a split second to reconsider the career-limiting move. If he'd seen them and called her out, it would've put an end to her promotion dreams. Maybe even her book deal would have been questioned.

She'd sent Ade a few messages, focusing on faculty deadlines and student updates. She'd agonized over every word, taking care to avoid any hint of hope or regret. But the memory of Ade's lips edging closer to Sylvie's replayed over and over. She'd spent the whole weekend shaking the vision of Ade's breath, forming in the cold air, blending with her own until the distance between them was imperceptible.

Her heart had raced like never before when she'd finally admitted her loosely defined feelings. Ade had mirrored Sylvie's own fear of being rejected, of being laughed off and discarded.

A tempest of questions stormed her mind, but she had no time to calm them. She adjusted the last of the cushions on her parents' couch and ignored the plume of dust which rose into the air. Country living was all very well, but it seemed to create much more mess.

A horn sounded, and Sylvie ran to the window to see Elda climbing out of the car. Grinning from ear to ear, she waved with both hands before a small child gripped her thigh.

Sylvie swung open the front door, and the whole Mason-Brown family poured into the cottage. "Guys, you're here." She enveloped Elda in a huge hug and planted kisses on the boys' cheeks.

Charlie brought up the rear with both hands full of gift bags.

"Hey, Sylvie. It's so good to see you." She blew her a kiss.

"In, in, in. I want to inspect these boys." Sylvie made a big deal of measuring them against herself. "Stand right there, Eli. Mm, just as I hypothesized. At least the length of a sausage."

Elijah giggled and leaned into her.

"How about you, Arlo? I'm not sure you've grown." Sylvie grimaced and sucked her breath between her teeth. "You seem just the same."

"I have grown!" Elda and Charlie's youngest son protested with a stamp of his foot. "Tell Sylvie, Mama."

"There's only one way to find out, little guy. Last time we got together you were up to this crease on my jeans." She pointed to her mid-thigh. "Shall we see what's happened?"

"I can already see he's grown a bit," Eli said, jumping on the spot.

"I think you might be right." Sylvie clapped her hands, and both boys cheered with glee.

"You are too much," Elda said, squeezing Sylvie's arm.

"Who wants lunch? You must be hungry from all that traveling."

"They're always hungry, Sylvie. It doesn't matter what we do." Charlie dropped the last of the bags in the hallway.

"Too early for champagne?" Sylvie drew her friends into the kitchen.

"It's Christmas, isn't it? We brought a couple of bottles with us. Charlie, will you grab the duty free?" Elda winked and peeled off her coat. "I love coming here. Thank you so much for the invitation."

"Thank my parents. They're the ones who've gone away and left us to it."

"We did bring them a little something as a thank you." Charlie handed over a perfectly wrapped box.

"Doggie!" Arlo made a beeline for the sleeping Labrador.

"Not while he's asleep, sweetheart." Elda intercepted her preschooler with a strong but gentle scoop. "You have to wait until he wakes up and then we must use gentle hands, okay?"

"Henri's quite deaf now, and he won't hear you coming, so we have to be careful not to frighten him." Sylvie bopped down to Arlo's level. "Otherwise he might get cross with us. Now, Charlie would you do the honors with drinks? There's a bottle chilling in the fridge. Boys, would you like to make your own pizza?"

The littlest boy screeched his delight as Sylvie brought out two chef's hats for him and his brother to wear. "First, we have to wash our hands."

"Good luck with that," Charlie said, pouring three large flutes.

"How were your travels?" Sylvie asked, attempting to minimize the splash from the kitchen sink.

Elda grabbed a towel. "All fine. Eli and Arlo love an airport breakfast, don't you, boys?"

"I had two sausages and three hash browns," Eli said.

Sylvie frowned, never having really grasped the concept of an English breakfast.

Charlie laughed. "Yep, smooth enough at the other end too. We picked up the car and made our way down here. Not much on the roads, to be honest."

"You're ahead of the usual rush." Sylvie set the boys the task of rolling out their balls of dough and bit her lip as they created a cloud of flour.

"Sorry," Elda mouthed from across the kitchen island.

"It's fine. It's all about keeping them entertained." Sylvie wiped her forehead, leaving a smudge of flour above her brow. "You two look tired."

"The joys of two under five." Charlie gulped at her champagne. "We were all ready for a break, hey, hon?"

"Absolutely. I've been busy gearing up for the exhibition launching in the new year." Elda tucked her hair behind her ear. "In fact, I was wondering if you'd come over for it."

Charlie coughed. "Elda's being modest. It's the biggest solo show she's ever produced."

"Oh, don't hype it up, Charlie." Elda threw a playful punch at her wife. "I'm trying to keep it low key, so I don't completely lose my mind."

Sylvie grinned. Elda had always been a talented artist, but since she'd found her confidence, she'd gone from a relative unknown to a pretty big deal. "Of course I'll be there. I love seeing your work."

"And we like those posh little snacks they serve with the drinks, don't we, boys?" Charlie asked. "They think Mama's work is all about the catering."

"And what about Mummy's work?" Sylvie asked.

Charlie laughed. "Hard to describe family law to a three-year-old. He's all cops and robbers and thinks I'm the judge."

"I wouldn't know where to start with European feminism. Mind you, I struggle to explain it to my class of twenty-one-year-olds, let alone a toddler." Sylvie placed three bowls of toppings in front of the boys. "These are to put on top of your circle."

Arlo tipped the entire bowl of cheese onto his blob of dough.

"Think we might need a bit more cheese grating," Elda said, trying to salvage her youngest's lunch.

"Now, once you're done building your pizza, we'll go outside and put them in the oven."

"Outside? Why is your oven outside?" Elijah asked.

"Because it's a special oven just for pizzas that gets super-hot." Sylvie beamed. "I lit it a couple of hours ago, so it would be toasty for when you got here."

"Aunty Sylvie is really spoiling you guys, isn't she?" Elda raised her glass in Sylvie's direction.

"I like pizza too. It's a win-win." Sylvie smirked. "Why don't you two put your feet up in the lounge, while I run the boys around the garden and cook pizza?"

"Absolutely not." Charlie stood firm. "We came here to see you, not to burden you with two live wires."

"But you're on your holidays. I want you to be able to relax."

"It's your time off too, Sylvie." Elda put her arm around her shoulders.

"In that case, bring the bottle outside. We'll all enjoy firing the pizzas." Sylvie ushered everyone out of the French doors to the terrace.

***

When the evening drew in, Charlie scooped up the boys by their little hands and led them up to bed. They both yawned widely before running back to beg for one last drink and to give their mama and Sylvie kisses.

"Good night, sweetheart. Sleep tight." Elda watched both her babies totter up the staircase, then stretched her legs out in the space they'd vacated on the couch. "And...relax."

A few more creases had gathered at the corner of Elda's eyes, but she was as beautiful as ever. Sylvie had witnessed her blossoming career as an artist, as well as her blooming relationship with Charlie.

"What are you thinking?" Elda asked.

"How far you've come since we were scrambling to pay our rent in Paris."

"We've both come a very long way."

"Well, you have." Sylvie swallowed back the regret. "Charlie by your side, the boys growing up. It's wonderful to see you all."

Elda frowned. "You've come far too. All the way south, with a fancy new job and another book on the way."

Sylvie tsked. The promise of future accomplishments mattered so much more than what she'd already achieved.

"What is it?" Elda asked.

"I can't get away with the new girl routine at work anymore, not in my second year." She rolled her head back against the sofa in defeat. "I feel stuck. Like I'm spinning my wheels at a roulette table, waiting for my number to come up."

Elda sat up. "That's not like you. What's going on?"

Sylvie put her hands to her burning cheeks, ashamed to put

words around her anguish. "There's a person. I can't get them out of my head."

"Now you have my attention." Elda edged closer on the sofa. "Tell me more."

"Her name is Adelaide. Ade." Goosebumps spread over Sylvie's arms. Just talking about Ade sent her body into overdrive. "We almost kissed."

"Interesting." Elda put her palm to her cheek, her eyes wide with intrigue. "Why almost?'

"My boss interrupted us." Sylvie groaned, covering her face with a cushion. "It was such bad timing. He dragged us off for Christmas drinks, and I could tell it was the last thing Ade wanted, but I had no idea how to get us out of it."

"What happened next?"

"We pretended it didn't happen." Disappointment rose in Sylvie's throat.

"Both of you?" Elda laughed. "Was she as into it as you were?"

"I think so. I mean...we haven't spoken about it. I was feeling pretty bold that night, but now I've completely lost my nerve. If he'd seen us, I don't know what would have happened."

Elda bit her lip. "Why? What's your boss's reaction got to do with anything?"

"She's a colleague," Sylvie said with as much clarity as she could muster. "A much younger colleague."

"How much younger?"

"Twelve years."

Elda's eyebrows flickered for just a second. "So what? Is there a rule against colleagues dating or something?"

"Not explicitly. But this feels ambiguous. She's a PhD leading an international cohort of students."

"But she's on the payroll, right, so she's not your student?"

Sylvie fidgeted. "Right."

"Then get over yourself. She's probably wondering why you left her hanging." Elda jumped off the couch. "If this was the other way around, you'd tell me to grow up and kiss her before she gets tired of waiting."

Charlie crept through the door. "El, keep your voice down; you'll wake the boys." Her gaze flicked between them. "What'd I miss?"

"Sylvie's got a hot woman on the go, and she's lost her bottle."

"That *is* news. Who is she?" Charlie poured herself a fresh glass of wine and sat next to Elda.

"We didn't get that far," Elda said with a huff.

"She's doing a PhD in marine conservation. She's over here for a year supervising a bunch of students from the US."

Charlie smiled. "She's American?"

"Yes. What's your point?" Sylvie asked.

"Nothing. Just that you're not known for your tolerance of other...cultures," Charlie said with a cheeky wink.

"I'm very tolerant. I put up with you two and your Britishisms, don't I?"

"You make it very well known when we frustrate you because we're not being French enough." Elda giggled and put her legs over her wife's lap. "We've spent two weeks negotiating the Christmas Eve menu."

Charlie nodded. "I don't know why anyone needs to buy that much fish for Christmas."

"You're in France for Christmas. The least you can do is respect our traditions," Sylvie said.

Elda mirrored her wife's baffled expression. "Anyway, you're distracting Sylvie from telling me all about the juicy bits. I want to know how you feel and exactly what's happening. Don't skimp on the details."

If only it was that easy. Sylvie couldn't describe the crushing disappointment of the almost-kiss, going from elation to despair in a single beat. She'd craved the resolution of that moment, her lips connecting with Ade's in a final crescendo of attraction.

But it had fallen to the cold, stone floor, along with her

expectations, leaving nothing but fear and shame in its wake. She wasn't only afraid of the consequences, but also of the strength of her feelings. She'd never obsessed over someone this much. No other person had gotten under her skin, leaving their mark on her, like Ade. "I feel desperate."

"Oh, jeez, she's got it bad." Charlie tipped her head in the air.

"There's only one thing for it." Elda sat bolt upright and took Sylvie's hands. "You need to see her. She needs to come over here."

The brakes inside Sylvie's brain threw her forward with inertia. But her heart stilled, as if it had emphatically known the answer all along. "Yeah. I think you're right." She excused herself and turned over what she might say. Ade needed a straight-forward message with no room for ambiguity.

Are you busy tomorrow? Would you like to come over? I know it's Christmas Eve, but I'd love to see you.

The interminable three dots blinking on and off the screen were enough to drive her to refill her wine glass. She never should have left the kiss hanging, and she was determined, more than ever, to put that right. But would Ade accept her invitation? Or leave her in a purgatory of not knowing if their lips would ever meet.

Chapter Twenty-Eight

ADE HAD WORRIED THAT the near-kiss at the Christmas fair was enough to put Sylvie off forever. The few messages they'd exchanged since had been courteous and functional, with Sylvie reminding Ade of her travel plans over the holidays. But the spark between them had been all but extinguished by Paul's interruption. And it seemed neither of them were brave enough to relight the flame.

When Sylvie messaged with a surprise invitation to her parents' house for Christmas Eve, Ade almost didn't believe it. But Steph had talked her into going, insisting that she didn't need babysitting, as long as Ade was back for Christmas morning.

Installed in the train carriage, Ade traced the line of her journey along the map and watched the coastline bend and break through the window, until it came to halt in a picturesque, tiny station about an hour down the track.

As promised, Sylvie was waiting when Ade jumped down onto the platform. Against the winter morning, Sylvie's radiance shone like the sun itself bounced off her. The days they'd been apart shrank in significance, and Ade wondered how she'd ever doubted Sylvie's sincere invitation.

She hoisted her bag crammed with gifts onto her shoulder; she'd already bought something for Sylvie but had run out for a couple of last-minute purchases for Elda and Charlie's two young boys. She'd figured a bottle of wine would suffice for the adult strangers. She wasn't used to buying gifts of any kind, especially for people she didn't know.

Butterflies erupted in her stomach as the idea of meeting new people dawned on her. That and the closing distance between her and Sylvie. What should she do? Should they hug? Not knowing whether to pick up from their chemistry-laden confession on Thursday night, she dipped her head, avoiding eye contact. If she didn't make the first move, Sylvie would, and Ade could happily follow.

"Happy Christmas Eve." Sylvie reached for Ade's bulging rucksack. "Here, let me put that in the car."

"Sure," Ade said.

No kiss. No hug. But the warmth of her greeting was more than she'd reserve for just a friend. Its intimacy promised something, even if Ade couldn't pin it down there and then. "Thank you. For the invitation, too. Thank you." *Smooth*.

"I'm glad you came." Sylvie held her gaze for a moment. "Let's get going."

Ade took the passenger seat, glad of a reason to face forward and avoid eye contact while she steadied her heart rate. She had no idea which route they'd take from here, but for once, the road ahead didn't cloud her mind. Ade lingered on the unfinished kiss which hung between them, and she breathed in the frisson of expectation in the air, like either could turn and make it right at any moment.

"I'm sorry it took me so long to message you," Sylvie said, putting her sunglasses on.

Ade tapped her foot in the well of the car. "I was wondering if I'd done something wrong on Thursday night."

Sylvie's flicked her gaze toward her. "Not at all." She took a deep breath. "It was a mis—"

"A mistake?" Ade's fears manifested, and she regretted making the journey just for Sylvie to let her down.

"No. A missed opportunity." Sylvie smiled. "Relax, Ade. I wanted to kiss you. Badly. I just didn't want to have to explain myself immediately to my boss. Our timing was off, that's all." She looked into Ade's eyes. "But I'm glad you're here now."

Ade's muscles eased, and she melted into the seat. "I wanted to kiss you too." She ran her hands across her hair, pulling at her frustration. Her desire didn't belong in the past tense. It was here and now.

Their sighs met in the middle. Sylvie rested her hand for a second on Ade's thigh, but it was back on the steering wheel and gone too quickly. It was like everything practical and logical conspired against their lips meeting.

"Tell me about what I'm walking into," Ade said. "You know I'm prone to shyness around strangers."

"I know." Sylvie nodded. "I don't want you to feel any pressure to perform or be anything but yourself around these guests. Elda and Charlie are good friends, and their little boys, Elijah and Arlo, are pretty special."

"Where did you meet?" Ade needed concrete details that she could bolt herself to like an anchor.

"Elda and I worked in Paris together very briefly. She was teaching art and English in my department, but she had to go back to England because she'd fallen in love with Charlie, even though she was kidding herself and everyone else about it." Sylvie filled their shared space with her laughter. "She'll deny it, but if it wasn't for me, they'd still be frustrated best friends."

"And Charlie? What's she like?"

"An esteemed barrister in family law. I like her a lot." Sylvie turned left into a narrow lane. "Elijah is five, and Arlo is three." She poked Ade's thigh gently. "You're going to love them."

Ade settled enough to enjoy Sylvie's profile and the softness of her cheek. Her gaze swept down Sylvie's body. What she'd give to lay her hands on Sylvie, to feel the heat of her body through the fabric of her clothes.

"We're here," said Sylvie.

Too soon. Too soon.

***

Ade's nerves didn't ease after the introductions were made. She gripped her spinning ring so hard, she worried it might buckle under her fingertips.

"How's the French way of life?" Elda asked, setting her wriggly three-year-old down on the tiled floor.

Ade considered her response. "There's so much paperwork for everything and too many people smoke. Including Sylvie, although she tries to hide it."

"Guilty as charged." Sylvie dipped her head, but Ade caught the glint in her eye.

"I've been trying to get Sylvie to quit smoking for years," Elda said. "If you manage it, you're a better person than I am."

"That wouldn't make me a better person, just a more convincing one," said Ade.

The falseness of Elda and Charlie's laughter rang with an untruth. Ade resisted the urge to cover her ears with her hands. She caught a frown pass between them, sign of a judgment.

Had she messed up already?

"Help me explain myself," Ade whispered to Sylvie.

"You're right: getting me to quit smoking is about encouragement, not taking the moral high ground." Sylvie pointed at Elda and stuck out her tongue, generating more knowing giggles between them.

Ade orbited the circle of old friends with a familiar envy. "Boys, would you like to play ball outside with me?" She had to escape. The room was so full of knowing looks, Ade couldn't interpret the conversation that she could actually hear above all the deafening subtext.

"Yes!" Elijah ran out first with his little brother not far behind him.

Ade grinned. The acceptance of little people was far easier to win than grown-ups. She followed them to the cottage garden and a patch of lawn big enough to throw a ball around. "Wait, what's happening?" Ade stopped in her tracks as the boys kicked a ball to each other.

"Football."

"That's not football, guys. It's soccer."

Elijah giggled. "Don't you know how to play football?"

"Of course." Ade ground her heel into the soft lawn, determined to make a good impression on at least half of this family. "We just call it something else." There was no point in getting into it. It didn't matter anyway; Arlo was now picking winter berries from a tree. "You okay there, buddy?"

"Smell nice," he said, lifting the tiny spheres to her nose.

Ade couldn't detect any scent. "Whatever you say, little dude. Don't eat them though. They won't taste nice, and they might make your tummy really sick." Ade did her best vomiting impression.

"Sadly, Arlo's at the age that if you tell him *not* to do something, it's like a green light to try it," Charlie said as she wandered out.

"Sorry about pretending to vomit." Ade stepped back. "You guys probably don't need a copycat of that kind of thing either."

"They've both done far worse, don't worry. Two boys, two years apart is a recipe for social humiliation of many and varied flavors. We're immune, in a way."

Ade stalled her reply while she digested Charlie's food-based metaphor. British people really did love a long and flowery sentence.

Charlie dropped her sweater in a pile on the grass. "Let's set up two goals, boys. We'll have a little match. Me and Arlo against you and Eli."

Grateful for the respite in conversation, Ade found a plastic pot for one of the makeshift goal posts.

They played for half an hour, kicking softly so that no one lost control of the ball. In the end, Arlo was running in faster and wider loops around the patch of grass.

"He's getting tired," Charlie said, stroking her hand through her cropped hair. "He probably needs a refuel and a little rest before all hell breaks loose."

Ade feared the worst. Her own meltdowns proved that the absence of food, hydration, and rest could spell disaster for anyone around her. She didn't want to mess with a three-year-old ticking time-bomb.

She wiped her brow.

"Have you worked up a bit of a sweat there with the preschoolers?" Sylvie stood against the open French doors, her hands on her hips.

"A little. It's harder than it looks." Ade's heartbeat spiked again.

"Come on into the den. I've made us a drink," said Sylvie, leading the way into a small living room which they had to themselves.

"I'm not doing well with Elda and Charlie, am I? Is it obvious?" Ade asked.

"You're fine. Those two are very British. Even if they noticed your nerves, they'd never say anything." Sylvie stepped forward. "Come here." She held out her arms, inviting Ade in.

Ade hesitated, not trusting herself with the moment. Every fiber of her being ached for Sylvie to hold her, to feel the warmth of her embrace, and to slow her heartbeat to match her rhythm. She moved closer, conscious of her own limbs and awkwardness.

"Shall I feed the dog, Sylvie?" Elda's voice carried through the adjoining hallway.

Sylvie's shoulders dropped with a sigh. "Sorry, I'd better go and sort Henri. He's only just woken up."

"Let me." Despite the spike of another interruption, Ade jumped at the chance to fuss over an animal. "I want to meet him."

"Come through." Sylvie took her by the hand, their connection reinstated and pulsing through Ade's arm.

"Here, boy." Ade knelt on the floor, allowing Henri to notice her and make his way over. He took his time, his old bones quivering as he steadied himself. "Look at you." As she locked eyes with the canine, a calm took over. The rush of blood slowed around Ade's temples, and her endless list of clarifying questions muted. The pair of them didn't need a shared language to understand each other's needs.

She patted his back with a firm stroke worthy of a dog of

Henri's breed and stature. She may not be great with humans, but she was a real gem with the animal kingdom. Her regret at not quite connecting with Sylvie's British friends faded a little as Henri inched closer and laid his head on her shoulder. Having gained his trust, she stroked his silky ears, and their smoothness brought an immediate quiet to her racing mind.

She lifted herself from the floor and beckoned Henri to follow her. "Here you go," she said, taking the food bowl from Sylvie. The pull to remain in Sylvie's family home was stronger than anything. If only she could stay here all night in the simple domesticity and the peace of Sylvie's embrace.

Closing the door, Ade held out her hand. "Charlie and Elda are settling the boys down," she said.

Sylvie bit her lip. "And Henri is busy eating his food."

Ade stepped forward, no longer feeling on the periphery of human experience but right in the middle of her own adventure. Her skin tingled with the anticipation of the kiss. Nothing existed except Sylvie, the flutter of her eyelashes, the arch of her brow, the softness of her cheek, and then...her lips. Ade trembled. A moment passed, and her world shrunk to their lips meeting. She held her breath, pausing in the beautiful tenderness that she'd dreamed of but never expected.

The promise of a kiss had been kept. And now she'd known its awesomeness, there was no going back, was there?

Chapter Twenty-Nine

SYLVIE CAUGHT ELDA'S EYE, and they shared a silent, knowing glance of the festive joy to come. The door opened, and a shaft of light stretched across the oak floorboards.

"Go on in, boys," Charlie said.

Arlo held Elda's hand and followed his older brother into the room. The floor creaked with each of their tiny footsteps.

"Has he been?" Sylvie whispered, knowing full well the tree was barricaded with gift boxes.

"He's been," Eli said, his tiny voice full of excitement.

Sylvie flicked the lamp on, bathing the room in the warm light that was usually reserved for the evening.

Wide-eyed, the boys rushed to the gifts which had been stacked like boulders against the Christmas tree. Tiny bows peeped above the boxes, glistening in the glow of the Christmas tree lights.

"I still don't know why we had to wait for the morning." Sylvie yawned. "No wonder the children can't sleep for excitement."

"Because that's what we do in England, Sylvie. It's tradition for Father Christmas to only come down the chimney once everyone is asleep." Elda glared at her, obviously not wishing to explain to her little ones why Santa might arrive earlier across the Channel.

"But you're all here, in France. You should be following my rules." Sylvie huffed, grabbed Eli and tickled him. "You're lucky I love you guys so much."

Charlie had arranged two indistinguishable piles of gifts overnight, sat at either side of the tree.

"Eli, it looks like these ones are for you." Charlie pointed at the left-hand side. "And these are yours, baby boy." She led her youngest son toward the first layer of wrapped boxes.

Arlo's face beamed, his eyes wide with disbelief.

"Want to see what's inside?" Elda asked. "Try this one."

He stroked the paper with just enough reverence before tearing it apart and bouncing with unbridled elation. "I wanted this one." Arlo's smile reached his bright blue eyes, and everyone in the room caught it like a common cold, unable to resist the contagious cheer. "Thank you, Father Christmas."

A lump of happiness stuck in Sylvie's throat, and she excused herself to make coffee. Having spent countless Christmas holidays in the company of adults, she'd forgotten the sheer magic of it all when seen through the eyes of small children.

The pot spluttered on the stove top, and her thoughts drifted to Ade and Steph enjoying their gift-giving this morning. An image of Ade in her pajamas, her long limbs stretched on her sofa, filled her mind and quickened her pulse.

Christmas morning, surrounded by the innocence of childhood, was no time to be humoring her wildest fantasies, but a huge part of her had wished that Ade had woken next to her in bed. What a Christmas gift that would have been. Their kiss, when it had finally come, had been everything. But she'd gone home last night because she'd made a promise to Steph.

"Earth to Sylvie?" Elda leaned against the door frame. "What are you thinking about?"

"Just enjoying the moment, that's all." Sylvie sniffed, caught in her reverie.

"Daydreaming about Ade, by any chance?" Elda asked.

"Maybe." Sylvie's cheeks flushed. "Did you like her?"

Elda stepped forward and gently gripped Sylvie's shoulders. "She was lovely. But you already know that."

"She gets nervous around new people." Sylvie returned the hug, baffled by the feelings swirling around her head.

"Hey, she was great with the boys. Anyone who gets them out of my hair for ten minutes is a win." Elda took over making the coffee. "Seriously, she had her quirks, but she seems like a good egg."

"Yeah. I really think so."

"Hot too. Smoking hot." Elda laughed. "So, what happened? I want all the details."

"Elda, I need your help." Charlie appeared at the doorway, shaking her head. "The boys are on gift number four. Arlo's more obsessed with unwrapping than actually playing with anything, and I need to find some batteries before Eli has a meltdown. Could you look in the suitcase?"

"I'm on it." Elda clapped her hands. "Operation battery-powered-toys has commenced earlier than I thought. Let's come back to our conversation as soon as I get five minutes to myself." She padded away.

As the sun rose, the early start made itself known with a second wave of fatigue, and Sylvie yawned and stretched her arms to the ceiling. "I might take a morning stroll before we start lunch. Anyone care to join me?"

Charlie looked up over a sea of wrapping paper. "Sounds delightful. You and Elda go, and I'll stay here with the boys."

Not needing to be told twice, they made their escape down the cobbled lane toward the village center. A couple of passersby wished them a Merry Christmas, and Sylvie reciprocated, sparing Elda the use of her rusty language skills. "Do you think you remember any French?"

"I doubt it. What is it they say about baby-brain? I think the last five years has robbed me of any ability to retain non-essential information. It's all been replaced by the names of Peppa Pig characters."

"You're happy though?" Sylvie asked.

"God, yeah. It's pretty perfect, isn't it?" Elda looped her arm through Sylvie's. "I mean, I don't want to be smug, but I really am living my best life."

Sylvie laughed, her breath puffing like clouds into the air. "That is pretty smug."

"But you have to really appreciate the good things when they come along. Like you and Ade. It's obvious she really likes you."

Sylvie drifted to the electricity that had sparked between their lips last night. "But she'll be going back to California in a few months. It can't last. Not like you and Charlie." Sylvie shivered, the cold air sneaking through the seams in her jacket.

"There were many times when I refused to believe in me and Charlie. Like when I moved to Paris for that job and met you. If I'd have stayed put, I would've been miserable and lonely. If you weren't around, that is." Elda nudged her. "And Charlie and I may never have got together."

"And when you left her, albeit briefly." Sylvie smirked.

"Yeah, well, that was a huge mistake, and I'd lost all faith in everything at that point." Elda tsked. "The point is, sometimes you have to believe that whatever's stacked against you will work itself out somehow."

"It's pretty stacked." Sylvie nodded. "But I can't get her out of my head."

"Oh, I know that feeling, Sylvie. You've got it bad, my lovely." Elda pulled her toward a bench and wiped the dew off the seat before she sat down. "Tell me what you like about her?"

"She's kind, without being over-the-top. She's dedicated. And gentle. I've never seen anyone move so deliberately. I don't know. She's magnetic. When she's in the room, I can't stop myself from getting closer just to hear what she says next, to feel her look at me." Sylvie screamed into her hands. "I'm going slowly mad."

"What would you say to me?" Elda asked.

"Calme-toi." Sylvie blew her cheeks out.

"Get a grip?" Elda asked.

"Exactly. Your French isn't so rusty after all." Sylvie winked. "You're right. I need to pull myself together. And do what?"

Elda steepled her fingers. "If you close your eyes, what's the best thing you see happening?"

"I drive back to the city. I surprise Ade. Somehow, she thinks my company is preferable to her sister's, she comes home with me and we pick up where we left off last night."

"So make it happen." Elda took her elbow and brought them both to a standstill.

"What, now?"

"Well, maybe after lunch. I can't handle a whole Christmas Day feast on my own, especially with all that fish you ordered. But after we're done, leave us here with Henri and go make your dreams come true."

"You're kidding." Sylvie slumped against her friend's shoulder, touching her lips where Ade had caressed her just a few hours ago. "Imagine if I just drove home and turned up on her doorstep."

"Don't imagine it. Just do it."

***

Sylvie couldn't pluck up the courage to knock on Ade's door. Or buzz her intercom. She sat for a short while until the jitters got to her, then she stood outside the five-story block for another twenty minutes.

The whole thing was madness. Elda and Charlie had her caught up in a fantasy where Ade would open the door and sweep her off her feet. The reality would be far more sobering, no doubt. Ade would be annoyed by the interruption in her routine, grumpy and awkward, until she got used to it.

Sylvie dared another look up toward the attic studio. The lights were on, that was something. Either she was in, or Steph was. Neither option made Sylvie feel any better. Perhaps she should just make her way home, settle in for the night. She had cheese, wine and good friends waiting for her

Her phone buzzed in her hand.

Hope you've had a great day. I wish we could have spent it together.

Sylvie's breath caught in her throat. So she hadn't conjured the whole thing in her imagination. It was all there for the taking, if one of them was brave enough.

Me too. It's been lovely with all the gang, but I've made my way back to the city. I missed you. Care to join me?

She wouldn't want to leave her sister alone, surely.

Where are you?

Right outside your apartment.

Oh, God, that was very firmly in the stalker behavior column. She hoped Ade wouldn't hold it against her. Although if the shoe was on the other foot, Sylvie most definitely would.

"I don't really buy all that manifesting shit, but I guess Christmas is a time for believing in something." Ade strode across the small square, filling it with her presence.

Sylvie couldn't meet her eye contact, a shyness overcoming her. "It's a bold move, I know. I hope you don't think I'm a stalker."

"Hey, I'm the one who took the train to the countryside for the afternoon yesterday." Ade smiled.

"It's like we can't keep away from each other."

"It's just like that." Ade stepped into her space and licked her lips. "But if we get interrupted again, I'm going to lose my shit."

Sylvie gave into her craving and met Ade's lips. This time it was tentative. She had tasted Ade, and she wanted more. She smiled into the kiss. "Me too." Her lips tingled with the contact, her ears buzzed with a rush of adrenaline, and for a moment, she might have left the floor.

Sylvie wanted the kiss to last for as long as possible. She burned with passion, growing bolder as they kissed.

Ade broke away, her eyes shining with the emotion. "I don't know what to say."

Sylvie pressed her finger to Ade's lips, desperate to reassure her that she didn't need the words to describe it. "I know."

"I've never done that before. Not like that." Ade cleared her throat.

"Me neither." Sylvie took Ade's hand and laced their fingers together. "Want to come over?"

"Absolutely, I do." Ade looked over her shoulder to her studio.

Sylvie's heart bounced. "Forget I asked. You'll want to stay with Steph." She'd known Ade would put her sister's feelings before her own, and she liked her even more for it. "Of course." But that kiss. She wanted more, and soon.

"I already told her not to wait up."

It was like Ade read her mind as she covered her lips once again with her soft, firm touch.

"Now look who's making bold moves." She rested in Ade's embrace, against her firm chest. "I could always come up and enjoy the company of two Poole sisters for the price of one?" She smirked, putting her hand on Ade's hips.

"That'd be weird." Ade frowned. "Oh, you're joking, right?"

"Come on, you." She cupped Ade's cheeks. "Could we just kiss again though, just to make sure I like it?"

Ade grinned and delivered a dozen tiny kisses along Sylvie's throat all the way to her earlobe. She liked it, more than anything she could think of. Desire rushed through her mind, fanning a heat through her veins and pumping blood to every inch of her body.

Time stopped while Sylvie surrendered to Ade's touch, before it sped up again, and they walked hand in hand toward her own apartment block. Sylvie hadn't thought through what would happen if Ade had actually come home with her. But one thing was sure: she didn't want to break away now that they'd finally come together.

At the main door, Sylvie looked to Ade for assurance. Did Ade want her too? Was this happening? Her heart raced as Ade undressed her with her eyes, peeling every layer of clothing from her right there in the shadows. Sylvie's knees buckled, wishing Ade would spare her the agonizing wait of climbing the staircase. Ade nodded as if the same filthy thoughts had run through her own mind. But just like they had to wait for their kiss, they'd wait for the rest. However achingly long that wait might be.

Chapter Thirty

EVERY SINGLE MOMENT HAD led them here. Ade brushed a strand of hair from Sylvie's temple, envying its curl around her earlobe. How she wished she could nestle that close to Sylvie's skin all day and all night. She touched her lips and came alive with the replay. Sylvie's taste, the stroke of her hand, the whisper of her smile against Ade's cheek, all in vivid color.

She no longer regretted the missed kiss: the one that should have been the night that Paul had met them in la Place de la Comédie. Because when it had finally arrived, it was everything it was meant to be.

Ade's breath caught in her throat as the anticipation of what might come next almost overwhelmed her. She scanned the bedroom, barely able to take in any details except the smooth landscape of the double bed that they were about to land on together. Every stolen gasp and arch of Sylvie's back promised one thing: that crisp sheet was about to get pretty crumpled.

Ade held Sylvie's shoulders for a second, creating a short but intolerable distance between them.

"What is it?" Sylvie asked, her brow furrowing with doubt and confusion.

"I just want to remember this," Ade said, trying to hold onto the moment for as long as possible in case this frenzied lust was all they had. She forced herself to take pictures for the memory book inside her brain, feeding that kernel of fear that once they were physically sated, Sylvie wouldn't need any more from her.

Sylvie peeled off her clothes, layer by layer, as if she was enjoying Ade's physical reaction. She kneeled on the edge of the bed, in her underwear. Her face softened, and she gazed at Ade with an understanding in her eyes. "Look at me." She tipped her chin with a stroke of her perfect finger. "I want you."

Ade's abdomen turned inside out, and her breath caught in her chest. How could Sylvie do these things to her body with just words? She had no idea before this moment that a look and a jumble of vowels and consonants could render her simultaneously immobile and trembling with unspent energy.

"Do you want me?" Sylvie asked, a flicker of doubt crossing her face.

Ade moaned, incapable of uttering a coherent sentence. She met Sylvie's parted lips with her own and Sylvie's back arched in response, inching closer until all that remained between them was the thinnest fabric of their underwear.

Ade stripped off her own tank top with one hand. "Can I?" She gestured to the thin strap of Sylvie's bra and peeled it off her shoulder.

Sylvie unhooked her own clasp with a single flick and revealed her breasts in their magnificence. Ade's breath stuttered again, and she blinked to commit the contours of Sylvie's body to her memory.

"Can I touch you?" Sylvie whispered. She peppered a line of kisses along Ade's neck and drew them both onto the mattress.

Ade resisted the urge to devour her and lingered in a kneeling position between Sylvie's legs, a smile forming as she imagined what might come next.

"Never mind rehearsing it, Ade. Just do it." Sylvie grabbed at the waistband of her shorts. "And take these off."

Obeying Sylvie's command, Ade rose from the bed just long enough to dispense with her own shorts and Sylvie's panties.

"I can't wait any longer," Sylvie said between shallow breaths.

The rise and fall of Sylvie's chest grew erratic as Ade covered her body with her own.

They kissed harder than ever. Ade had never wanted someone so much in all her life. She cried out with frustration that she couldn't put the strength of her desire into words.

"Are you okay?" Sylvie asked, drawing back against the pillow. "What is it?"

"It hurts." It was all Ade could say, pulling Sylvie back to her.

"What hurts, Ade?" Sylvie raised herself up onto her elbow. "Where am I hurting you?"

Ade rose onto her knees and held Sylvie's gaze for a moment. "Here." She pulled Sylvie's hand to her center, wet with need and anticipation. "I can't stand it."

Sylvie's smile played on her lips as she parted Ade and found the core of her pleasure, stroking slowly and deliberately until she found a rhythm that forced another groan from deep in Ade's lungs.

"Tell me where." Sylvie bit her lip, causing another wave of desire to crush Ade's ribs.

"There." Ade angled her hips, offering Sylvie all the access she needed to maintain her touch. Her hips jerked with the rise and fall of her need. She leaned back, opening herself up to Sylvie, edging closer to the climax she craved.

Wedged between Ade's knees, Sylvie looked like she'd abandoned her everyday mask. With every stroke of her nimble fingers, she played another note of desire on Ade's body until a key change built to a crescendo.

Naked, the pair discovered a nighttime of blissful revelry. Whether she knew it or not, Sylvie held a whole new and different power in her hands: the power to undo Ade with a single caress, a firm touch, creating a cadence that intensified and waned until it was almost unbearable. So close to pain yet brimming with pleasure.

Their gaze locked, and Sylvie turned the key on all the feelings Ade had hidden. Could Sylvie see her for what she was? Complicated to the point of seeming plain and simple? A melody so perplexing, she was white noise to most people. Ade bit down on the refrain which hummed from the depths of her core to the edge of her brain.

She screamed out, reaching the heights of a wordless descant as she was understood completely for the first time. Sylvie held her until the wave of her orgasm crashed and grew again. Ade quivered with the release of giving herself to another, of letting go of her trapped thoughts and taut muscles.

Rattled by the vulnerability of it all, she sank down on top of Sylvie in a mess of sweat and sex. It was almost unbearable to be so undone by someone else, to lose control of her anatomy, for even a few seconds, to be so transparent that Sylvie could judge her every need. What had happened between them was magical and scary, like she was learning a new language with Sylvie, but she was already fluent. Ade had learned one thing for certain: she wanted more of it.

***

Ade breathed deeply and loudly, the echoes of Christmas night ricocheting off the spongy walls of her brain. She couldn't get a grip on her memories. Everything was a fabulous riptide of blood rushing against her skull and pulling her under, back into the slumber.

She blinked, and the walls of Sylvie's bedroom embraced her. It was everything she'd imagined: a soft blush color painted on three sides, and the fourth was a flash of gigantic floral print in shades of forest green and fuchsia. Confident yet tender, like Sylvie.

Their first night together had smashed through every one of Ade's expectations. She touched her lips, sore from their famished embrace, and recalled the taste of Sylvie's skin on her tongue.

Closing her eyes, Ade breathed in the scent of Sylvie, the drifting notes of lavender and bergamot that drove her crazy. She couldn't pin it down in their previous encounters, but now, laying in the crumpled sheets of Sylvie's bed, her signature filled the room. Ade stroked her lower back.

As if sensing Ade's reignited desire, Sylvie stirred. "Good morning, you."

Ade couldn't speak, unable to break into this moment that she wanted to preserve in her memory forever. She buried her head in the curve of Sylvie's neck and kissed her earlobe.

"Are you okay?" Sylvie asked.

The euphoria of holding Sylvie in her arms was too much. Ade pressed against the weight of Sylvie's nakedness, drawing their legs together in a tangled heap. "I'm okay." It was all she could manage.

Sylvie arched her back, and her rumble of laughter vibrated against Ade's chest. "I can't believe we bailed on Steph last night."

Ade grinned. "She figured what was up. She did a whole bit about being so wiped, she needed to go to bed early. She gave me an out." Ade shook her head, recalling her sister's acting skills. "I'll face the consequences later."

The absurdity of the moment hit them both as they collapsed against each other in a fit of shared giggles. Of course, Steph had seen all the way through Ade's list of excuses. She always could read her like a book. In a way, Sylvie was the same, able to decipher her thoughts before she'd even formulated them in her mind, before she'd wrapped enough vocabulary around them.

"She's a good sister," Sylvie said.

"Tell me about it," Ade said. "All I wanted in that moment was a two-bedroom apartment."

"Really? How practical of you." Sylvie tickled her ribs. "And what were your plans with this extended floorplan?"

"I guess I'd have sent Steph to her room," Ade said.

"Oh, yeah? I'm sure she would've loved that."

"I would've loved it." Ade stroked Sylvie's cheek. "I would've taken you to my room and laid you down on the crumpled sheets that I wished I'd taken the time to steam. I would've kissed every part of you that's been hidden from me by sweaters and jackets for so many weeks."

Sylvie ran her tongue along her lips, and Ade followed its

journey back into her mouth with envy. Beads of sweat formed at Ade's underarms as adrenaline pumped through her body. For a moment, a dizziness threatened to overwhelm her, and she was unable to act on her impulse. Instead, she detached from her own body and watched a reel play of what she'd like to do to Sylvie. "I wish you could see what's inside my head," Ade said, breathless, even though a little part of her worried that Sylvie might turn away.

But the tiny space between them was blazing with unspent fuel, and Ade breached it, meeting Sylvie's lips with her own and covering her cheek with a tenderness that she wasn't sure she was capable of, holding as if she'd never let go.

A greed filled their kiss, and Ade ran her hands through Sylvie's hair, relishing its silky feel. The moment was as charged as their first kiss, and the beat of desire pulsing between them.

"Hello, again." Sylvie wrapped her legs around Ade's thighs and drew her closer.

Ade met Sylvie's body, and they eased into each other, fitting together as if they'd been making love like this forever. She contemplated the shift in her reality over the past couple of days. She'd acted on her deepest fantasy, and it had come true. What else could come true if she allowed it to?

Chapter Thirty-One

STUDENTS FILED IN WITH their January blues, while Sylvie slowed down to avoid skipping into the staff room. The Christmas week had transformed her from the inside out. She smiled at the memory of Ade's tongue on her skin and blushed as the reverb of the touch sent her pulse skyward. She rejoined her colleagues with an ache in her center, missing the solid weight of Ade's body between her legs.

How could normal life continue when they'd been wrapped in each other's arms just a few short hours ago? Sylvie had left Ade in her apartment, insisting they arrive at the campus separately to avoid suspicion. Not that she was ashamed, and she'd made that more than clear this morning, as she'd knelt at Ade's feet, planting sleepy, tender kisses to her thighs. It was just easier to avoid the questions and protocols of having a relationship at work—if that's what it was. They hadn't discussed labeling what they had.

The only thing that Sylvie was certain of was the physical yearning she couldn't satiate, no matter how many hours she'd spent on her back trying to.

Isa scrutinized Sylvie's face more thoroughly than usual. "Good morning, Professor Boucher. Looking very perky for a January morning."

Sylvie braced for an interrogation, as if last night's sex was written all over her face. Not much escaped Isa's notice. "Happy New Year to you. How was your break?"

"Marvelous, and over far too quickly. How is it we're back here so soon, responsible for the education of our wayward young adults?"

"Time flies..." Sylvie left the sentence hanging, not wishing to describe exactly how much fun she had been having.

"You seem different. Have you done something with your hair?"

She'd been combatting bedhead for the last four days, but she didn't think that was a suitable answer.

"What's with you?" Isa asked, her brow furrowing so far it almost met in the center. "Why are you silent?"

Sylvie wasn't sure how long she could keep this up. "I'm simply strolling into campus with my work bestie. Nothing more, nothing less." She wasn't ready to share the details with anyone, wanting to keep the ecstasy that Ade had brought all to herself for now. Her breath caught when she saw Ade striding toward the science block. She wasn't near enough to warrant a conversation, but her proximity sent a rush of fiery wanting through her, heating her cheeks.

"Oh my. Have you?" Isa sidestepped a group of students coming toward them and dragged Sylvie by the elbow into a quiet alcove. She looked upward, as if to check if anyone could eavesdrop. "Have you and Ade been...you know?"

Sylvie closed her eyes against the glare of Ade's scrutiny. She couldn't lie. And she didn't want to deny Ade. "Yes. We have."

"What the fuck?" Isa whispered, her face animated with confusion, curiosity, and glee. "Well, this makes the January return much more fun."

"It made Christmas pretty interesting too." Sylvie clamped her hand to her mouth.

"Tell me *everything*."

Sylvie snuck a look around her, checking for wayward students. Telling Isa the truth was one thing, declaring it to the whole campus was quite another. "I don't know where to start."

"Don't give me that. You know the start, middle, and ending of everything. Now don't spare any details. I want to know exactly how hot that mysterious post-grad is."

Sylvie cringed. She didn't want to reduce Ade to gossip. What they'd experienced over the holidays was so much more than that. "Ade is pretty special."

"Yeah. Special and hot as fuck. Come on: scale of one to ten." Isa folded her arms.

"Ten," said Sylvie, without hesitation.

"Whoa," Isa stepped back in surprise. "You're serious then. She's that special?"

Sylvie wasn't sure how serious they were, but she couldn't dismiss their connection as anything frivolous or trivial. "We've had an amazing few days together."

Isa leaned back against the wall, as if they were teenagers hiding during their break. "What now though? You're both back at work. Are you going to tell Paul?"

Sylvie rested against the building, unable to hold the weight of expectation and responsibilities she now faced. Why couldn't she and Ade have carried on just as they were, hidden in the fog of festivity, with no reason to leave her apartment except for the odd pastry and fresh baguette. "I haven't thought about it. I wanted to get through today and talk to Ade."

"So it's an 'us' problem, is it?" Isa smirked.

Maybe it was. Sylvie didn't think it would be fair to go to the head of their department without consulting Ade, not that she'd really care either way since she was a temporary member of university staff. It was Sylvie with the bigger stake in all this.

"I knew there was something about you this morning." Isa winked before wrapping her arm around Sylvie's shoulders. "Don't have too much fun and forget your friends though, will you? We have that quiz night this week."

The date had fallen from Sylvie's memory. Perhaps Ade could come along. It was a faculty event, and she was part of the team. "I won't. But I'd better get to class. See you later."

"Absolutely, you will. Don't think I'm letting you get away with keeping the rest of the story to yourself." Isa waved her off with an extra flourish.

A few hours of teaching and coaching passed before Sylvie sat down to her to-do list and opened her laptop to a sea of unopened emails. What she should be doing was editing her book. The publisher had been in touch over the holidays to grant her another extension. Only this one came with an ultimatum: cough up the goods or pay back the advance. It wasn't that explicit, but she could read between the passive-aggressive lines of her commissioning editor. She'd really pushed her luck, ignoring deadlines and procrastinating for weeks. Her sex life had become a major distraction too.

Scrolling through the endless messages she'd ignored before they broke up for Christmas, she didn't notice the sun set until her eyes watered from the blue glare of the screen. She turned her silenced cell phone over, wondering if Ade had been in touch. They'd promised each other time to focus, but that was easier said than done.

Maybe she could drop Ade a quick note. She wanted to see her tonight, even though a good night's sleep in her own bed—alone—would be the best thing for her mind and body. Ade had reawakened a passion deep inside, but the fatigue from their midnight sessions was starting to show in the shadows under her eyes.

Right on cue, Sylvie heard Ade's telltale footsteps in the corridor. She bit the lid of her pen, awaiting Ade's appearance. As the door creaked ajar, Sylvie's heart skipped a beat. They'd barely made it through a whole day without seeing each other. She didn't know whether to despair or rejoice.

"Can I disturb you, ma'am?" Ade grinned, looking every bit the grad student, sporting her washed-out hoodie and jeans.

"Well, it's past my office hours, but I *could* make an exception."

Ade sauntered to the edge of the desk and leaned against it.

"I can't promise any special treatment." Sylvie pursed her lips, hiding her smile behind the pretense of her strict principal routine.

"Well, that's a real shame." Ade stuck out her bottom lip. "I was hoping for some *special* treatment." She spun the chair around and positioned herself between Sylvie's knees.

Sylvie's throat dried out so much she worried she wouldn't be able to form her next line. "What kind of thing did you have in mind?"

Ade held her gaze, giving nothing away. Perched against the desk, with a clear height advantage, Ade's gaze dropped to Sylvie's breasts. She raised her eyebrow, clocking the widening of Ade's pupils as she began to open the top button, and the next, and each one until her blouse fell open.

Ade froze in her spot.

"Is this the kind of special treatment you're used to?" Sylvie asked.

Ade's lips twitched in an almost-smile. "Not quite."

A dare? Sylvie flicked her eyes to the door, closed but unlocked. She paused for a second, weighing the possibility of someone coming by this late in the day. She'd heard all the students leave an hour ago, and most of the staff would be gone by now. They had at least two hours until the final sweep by security.

Rising, Sylvie slipped her shirt to the floor, bracing herself for the chill around her bare shoulders. She stood at eye-level with Ade but didn't move closer. She longed to be touched, but the lack of it intensified every nerve ending.

She removed her shoes and socks and stepped out of her pants. Standing there, in nothing but her lacy underwear was a real turn-on, and the evidence pooled between her legs. As if she knew, Ade's gaze flicked up and down her abdomen, and she licked her lips.

Sylvie held herself back, resisting the strong urge to collapse into the gap between Ade's thighs and succumb to her lips. "What do you want?"

Ade gripped Sylvie's hips, moving her around so they swapped places, then she took the vacant seat. Her breath came fast against Sylvie's breasts before she leaned back into the chair. "Touch yourself for me."

Sylvie almost came at the instruction. No one had ever commanded her with such direct tenderness. Conscious of every inch of her bare skin, she shivered. Her breath was barely a whisper as she ran her fingers over her beating heart, between the channel of her breasts and down the center of her ribs. She stopped at her lace waistband, awaiting further instruction.

"Go on." Ade swallowed.

Sylvie could barely contain the urge to straddle Ade's lap and rub her center against her thigh. She wished the charge between them would last forever. Her hand traveled further down, dipping beneath the sheer fabric, the only barrier between her sex and Ade's loving gaze. "Please, Ade."

"What do you want?" Ade whispered.

Sylvie's knees buckled and she breached the space between them, falling until Ade wrapped her strong arms around her and looked up.

Ade bit her lip. "Tell me. Let me give you everything you want."

"Touch me, please." Sylvie straddled Ade's lap, her thighs shaking with need.

Ade grinned. "You still have too many layers on." She grabbed a pair of scissors from the pencil cup. "Let me get rid of these." She cut through the seam of Sylvie's panties and let them drop to the side, giving her full access to Sylvie's pulsing desire.

Fuck. Sylvie couldn't focus on anything except Ade's fingers on her throbbing body. She glanced down at Ade's fully clothed body and dropped her head in a moment of vulnerability.

"No." Ade tipped her chin up. "You're perfect. I want you to see yourself in my arms, feeling every single thing."

Sylvie ground herself into Ade, building to a crest. Ade held her in the palm of her hand, gently edging her to a blissful release. Every part of their bodies, clothed or naked, communicated with each movement. Words weren't needed right now; Sylvie simply trusted in Ade's touch.

And when it came, it shook her to the core. A raging explosion of chemistry, and then Sylvie collapsed against Ade's chest, desperate for breath.

Ade stroked Sylvie's back. She couldn't move, her legs paralyzed with ecstasy and affection. "Thank you," she said into the crook of Ade's collar.

"You're beautiful, you know?"

Ade only ever spoke the truth, and Sylvie allowed the compliment to penetrate her armor, before the exposure tipped the scales and she shrank away, hiding her face.

"Don't do that." Ade stroked her cheek. "Don't hide from me."

She guided Sylvie back to her chest where she lay, counting the beats. How could Ade have stepped into her life and made such a tremendous impact in so short a time? Sylvie's entire world had been upended by this unquenchable thirst for her. She began to imagine a future she'd never thought could be hers, one where she and Ade were together.

The alternative was starting to become unthinkable.

Chapter Thirty-Two

"IT'S A FEW SHIFTS at the bar," said Steph, dragging Ade by the sleeve down the tall, thin alley.

Ade blinked away the glare of the streetlamp. "So you'll be sticking around for a while?" She'd do just about anything to escape Steph's clutches and head back to Sylvie's for a quiet evening in.

"Yeah, for as long as they'll have me."

"But you're supposed to be traveling this year, not working in a bar. What's Dad going to say?"

"He'll have to find out first, won't he?" Steph glared. "It's just a few weeks to top up my travel fund, and then I'll be out of here. Maybe less if I can pull in some tips."

Ade counted the paving slabs until they reached the threshold of the Irish Tavern.

"What's up? Think I'll cramp your style with Sylvie?" Steph approached the bar. "Hey, Dermot."

The oversized bartender's face lit up. "Hello there, Stephanie." He looked at Ade. "This must be your twin."

"It sure is."

"Two of you? Jesus, what a package." He extended his chubby hand to Ade. "Nice to meet you. Welcome to our little slice of Ireland."

"Thank you," Ade said, enjoying his warm and kind voice.

"So your sister here is joining us for a few weeks. Will we be seeing you too?" Dermot asked and gave a kind smile.

"I'm here now," Ade said.

"Well, that's grand." He chuckled and filled another glass from the large brass pump. "What can I get you both?"

"A diet Coke and a pint of Guinness, please," Steph said.

"Grab yourselves a booth, and I'll bring them over."

Ade followed Steph to the back of the bar, grateful that the evening crowds had not yet gathered. "I'd like to invite Sylvie up to my place, and I'd rather you and I weren't sharing a bed."

"Well, that told me." Steph laughed, brushing off Ade's concern. "I'll make myself scarce, I promise. Plus most of the shifts are evenings and weekends, so you'll have plenty of time to entertain your new friend."

"She's not a friend." The word stuck in Ade's throat. It wasn't nearly adequate to describe the depth of the feelings she had for Sylvie.

Steph squinted. "What do you mean?"

"What does love feel like?" Ade asked. "Romantic love, I mean. Not like Dad and Pops."

Steph's mouth hung open. It was a rare moment that her sister was lost for words.

"I need a real drink for this, Ade. Hang on." She turned as Dermot set down the pint of Guinness on a flimsy coaster, then she lifted the glass to her lips and gulped four times. "What the fuck is happening with you?"

"What do you mean, happening?" Ade scratched her head. "I just asked you a question, and you haven't answered it."

Steph leaned back, smiling. "Okay. Romantic love?" She picked at the cardboard coaster. "I'm no expert. I've only really had one serious, and seriously flawed, relationship. But I can tell you how I felt."

"I'd be grateful." Ade nodded.

"Initially, pretty intoxicating. Like I was addicted to her. I had a thirst that I just couldn't quench."

Ade nodded. "Yes. That's it."

"That's not it." Steph touched her hand across the table. "That's desire and attraction; it's not love."

"Why are you telling me what isn't love? You're not answering the question."

"I'm sorry, I was getting to it." Steph held her hands up. "Love is...wanting to be with someone so much that you think you might fade away without them. When you're not with them, you *do* fade a little. Then they walk into the room, and your whole body and mind is turned on like a light switch."

"Is it like you didn't know you had something inside you, like a treasure chest? And when you see that person, it's like they're the only one with the key? No one else could have unlocked it." Ade wasn't good with metaphors, but that was the best she could do.

"Is that how you feel?" Steph asked, taking another gulp of her drink.

"Maybe. I'm trying to put it into words, but the concepts are tricky." Ade spun her ring. "Is it like finally being understood without having to say anything?"

"Yeah. I think it might be." Steph rubbed her eye.

"Are you crying?"

"No, you idiot." She giggled. "Is it that serious between you and Sylvie? Aren't you just hanging out?"

Ade laced her fingers together. "We have been hanging out. But the more we hang, the harder it gets to leave."

"Have you told her any of this?" Steph asked.

"With my words? No." Ade was pretty certain that her body had communicated all of it, and more.

"What has she said?"

Everything. She'd said everything and nothing. "I can't work it out. When we're together, it's amazing. But we haven't talked about how we're feeling. Not really."

"So it could be casual for her?"

Ade flinched. "I really hope not."

"What's her story? Is she a serial monogamist or a casual fling kinda gal?"

Ade didn't know. How did she not know? Doubt sprouted in her mind, growing rapid, tangling roots. "Do you think I'm just a casual hook-up for her?"

Steph blew out her cheeks. "I don't know Sylvie all that well. She's much older than you, and she lives here. I mean, what could a future look like? It's not like she's going to come back to Monterey and live in the annex with us, is it?"

"Fuck." Ade hadn't thought the logistics through.

"Sounds like you have some talking to do with your new gal pal." Steph swirled the diminishing black liquid in her glass. "Hey," she reached for Ade's hand, "I like Sylvie. I think she's special too."

They were joined by two more of Steph's new bar friends. Ade wondered at how her sister could collect acquaintances like ticket stubs, accumulating several for each city she visited. When the crowd and the decibels increased, Ade made her excuses and headed back to the apartment. At the Place St Roch, her feet took her toward Sylvie's apartment. She buzzed the intercom, desperate for Sylvie to be in so she could satisfy her latest craving.

Sylvie waited at the entrance, her hip cocked, a wide smile, and her hair tumbling out of place. "I thought we were having a night off?"

Ade looked at the floor, not proud of her inability to abstain for just a single evening. "That's a lot harder than I thought it'd be."

"Oh, yeah?" Sylvie swayed her hips on the way inside. "Lucky I was in. I have a packed social calendar."

"You do?" Ade hovered. Should she leave Sylvie to it?

"No." Sylvie turned and put her arms around Ade, pulling her into a long kiss. "I'm kidding. The truth is I've been pining for you and trying to distract myself with polishing furniture."

The chemical smell made Ade's eyes sting. "It's kinda strong."

"Is it? I haven't sprayed it in the bedroom." Sylvie took her hand and led the way.

Ade willingly followed, aching for Sylvie's mouth against hers again. But she also wanted to talk. Steph's words twisted like a corkscrew inside her head. She perched on the edge of Sylvie's bed, kicked off her shoes and pulled off her heavy winter coat.

"Can we talk first?"

Sylvie kneeled on the bed behind Ade and slipped her arms around Ade's torso. "Of course. What's on your mind?"

"Stephanie." Ade swiveled onto the bed to face Sylvie and took her hands.

"You want to talk about your sister right now?" Sylvie smirked. "You never fail to surprise me. Just when I think you're the most consistent person in my whole world."

"I've just been with Steph, and I was asking her about..." Ade stumbled on the right words. Could she admit the strength of her feelings to Sylvie without her running from them?

"You can tell me." Sylvie stroked the back of her hand, leaving a warm trail.

"I was asking about how you know when you feel something for someone."

An understanding silence hung in the few inches between them.

"What are you feeling?" Sylvie asked.

"I can't put the rights words together," said Ade. "But it's unfamiliar. I haven't felt it before. Steph said it's like an addiction."

"I get that. I couldn't give you up right now."

"Really? Me too." Ade released the air from her lungs and the tightness from her body with a long breath. "What does it mean?"

"I don't know. This is a first for me too." Sylvie folded her arms. "I know you think I'm the older and wiser one here, but the reality is I've never allowed myself to get close enough to someone to feel this way about them."

Ade followed the lines of stitching on the bedspread, grappling with her feelings like they were a math problem that could be solved. "It's new for both of us?"

"I guess so." Sylvie caressed Ade's cheek. "We might need to work it out together. What are you thinking right now?"

"I want to kiss you so bad. Like all the time." Ade grinned. "I want to wake up with you. I want to walk into campus with you. I never want to be away from you." Out loud, all that sounded crazy. But it was the truth.

Sylvie looked away. "What about the summer when you have to go home? The odds are stacked against us."

"What do you mean?" Ade asked.

"We live on different continents. The clock is ticking on your time here."

"You could come home with me."

A raspy, almost bitter laugh escaped from Sylvie. "That's exactly my point. You live your life exactly as you should: you're young, and life is about you."

"You're young too." Ade put her finger to Sylvie's lips, wanting to hush any more barriers.

"I'm closing in on forty, and my career is here. In many ways, we're on different tracks, and we have to think about the future."

"But I want you." Ade cupped her cheek. "I want you now. I don't know about the future, but what's in this moment matters to me."

"You have me for now," Sylvie tapped a line of kisses on her fingers, "if not forever."

"That can't be enough." Tears pricked at Ade's eyes. Had she found the love of her life only for it to be fleeting?

"It might have to be, darling." Sylvie kissed her lips.

Ade dropped her gaze. "That makes me so sad."

"Why? You're the one that tells me to live in the present, not the past, nor the future. We can enjoy every single moment from now until you go home." Sylvie walked her fingers down the buttons of Ade's shirt until she reached the waist of her jeans. "Every. Single. Moment."

Sylvie was right. If this was all they had, Ade couldn't waste it. It's not like she could uproot her life and move to California. And Ade couldn't fathom a permanent move away from her support network. She leaned into the welcome kiss and tried to banish the future from her mind. The present was here to be enjoyed.

Chapter Thirty-Three

SHIELDING HER CHEEKS FROM the bite of January's wind, Sylvie shrank from the harsh truths of last night. The walk to work had been longer than usual, as she went over their conversation. She entered the cocoon of the staff room grateful for the sharp change in temperature and the familiar aroma of milk and burned coffee. With everything else up in the air, the coziness of the staff room was like a warm hug.

She checked her watch: the faculty meeting was due to start in ten minutes. Hoping to keep a low profile, she made for the corner. With the meeting done, she could retreat to her classroom to overthink.

She didn't regret what she'd said to Ade, but she wished it were different. If only it was a lie to protect both their feelings from the eventual hurt. Deep down, she knew that Ade would leave, and that would scar her heart. She'd held Ade extra tight after a night of satisfying each other's desires, but there'd been a hint of sadness. Despite their promises to live in the moment, Sylvie had started to grieve the loss already.

"Damn." She burned her tongue on the university's poor excuse for coffee.

At the other end of the room, Isa's raised voice attracted Sylvie's attention. She straightened to see what the matter was and caught the undeniable fear in Ade's eyes as she stared upwind into Isa's torrent.

Sylvie sighed, curiosity simmering beneath her wish to stay put and stay out of it. She risked another glance in their direction. What was Isa talking about? Was it about her and Ade? It couldn't be.

Even Isa wouldn't risk the whole faculty listening into their private affairs.

Ade froze, as if she was unable to process what was happening. Sylvie had seen that terror before, when Ade was new to the city and every conversation had been a strange encounter for her. *Christ.* She had to do something. The urge to rescue Ade from what looked like an impossible-to-read situation was too strong, and she strode across to them.

Isa regarded her with a strange mix of concern and irritation. "Don't get involved, Sylvie."

"What are you talking about?" Sylvie whispered, not wishing to attract any more onlookers. "I'm Ade's supervisor. If something's wrong then I need to be involved."

Isa rolled her eyes. "Oh, really? You're Ade's supervisor today?"

"Isa, please." Sylvie couldn't say anymore without drawing more onlookers. She begged Isa to tone it down with a pleading glare.

Ade stared at the floor, shuffling from foot to foot as if she was waiting outside the principal's office.

"What's going on, Ade?" Sylvie asked, resisting the temptation to take Ade's hand.

Isa crossed her arms. "I didn't want to embroil you, but if you must know, I was enquiring about the faked attestation that I've just received reports of."

So this was faculty business catching up with Ade and not their personal lives. Relieved, Sylvie almost laughed. *Damn it.* Did Isa think that Ade had encouraged it? Sylvie had a split second to weigh the ethics. She'd known about the risk of faked reports and had decided not to do anything about it. Did that make her as guilty as Madison, who'd obviously gone through with the forgery?

"Did you know about this?" Isa asked, already reading Sylvie's silence as guilt.

"Why don't we go somewhere quieter?" Sylvie asked, desperate to take the sting out of the moment.

Isa's face reddened with her obvious fury. "Don't try to protect her, Sylvie, just because you two are—"

"Please." Sylvie grabbed Isa by the arm and led her into the corridor. It was no less busy, but the hum of activity masked the volume of their emerging scandal. "It's not like that."

Ade followed, still rendered mute by the accusation.

Sylvie took a breath and steeled herself. This was going to take some ironing out, especially if Ade was unwilling to explain herself. "Ade told me that one of her students had suggested something about faking signatures to pass their modules, and she explicitly told them not to do it."

"How come there's a rumor that Ade encouraged it?" Isa asked. "Well?" She turned back to the wide-eyed statue of Ade.

"Madison…" Ade cleared her throat. "Madison mentioned it. She was clearly distressed and needed some support. But I told her not to do it."

"I can vouch for her," said Sylvie, hoping that her own integrity wasn't about to unravel.

Isa's jaw stiffened, and she looked between them. "Listen, Adelaide, I don't know you all that well. But I do know that Professor Boucher is one of the most respected academics in the country. She sets high standards and demands professional ethics. If she's in your corner, that's enough for me." She stepped forward. "But you need to know that the students you brought over from California are in your care. Faking reports undermines the efforts of every single student here, not to mention the staff working hard to keep them on track. You're responsible for their behavior and conduct, as well as your own. I don't want to hear about this kind of thing again. And neither does Paul."

Sylvie placed her hand on Isa's upper arm. "Absolutely. We're all agreed on that. Ade told me about this straight away. As her supervisor, I made the judgment not to take it further at the time. If some evidence has come to light now that suggests one of the students has acted inappropriately, then Ade and I will deal with it."

"I don't want rumors flying around that teachers are encouraging grade fraud. It's the last thing we need as a faculty. Get your house in order, Sylvie, before people start to really question our ethics." Isa turned and went back to the staff room.

Sylvie rounded on Ade. "You knew about this?"

"No!" Ade's face fell. "I told you what happened before Christmas. I had no idea that Madison had gone through with it."

"Jesus Christ, this is all we need."

"What?" Ade reached for Sylvie's hand but withdrew before they touched.

"More paperwork. We'll have to investigate what happened and make a report to the faculty here and your leadership team at home." Sylvie groaned. "Bring Madison in for a meeting this week, and we'll try to get to the bottom of it."

"Sure." Ade's shoulders sank.

"I'm sorry I'm worked up about this, Ade." Sylvie released a heavy sigh. "But if Isabelle has heard about Madison, then other members of the staff might have too. This isn't just about the rights and wrongs of it, it's about my reputation."

Ade gave nothing away. Her body swayed a little, but her face remained unreadable.

"Are you going to talk to me?" Sylvie stamped her foot in frustration. How could Ade just stand there with all this going on?

Ade swallowed what looked like a lump of emotion. "I can't right now. I've got to get to the marine center for a shift."

"Great. You get to your safe space." *Leave me to clear up your mess.* Sylvie ran her hands through her hair, struggling to keep her cool. "I want to protect you, but this is the job. This is exactly what I was talking about last night."

"What do you mean?" Ade's mouth gaped slightly.

Sylvie hesitated. Maybe Ade just needed to hear the truth. "I'd love it if you could see this from my perspective. But that's tricky for you, and I should know that by now."

Ade blinked. "I do struggle with that, yeah. My bad."

Sylvie glanced at her watch. She couldn't stand there any

longer. "The meeting is about to start." She walked away, kicking herself for her outburst. If Ade had been firmer with Madison in the first place, this wouldn't have escalated. Anger rose inside Sylvie's chest, and tears threatened to give her away. She was furious, not with Ade but with the whole ridiculous situation. This was exactly the kind of silly trivial error which could blow up in her face and destroy her chances of promotion next time round. But back in the staff room, with Ade under attack for her mistake, Sylvie was more certain than ever that she'd do anything for her. How could she be so frustrated with someone and feel so much for them at the same time?

Chapter Thirty-Four

ADE HID UNDER HER comforter, shutting out the world. She'd had enough of other people's opinions. She didn't always get things right. God knows she'd known that since she'd been conscious of her place in the world. But she didn't mean to hurt anyone or break any rules.

Her skin itched with the injustice of it all. She threw off the cover and counted the cracks in the ceiling, but it did nothing to tame the feeling of ants crawling over her skin. She could've yelled back at Isabelle and Sylvie yesterday. Instead, the tormenting scream stayed locked inside her mind. She hadn't even heard half of what Sylvie said. But the other half was enough. Ade had let her down in a big way. She'd been winging it for far too long in this job, thinking she could get away with the bare minimum.

It'd all started to unravel at the worst possible time. Just when she was desperate to show Sylvie she could make a real try at something and that she was serious about their relationship. Maybe even be ready for a commitment, whatever that could look like on either side of the Atlantic.

The door cracked open, and Steph came in from her early shift at the bar. "You're still in bed? Have you even moved today?"

The clock ticked past four. "Not much."

"You still sore over Sylvie's takedown?"

Ade grunted. She'd explained as best she could, but Steph only grasped the simplicity of the problem.

"She'll get over it," Steph said. "But not if you insist on dwelling in your self-pity over here."

"It's not self-pity. I'm worried. Everything was going great, but then she started talking about enjoying the next few months and not looking too far ahead." Ade launched backward into her pillows with a frustrated scream. "Then this happened, and I'm not sure she's even up for enjoying the time we have left."

"If she drops you at the first hurdle, she's not worth it. You deserve better."

Ade rolled over and planted her face against the mattress. "You don't get it."

"Help me then. Talk to me." Steph sat on the bed. "Hey, why don't we hit the bar tonight and take your mind off it?"

"That's not going to help. I need to be more responsible, not go out drinking on a school night."

"We're young, Ade. Don't waste your year abroad pining after some professor with a stick up her ass about something minor."

"Don't say that. Sylvie was right to be annoyed."

"So get your act together and apologize clearly. Then you can both move on. If she's the mature adult she claims to be, she'll have no problem in putting it all behind her. Am I right?"

"I guess so." Ade rubbed the pulse at her temple. How could she say sorry to Sylvie?

"Come out with me, and we'll figure something out," said Steph, a familiar twinkle in her eye that promised nothing but trouble.

An hour later, Ade's world swayed from one side to another, like the spirit level in her abdomen was off kilter. If Ade didn't know better, she'd swear she was on a sailboat off the coast of Monterey.

"Here." Steph passed her another shot of tequila and tipped salt on her hand.

Ade lost her balance, and the white grains spilled over the bar. "I can't take any more."

"Of course you can. I'll look after you Ady-baby." Steph slurred her words and draped her arm like a dead weight across Ade's shoulders.

"I can't believe you two are twins."

The greasy hanger-on they'd attracted had been with them for an hour. Ade had blocked out much of the conversation, choosing to slip her earbuds in and play her favorite tunes.

The evening had been predictably fueled by strong liquor and extrovert energy, neither of which Ade could stomach at the best of times. Pulled along by Steph's enthusiasm for random strangers and their anecdotes, Ade sat like a spare part on bar stool after bar stool. "I'm heading home after this one, Steph." She slapped her hand on the bar to emphasize her intention.

"Hey, you want to get out of here? My place is just around the corner."

The slimy guy leaned in too close, and she backed away from the stench of liquor on his breath.

"Trust me, you're not her type." Steph stepped between them.

"Oh, yeah?" He stood up, leering over them both. "How about you then, sweetheart? The three of us could have a good time."

"Fuck off, loser." Steph slammed another shot and turned her back on him.

"Steph—"

The guy pushed Steph against the bar, sending their glasses shattering against the floor. "Bitches like you don't deserve my attention." He spat in their direction and stood even taller.

Ade's vision shrank to the space between them. She grabbed his forearm and bent it just enough to send a shockwave of pain through to his shoulder, rendering him weak and willing to follow her lead to the open door.

"You show him, Ade," Steph shouted and beckoned another round from the bar staff.

It wasn't the first time Ade had pulled this move on guys that bothered them. It wasn't often that she needed to show her strength, but it came in handy on occasion. "I really don't like people treating my sister like she's an object. So please leave us to our evening." Ade ejected the guy onto the pavement, where the security for the bar across the street nodded in her direction. "And don't put your hands on people. It's rude."

"Fuck you," he said and sneered until he rounded the corner. Ade strolled back into the bar.

Bruce carried a barrel up from the cellar. "You okay there?"

"Yeah, I'm fine," she said, willing the night to be over. *Why did I think this would help my bad mood?* Nights like this only ever ended in one thing: drama. "I'm heading home now though. Will you keep an eye on Steph and send her back when she's ready?"

"Sure thing," Bruce said, hooking up the beer to the pump. "See you around."

Back home, Ade peeled off her clothes and climbed into bed. She stared at her phone, willing another of Sylvie's messages to flash across the screen. She thought about the last couple of days and tried to decipher what she could have done differently to avoid Sylvie's anger.

She sighed, tired of raking over the same scenes in her head, hoping to unearth a different outcome. She needed to work out what to do right now to make it better. What was Sylvie expecting? A grand apology? Ade gritted her teeth, resenting her inability to read the world and its norms. Would she ever find peace when the sands continued to shift beneath her?

Chapter Thirty-Five

THE ROTATION OF THE washer threw another sock at the drum, its wrung out, distended shape ready for another trip around the steel cylinder. Sylvie sympathized with the sopping wet cotton. She'd traveled another rotation of optimism and panic since breakfast, doubting that anything she wanted would ever come to pass.

"Penny for your thoughts?" Colette asked, her arms full of napkins and tablecloths.

"They're not worth that much." Sylvie moved along to make space for her neighbor. "Have you abandoned your post at the café?"

"Just for a while. We've run short of linen, so here I am." Colette cocked her head. "You don't seem your usual self."

"No."

Colette raised her eyebrows. "If I was a betting woman I'd guess it's trouble of the heart?"

Sylvie couldn't deny her heart was troubled, but the pain and panic was so much more complex. "You're not wrong."

"Girlfriend?"

"That's a strong word."

"Is it?" Colette asked.

To Sylvie it was. Maybe not for others. "It's not just her. I'm drifting along with a lack of purpose. I'm thirty-six years old, I've got two days to make another book deadline that I'm probably going to miss, I have a thigh-high stack of marking to do, and I've no food in for dinner. I don't know what's wrong with me."

Colette bumped against her. "I'm going to circle back to the girlfriend. How's it going?"

"I'm in too deep. I'm doubting myself more than ever, but I can't stop. Sorry, I'm waffling on."

"It sounds pretty typical," Colette said.

"Of what?"

"Falling in love, silly." Colette laughed her innocent, casual laugh.

Sylvia juggled the grenade of truth that threw in her lap. "I'm not in love." It sounded like a lie, even to her.

"You can't stop thinking about someone, even though you're a rational and responsible adult with duties and deadlines. You can't even buy food. You look tired and ragged. They call it lovesick for a reason, you know."

Sylvie scanned her untidy appearance. Of course she'd thrown on some old joggers and a T-shirt for a visit to the launderette. That didn't make her a lovesick puppy.

"I've watched you guys, you know?"

Sylvie pursed her lips. "Now you sound creepy."

"I see how you look at your not-girlfriend." Colette stretched her legs across the linoleum. "You don't see anyone else when she's in the room. The city could be on fire, and your only concern would be making sure she was safe."

Sylvie's jaw dropped. Had her feelings been there for everyone to see, or did Colette have some kind of magical ability?

"I like her," Colette said. "She sees you too."

"She does?"

"She reads your lips, she mirrors your movements. It's like you're her whole world."

"How do you know all this?"

"I suck up the vibe at the café. I know when people need something and when they should be left alone. It's a talent, being able to read the room."

Unsettled by Colette's revelation, Sylvie loaded a dryer and made her excuses to get some air. When her cell rang, she almost ignored it, wishing away the interruption. But Ade's name across her blank screen made her heart leap. "Hi."

"I wanted to see you," Ade said. "Can you come over to the marine center?"

"I'm in the middle of some chores." Sylvie looked to the sky for an answer. "And I'm meant to be working on my book this afternoon."

"I don't want to disturb you, but..." Ade said, "I've been thinking. You'll be away in England soon for Elda's exhibition and then I'll be away with Steph for our birthday."

"I know that." Sylvie had dreaded the time apart too...until they'd argued.

"Maybe bring your edits with you. I have jobs to do, and we can work down here together. It's quiet, and I won't disturb you, I promise. I just need to see your face."

Sylvie swallowed back the trepidation she'd been feeding all day. "Okay. I'll see you soon."

The last time they'd spoken, Sylvie had worried she'd said too much, been too abrupt. But Ade's invitation seemed like an attempt to wipe the slate clean, and with no real reason to delay, Sylvie headed for the marine center as soon as she'd dropped her laundry back at her apartment.

She swiped her entry pass at the front of the building, and Ade was already there, waiting to meet her in the foyer. Their eyes met through the rotating doors, and Sylvie's whole body responded, a thrill coursing through her veins.

"Close your eyes," Ade said and gave her a cheeky smile.

"What are you up to?" Sylvie asked.

Ade took Sylvie's hand. "Come with me."

She'd missed the warm softness of Ade's palm against hers, and she allowed herself to be led through the center's corridors to its main labs.

"Here we are." Ade stopped and held both Sylvie's hands. "Don't open your eyes yet. Just listen."

Sylvie focused on what she could hear: a gentle lap of water and the deep moan of something animal.

"Feel better yet?" Ade asked.

Sylvie hummed her response in tune with the calm, restful melody of the marine life around her.

"Okay, you can open your eyes. Come, sit." Ade led her to a desk station, adorned with blankets and cushions, where there was a flask full of coffee and homemade cookies. "You could work here for the afternoon, while I get the rest of my jobs done."

"You did all this?"

"Sure." Ade rested her hands on Sylvie's shoulders and gently eased her into a seated position. She removed her jacket and began to massage Sylvie's shoulders.

Sylvie leaned into the touch, enjoying the firm roll of her muscles under Ade's fingers. "I won't get much work done this way."

"I know, but it would be good to relax."

"Relaxing is one word for it." Sylvie bit her lip, the sensation in her shoulders traveling all the way to her core.

"Hey," Ade said, swiveling the chair around so that she faced Sylvie. "I fucked up this week. I embarrassed you, and that's not okay. I'm trying to signal here that I will do just about anything to put that right. And that means creating an environment where you can relax, get some work done, and we can enjoy each other's company."

"It beats working at my kitchen table, which is what I had planned." Sylvie smiled, grateful for the simple gesture. "You know, you're like a different person when you're here."

"What do you mean?" Ade frowned. "I'm the same person I always am."

"Not like that. You have a calm, which is kind of catching. I feel more relaxed already." Sylvie put her head against Ade's stomach. "I'm really worried about this work stuff."

"I know you are. What can I do to help?"

"Just this," said Sylvie. "Giving me time and space to focus on it. I've been distracted lately."

"Because of me?" Ade asked.

"Not at all. I'm a grown-up. I should be able to sort my schedule and meet my own deadlines."

"What's getting in your way?"

"Me." Sylvie sighed. "I'm my own worst enemy sometimes. All I can think is that the next book won't be good enough. That the publishers will drop me. That Paul will fire me."

"What evidence do you have that the book won't be good enough? Has your editor said something already?"

"God, no. She's pretty content with what she's seen so far." Sylvie stroked Ade's palm. "It's all in my head."

"This head here?" Ade tapped lightly on her scalp. "This beautiful head is full of thoughts that aren't true?"

Sylvie nodded.

"How about I fill them with things that are true?"

"Like what?"

"You're one of the most intelligent, thought-provoking people I've ever met. You're open and honest in a way most people aren't. You're kind and see the best in people, even when that's hard. You see the flaws in society and want to make it better."

"Stop it." Sylvie dropped her gaze, unable to meet the glare of Ade's compliments.

"You can't take it?" Ade tipped Sylvie's chin up.

"No one has ever spoken to me like that."

"Never? No one has ever told you how utterly brilliant you are?" Ade shook her head. "I want to tell you those things every single day. I want to tell you that you light up the room, that your students hang on your every word, and that people in cafés look your way whenever you glide past them. You have an aura that I've never known anyone else to have."

If Sylvie had an aura, she'd found her match. Not brave enough to say the words aloud, she pulled Ade closer and snuggled into her abdomen. "I don't deserve all of that."

"Why not?"

"I was pretty horrible to you on Friday."

"I let you down. We both know that," Ade said. "But I want to be better. I think I know what went wrong with Madison, and it won't happen again."

Sylvie pushed up from the chair and pressed her lips to Ade's, hoping to silence her self-doubt. They kissed, a longing, loving exchange that meant more than she could describe with the language she had.

Sylvie wished she could articulate the enormity of her feelings for Ade, but she grappled with the scale of something so personal yet so universal. How could she pretend to write about the human existence when she couldn't understand her own basic emotions?

Chapter Thirty-Six

SHE MIGHT HAVE SAID too much. But for once, regret didn't hang around in Ade's consciousness. She was glad to have created a cocoon of calm in which Sylvie could focus, and after they'd peeled themselves away from each other's lips, they both got some work done. By Monday, the equilibrium of their fragile in-the-moment relationship was back on track. The successful afternoon at the marine center had been followed by a weekend of easy contentment.

Ade was dreading the latest of her student counseling windows, but she settled in her office, ready for the first of her appointments. Her misgivings about her own abilities clung on, but this was a chance to show up for her students and quiet her self-doubt.

Madison turned up twenty minutes late. Having already begun to worry, Ade's concern tripled when she saw the state of her. Her limp, greasy hair fell against her shoulders, and her eyes were red, with dark shadows hanging above her gaunt cheeks.

"What's going on with you?" Ade feared that the reprimands for the faked attestations had been worse than expected. "Are you okay?" Silly question, given the obvious physical evidence.

"Just tired," Madison said, her voice croaking with a clear lack of rest.

"Please, come and sit down. I'm worried about you." Ade immediately clocked the red lines on Madison's arms: a sign that she'd been cutting herself. Helping her with that was way beyond Ade's expertise and pay grade. But she couldn't abandon her right now; she was obviously in crisis. "Hey, I'm going to ask you some questions. You don't need to answer me, but if you want to talk to me, it's just between us. Though I do need to tell you that if I think you might be at risk of any harm, I'm gonna need to tell someone else about it, okay?"

Madison nodded, as if she'd resigned herself to the conditions of their meeting, and that might just be the reason she showed up.

Ade nodded at the marks on her arm. "Have you hurt yourself, Madison?"

Madison gave a whimper of acknowledgment.

"You want to talk about why?"

"Not really."

"You planning on doing something more serious?" Ade asked, not really wanting the answer.

Madison met her eye contact. "No."

Ade believed her. But she had to make sure. "Are you thinking about it?"

Madison shrugged. "If I wanted to, I would've done it by now. Trust me."

That did not make Ade feel a ton better. "What can I do to help?"

"I want to go home, but my folks say they're not willing to pay the airfare, and I need to suck it up. They said I'm homesick, and I'll feel better when the weather improves."

Sounded like something her dad would say, and her pops would get mad about. "How do you feel about all that?"

Madison stared at her filthy shoes. "Trapped in this shitty place with no real friends and no one to talk to. I can't understand half of what people say to me. The work is too hard, and the schedule is almost double what we had last semester."

Ade's computer of a brain returned a blank file. *Damn it.* Madison was sitting right there in front of her, expecting her to solve her problems. What would Sylvie do? Ade cleared her throat again. "I don't think I have an answer right now."

Madison rolled her eyes. "Great. Thanks."

"Wait." Ade started to pace and flapped her hands, which helped clear the fog in her mind. "I don't think either of us need to have all the answers."

Madison screwed her nose up.

"It sounds like you're feeling really lonely out here," Ade said.

"I miss home."

"And the pressure of classes is mounting." Ade practiced the reflection technique her therapist had taught her to clarify meaning when she struggled to grip a social situation.

Madison nodded.

So far, so good. "What do you think the options are?"

Madison picked at her pink nail gels. "Go home."

"That's one option. Are there any others?"

"I guess I could reduce my class load. We talked about that before Christmas."

Ade didn't want to get into what had happened before Christmas, fearing the guilt about the faked report cards would worsen Madison's current mood. But tweaking her schedule was pretty safe ground. Even Sylvie couldn't deny that. "I can definitely help with your schedule. I'll speak to the faculty admin today, and we'll see what we can do. What else? Have you spoken to anyone about how you're feeling?"

"Nuh-uh." Madison shook her head. "But I think Greg is a good guy. The others are pretty toxic."

"Greg is solid, I can attest to that." Ade nodded, finally on firm ground. She sat back down, leaning back, not wishing to crowd Madison and cause her to panic. "What about the cutting? Can we do anything about that?"

"I've always done it. It's nothing new." Madison pulled her bag on her lap. "I'll try not to, but I can't make promises."

"I get that." Ade was out of her depth with this, but she pressed on. "Promise me one thing, okay? Stay safe. Keep it clean and try not to get infected. And if you do feel worse... I mean, if you think about hurting yourself, come and talk to me or someone else. I'll make a referral to the well-being team."

Ade continued her sessions, pushing the worry about Madison

to the back of her mind until the end of the day, when she downloaded to Sylvie on their way home.

"It sounds like you handled that really well," said Sylvie.

"I just asked myself: what would you do in this situation?" Ade shrugged.

Sylvie grimaced. "I'm not sure you should stake all your hard conversations on what I would do. I often get things spectacularly wrong."

"I don't think so." Ade squeezed Sylvie's hip, enjoying the proximity on their commute home by tram. "Once I tracked your voice in my head, I just leaned into my instincts."

"Sounds like a tough session. Did you report it to the well-being team?"

"I filed a report right away." Ade flicked the screen on her phone. "They got back to me with a referral link that I can send onto Madison."

"Good. Tell her I'd be more than happy to talk to her too, if that would help." Sylvie rested her hand on Ade's thigh. "Not that I want to step on your toes. You're doing a good job."

Ade looked down at her toes and the clear gap between her feet and Sylvie's. "I know." She closed her eyes to the crowded tram and focused on the gentle sway of the car. When she opened them, the orange lights of the city's street lamps were speeding past the windows.

"You okay?" Sylvie asked.

"I'm going to miss you while we're away." Her head pounded with the heaviness of the day, but the flicker of pride in her chest was enough to keep her going. Rather than retreat to the solitude of the marine lab, today she'd faced her fears and dealt with the most human of problems: someone in pain, hurting from loneliness and overwhelm.

Ade had been there. She'd climbed the spiral that Madison was trying to clamber out of. She wanted to be there when Madison needed her most. She wanted to prove to herself and others that she could stand on her own two feet and not just be a grown-up but also a helpful person.

But most of all, she wanted Sylvie to see her and value her. Ade already ached from Sylvie's impending absence. Would Sylvie's essence stay in her heart when she wasn't by her side?

Chapter Thirty-Seven

"I TOLD HER THAT one best friend was more than enough, but Elda's greedy." Jack threw Sylvie's holdall across his slim shoulder and winked.

"Elda is one of the most demanding people I know when it comes to love and affection. She has it in spades and still wants more." Sylvie giggled. "I'm sorry to usurp your position, but I promised I'd come for the exhibition launch, and I missed the last one."

"Yeah, she wouldn't stop complaining when you didn't show up in Edinburgh. I never thought she'd forgive you."

Sylvie winked. "I have my ways."

"I bet you do, you minx." Jack held open the door to their hotel.

He'd lost none of his British charm since she'd last seen him. His previously skinny frame had filled out with muscle, and he boasted a healthy glow on his fair skin, which reassured Sylvie that all was well, despite Jack's years of hedonism with Elda as his sidekick. He was a magnet for fun and laughter, attracting like-minded people who found joy in life, even in its darkest moments. Sylvie loved him all the more because he could be there for Elda when she couldn't.

"Now," Jack said, "I need to warn you that my new boyfriend is super stylish and will give your Parisian ways a little run for your money."

Sylvie doubted that. Jack's last beau had been a fleeting guest at their dinner table one hot summer afternoon a couple of years ago. He was tall and handsome, no denying that, but had all the grace of a baby giraffe. "What's his name?"

"Julius."

Sylvie stifled her laughter. "As in Caesar?"

"As in, Smith. Julius Smith." He shrugged.

"I look forward to meeting him."

"Good, because there he is at the bar. I messaged him our order." Jack pulled her suitcase through the grand foyer of the hotel. "Darling, this is Sylvie Boucher, Elda's *second* best friend. She's French, and she looks down on most people, but I've warned her that you have a sense of style to rival Dior himself."

Sylvie smirked at the introduction, used to Jack's unique sense of humor. "Delighted to meet you, Julius. I've heard very little about you, but I get the sense that by the end of the evening, we shall be the best of acquaintances."

Julius took a ridiculous bow, dipping his perfectly coiffed hairline. Sylvie wasn't sure whether he was greeting her or beginning a performance.

"Enchanted to meet you." He took her hand and kissed the back of it gently.

"Such a gentleman." Sylvie grinned at Jack. "What do you see in our friend Jack the lad?"

Julius winked. "He has his moments."

"Don't I just." Jack nudged him in the ribs. "I'll pop your bag at reception, Sylvie. We'd better get a wriggle on if we're going to make it in time for the canapés." Jack passed Sylvie a flute of champagne and drank his own.

Sylvie and Julius tsked in tandem. Reunited with Jack and already finding a fellow comrade in Julius, Sylvie looked forward to the evening, despite Ade's absence nagging at her.

By the time they reached the gallery, Jack was in full swing, regaling Sylvie of tales of more travels across Europe and his journey back to England where he'd met the current love of his life, Mr. Julius Smith. "I've got an apartment now, not far from Elda's old man. She pops in every week or so with Arlo."

"Does she see much of her mother?" Sylvie pondered every now and again on the pain that Elda suffered.

"Now and again. They keep it civil, but there's a bit too much scar tissue in that relationship for it all to be plain sailing." He held the door of the cab open for her.

She breathed in the scent of taxi fumes and street food. Every shop front was illuminated, and lamps glowed with optimism, even in January's darkest days.

They pulled up to the grand venue, and Julius offered his arm while Jack skipped ahead like a kid wanting to beat the queues.

"She's here," Jack said at the entrance doors.

This was bigger than any exhibition Elda had staged before. The venue dwarfed the last event Sylvie had made it to, and its bespoke signs and finishing touches would've blown a modest budget.

Anticipation and pride tingled in Sylvie's belly. "This is fabulous." Her cheeks ached with a wide smile. "You look stunning."

Elda gave her a little twirl, revealing the glamor of her golden dress. "Thank you." She planted a kiss on Sylvie's cheek. "I'm so pleased you could come."

"What about me?" Jack wriggled between them. "I came all the way from East London."

"Forever grateful to you too." Elda kissed him on the cheek and rubbed his hair like a big sister. "You're my angel."

Jack blushed. For all his bluster, he was a softie at heart. Before Elda could finish her greetings, she was whisked away by someone looking efficient and fashionable.

"Her publicist," Jack said. "She has an actual publicist now. I remember when she was hiding in the store room drinking vodka with me."

"You've both flourished." Sylvie brushed dust from his collar. "I like Julius. You're right; he's civilized and beautiful."

"And how about you, my little chérie? Elda tells me you had a special friend for Christmas." His cheeky smile burst into a lewd expression.

"Put your tongue away." Sylvie chastised. "If you're referring to

Ade, then yes, she came for Christmas."

"I bet she did."

Even Julius laughed out loud. Sylvie was surrounded by school boys.

"Where is she then?" Jack asked. "Why isn't she dripping from your arm?"

Sylvie wished for that, already missing Ade's body next to hers. "She's working this week and then has birthday plans with her family. It was arranged months ago, and we couldn't make the dates work."

"Oh, that's sad. Elda said it's hotting up between you two." Jack extended his hands in a theatrical stance. "I mean in a Sylvie way. With plenty of yearning, overthinking, doubling back to make sure—"

"Did Elda tell you all that?" Sylvie twisted her hair between her fingers.

"She didn't need to. That's how you move through the world, Sylvie. All furrowed brow and disapproving of everyone, especially yourself."

"Jack!" Julius slapped him gently on the arm.

"There's no need to intervene," Sylvie said, patting Julius. "Our little friend here spends most of his life enjoying other people's drama. Whether it bears any resemblance to the truth is neither here nor there."

Julius still looked horrified. "Are you two always like this?"

"Oh, we're worse than this, darling. Wait until we've had a few more glasses of Sylvie's favorite wine." Jack draped his arm around her shoulders and took Julius by the waist. "For now, let's go and see what Elda has painted for us, the talented little witch."

The evening was a roaring success. The glitterati of the art world had turned out for Elda's latest show. Critics had nodded and idled for the appropriate amount of time. Red dots had even appeared on a couple of pieces, which delighted Elda.

Charlie had graced the audience with her presence just before it started, blaming Arlo for needing another story before he'd settle with Grandad. Now, in the after-hours hotel bar, the gang debriefed on the evening and reminisced on old times.

"Elda was undoubtedly a lovesick puppy when she turned up at my doorstep." Sylvie wiped away her tears of laughter.

"Charlie was no better. She was wasting away with all the pining," Jack said, fanning his face.

Elda put her hands on her hips. "Okay, you two. I think I prefer it when you're sparring with each other rather than ganging up on me."

"We probably wouldn't have made it, if it weren't for you two." Charlie raised her glass. "Jack practically pushed me into the Channel Tunnel, and Sylvie gave me a good talking to."

"Liar. You trot out that tired old line every time we're all together." Jack tipped his chin. "We all know you were desperate for Elda, and you would've followed her to the ends of the earth."

Charlie kissed Elda. "Fine. You two had nothing to do with it."

Julius rose. "Who wants another drink?"

They all nodded and raised their empty glasses.

"Isn't he a keeper?" Jack said, his gaze following Julius to the bar.

"He is. Don't fuck it up." Elda shot him a warning look, then followed it with a comedy smile.

"Hey, I'm a changed man. The only one of us who's still single is Sylvie." Jack pretended to play a tiny violin. "When are you going to make it official with your California girl?"

Official was a funny word. Were they official, for now? She squirmed beneath the scrutiny of three pairs of eyes. "We're just having fun."

Jack's eyes sparkled. "Fun for now, or fun forever?"

Elda laid her hand across Sylvie's. "Leave her be, Jack. It's not that simple for everyone, is it?"

The sympathy only served to remind her how sad it would be when Ade was no longer around. Her jaw tightened. "I wish it was forever, but I can't make her stay."

"Can't you go?" Jack asked.

The question so simple, but the answer was so very complicated.

"We can't all upend our lives for love." Charlie twisted a coaster in her fingers.

"You would've done for Elda, though, wouldn't you?" Sylvie asked.

Charlie glanced at Elda with a tenderness. "Yeah. But giving up your life's purpose for love isn't the only option. If you two are meant to be, then you'll find a way." She took Elda's hand. "We made it work, didn't we?"

"We absolutely did. But I get where Sylvie's coming from. California is so much further away. We didn't have the Atlantic between us." Elda twisted in her seat. "Are you really serious about her?"

Sylvie resisted the shrug that would casually brush off the question. If she couldn't be honest with her closest group of friends, who was she kidding? "I've never really trodden this path before. The only blueprint I have for this kind of whirlwind is you two."

"Praise indeed." Jack whistled into the remains of his cocktail. "I'm with you though, Sylvie. These two have created a pretty high bar when it comes to finding love."

"But that's it." Sylvie cleared her throat. "I think I've reached that bar. Ade is everything. I'm just not sure where that leaves us in a few months' time."

Julius returned with a tray of drinks. "Who died?"

"Sylvie's love life."

"Not yet." Sylvie punched Jack's arm. "Plenty of juice in the tank for now."

"That's what she said." Jack guffawed, leaning on Elda for support.

"Don't change, Jack. Never change," said Sylvie.

Elda rolled her eyes. "No chance of that. He's been like this since we were at school. At least Eli and Arlo are out of earshot tonight."

"What a slur on my name. Those boys adore me." Jack protested with a wave of his hands.

"Of course they do. No one else will indulge their passion for breaking the rules," Charlie said, swallowing a yawn and evidence of her parental candle-burning at both ends. "I think we'd better head back soon."

The bar was beginning to close around them. Sylvie wished she'd asked Ade to join her. A night in London together would have been perfect. She said her goodbyes to old friends and took herself to bed with her fantasy that next time she booked a hotel for the night, Ade would be sharing her bed. Whether or not she could share her life—or her future—was another question.

A bigger, thornier, harder question. And one she didn't have an answer for. Not yet.

Chapter Thirty-Eight

ADE BOUNCED INTO CAMPUS. With a newfound confidence, she no longer shrank into her jacket and retreated to her comfort zone at the marine center. In fact, she'd accepted a whole slew of back-to-back appointments with her students, all of whom seemed to have entered the Spring semester with a bag of worries and a list of ailments.

Scott hovered at her classroom door. "Good morning. I brought you a coffee."

"Really?" Ade eyed him suspiciously. The gesture was uncharacteristic. "How come?"

"I went by the coffee shop and figured you might be in need of a caffeine fix too."

She took the cup. "Thanks. I appreciate it." She sat in her usual spot and gestured to the seat opposite. "How're things with you?"

"It's not me I'm here for actually. I know Madison's in hot water because she faked some reports. I'm low-key worried about her."

Scott's concern about the well-being of another student demonstrated some real growth. Maybe Ade had underestimated the jock. He sat with his arms folded. She'd come to learn this signaled his discomfort with the subject. But he'd had the balls to come and see her about it. "If you're worried, *I'm* worried." Ade chewed the inside of her cheek. "Tell me more."

"She skipped a bunch of classes last week. We had a joint assignment, so I messaged her but got the brush off."

"Has anyone else heard from her?"

"Not that I know of." Scott shrugged, his familiar nonchalance poking through. "I could ask, I guess. But she's been acting really weird. When she does show up for class, sometimes she's been drinking or something."

That was news. Madison was fast becoming Ade's number one priority. "Thank you for telling me all that. I'll check in with her today." She made a note on her laptop. "Will you let me know if you hear anything else?"

"I guess."

That would have to do. "How about you? How're things going?"

Scott wrinkled his nose. "Classes are tough, man. The language barrier is like doing the pole vault sometimes."

"Yeah, I know." Ade sympathized, but her sticky brain was better with languages than all of her students put together. "Just focus on the practical classes. Spend more time at the lab."

"And less time in the Latin class. It's crazy that anyone's learning that shit these days." He ran his hand through his hair, which had dulled with the lack of winter sun these past few weeks. "Anyway, I'll let you get on with it. Later, Ade." He laughed. "Sounds like Gatorade."

"Thank you for coming by, Scott." Ade blinked away her confusion as he left. "How're you doing?" she asked as Greg strode through the open door.

"All good. I recalibrated some of the instruments back at the lab. Everything should be in order." He grinned and sat down.

"Sounds great. Thank you for your work on that." She loved his enthusiasm for lab time. His passion almost rivaled her own. "Tell me how your other studies are going."

"Fine. I'm on top of the assignments and ahead in marine biology. I've asked the professor for some extra credits to do during this semester's reading week."

Ade nodded. "You can pick up some extra maintenance shifts too, if you'd like."

"Absolutely. I'd love to. Just say the word."

Ade frowned; she'd just done that, hadn't she? But she let it pass because she liked Greg, and she didn't want to make him feel uncomfortable.

Their conversation wound up, and she handled two more appointments: one of the students had damp in her room that she needed help with, and the other couldn't work out how to pay their phone bill.

Ade scanned her task list: she'd called a housing company and made an online payment but still had to make a call to Madison. She stalled, her cell in her hand, staring at Madison's name. Maybe she should write up her supervision notes while they were fresh in her mind. She didn't want to blow all that progress with shoddy record-keeping.

She typed her notes into the university's student system, diligently logging her students' concerns and resolutions. She was pretty proud of her progress today. There'd been no meltdowns, and she hadn't had to put herself into Steph's or Sylvie's shoes to fix anyone's problems. Without thinking, she picked up her cell and scrolled to messages she'd shared with Sylvie.

Hey. Missing you. How's it going?

Having fun, but wish you were here. The bed is far too big for one person.

I bet. I could really help with that.

She was putting off the call to Madison. And she wasn't so proud of that. She was really trying to be the person who got things done, and did them well, rather than relying on anyone else to take care of matters. She sighed, and her finger hovered over the call button.

Convincing herself that it'd be so much worse if she didn't make contact, she pressed the button. It rang a few times, and she almost hung up until the connection clicked into place. "Madison? Is that you?"

"Hi, Ade," she almost whispered.

Now what? "I wanted to check in and see how you're doing. You know, after the last few weeks and all."

"Yeah, I know. I'm okay." Madison sniffed. "Are personal

check-ins part of the service now?"

So, she'd figured out that Ade's call was unusual. "They are for people I'm beginning to worry about. It's my job to be here for you when you need extra support."

"You don't need to worry about me. Everything is great. I've sorted out my report cards, and my schedule is so much lighter since you fixed it for me."

They were the right words in the right order, but they rang hollow. Ade drummed her fingers. "Are you sure? I heard you've missed a few classes?"

"Yeah, but only the ones we talked about me dropping, right?"

That threw Ade off. Had she given Madison permission to skip class? She'd arranged for her schedule to be modified, but that wasn't a carte blanche for her absence. "Right. So you're attending the classes you're supposed to be going to? Just reassure me of that. We don't want to be getting in any more trouble with the faculty this semester."

"No, we wouldn't want that." Madison sounded detached, like she was staring into space, speaking words that Ade might want to hear. "I gotta go; someone's at my door."

She hung up before Ade could wish her well. At least she had company, but Madison's dead tone played in her mind all the way home.

Back at her apartment, she had no time to dwell on the interaction. Steph was home and itching to hit the bars.

"Come on, you know you want to." Steph threw a towel in Ade's lap. "Get yourself ready. It'll take your mind off missing Sylvie and whatever the hell happened in class today."

Ade had downloaded a summary of what happened with Madison, but as usual, her sister had brushed off her worries with a flick of her hand and the offer of a quick drink to soak up the misery.

"I don't feel like it tonight." She almost never wanted to go out with Steph. Most times, she tagged along with the hope that this one time would be the night of her dreams. She would morph into the social being she fantasized about, easily moving through a crowded room, unconcerned by the lights and the noise piercing her eyes and ears.

"I don't want to go out alone, Ade." Steph stuck out her bottom lip.

"I need a quiet night." She missed Sylvie terribly. The day's work had been a good distraction, but they were about to spend more time apart than they had in a long while, and it hurt.

"But we have birthday plans to polish. How am I going to plan dinner and dancing if you're not around to sign off on the plans?"

Ade rolled her eyes. "We both know that I have no real power in that decision-making process." She hadn't spent a birthday on this earth without her twin on center stage.

Steph tilted her head, throwing Ade a pity look. "You sure Sylvie can't come? It's a shame you won't be together on our birthday."

That fact sat heavy in Ade's heart. But plans to meet her parents had been made months ago. They were enjoying the finale to their European tour by adding a trip to Morocco, where she and Steph were going to meet them for a few days. "She can't take any more personal time off." What Ade really wanted was to stay in the city and celebrate with Sylvie. But breaking her promise to her family was unimaginable.

"Bummer." Steph adjusted the waistband of her miniskirt. "Do you think this is too long?"

"I have absolutely no opinion on the length of your hem," Ade said without looking up.

"You could pretend. Just this once."

"That would be dishonest of me." Ade sat taller. "You don't really care about what I think, you're going to wear it anyway."

Steph chuckled. "So true, sister. So very perceptive."

Ade blocked out the remainder of Steph's getting ready routine with a pair of noise-cancelling headphones and her go-to playlist. She stretched on the sofa and drifted into a fantasy where Sylvie came along to Morocco for their birthday trip. Her absence gnawed a hole in her heart like nothing else. When they were back together, she'd make up for it.

Chapter Thirty-Nine

A TAP TAP INSIDE her skull wrenched Ade from another pleasant dream involving a half-naked Sylvie in the supply closet. She protested the transition to waking state with a groan. "What's happening?" The incessant pounding was coming from directly behind. Ade unstrapped herself from the airline seat and leaned over to meet the eyes of a small child, holding his index finger in a decisive point. "What are you pressing back there?"

"I'm so sorry." His mother met Ade's blurry gaze. "He's playing a game on the screen."

"Sure." Ade took a deep, calming breath. "Could he play a little more gently?"

"Of course."

Ade settled back in her chair. If she was going to make it through the next few lonely days, she needed maximum reserves of patience with other people.

Flying above the puffs of clouds soothed Ade's racing heart. She'd long ago rationalized that airplanes were safe enough to endure, but it didn't diminish the primal fear that seized her in the moments of take-off and landing.

In the next seat, Steph chugged another beer. "You sure you don't want to start our birthday celebration yet?"

Ade shook her head, content to remain sober for another few hours before a boozy flavor of anxiety replaced her usual kind. "I don't see why we need to have a whole weekend of drinking."

"We're a quarter century. Don't be such a bummer," Steph said. "Do you think Dad will just send a cab to pick us up from the airport? By the time we get to the hotel, it'll be siesta time for those two."

"Do they have a siesta in Morocco?" Ade questioned another of her sister's throwaway cultural references.

"Whatever it is, Dad and Pops won't make it through the afternoon without a nap."

By the time they made it through customs, both their fathers were standing expectantly in arrivals, beaming with excitement and proving Steph's assumptions wrong.

"Girls!" Their pops burst through the barrier, wrapping them both in his linen-clad arms. "I've missed you both."

"Me too," said their dad, exchanging kisses and hugs all round. "This is Aamir; he's our driver for today."

Steph and Ade exchanged a look, disapproving of their fathers' privilege, and followed them through the revolving doors into a wall of heat. The North African breeze warmed Ade's bones, and she rolled her shoulders. Maybe this was the break she needed from Europe's wintry skies.

They clambered into Aamir's SUV and set out onto the dusty highways, twisting and turning through the rust-colored landscape until they reached a settlement just north of Marrakesh.

"You sure splashed out on our birthday pad, guys," Steph said, accepting Aamir's hand as she stepped from the tall SUV.

Ade jumped out, creating a dust cloud which landed back on her boots. She squinted at the unassuming doorway.

Pops slipped his arm around her and squeezed. "Happy birthday weekend."

"Thanks. You didn't need to go to all this trouble." She leaned against his chest.

"For my girls? Anything." He grinned. "It didn't take much to convince your dad to splurge."

"Go on ahead," said Pops, reaching for their weekend bags. "Behind that door is an oasis of luxury."

Steph strode to the house, while Ade wandered through the inner courtyard until she came to a small swimming pool. "Do we have it all to ourselves?" she asked, her voice carrying though the lush gardens.

"Affirmative, honey. We have the whole place to relax and celebrate." Her dad reclined on a nearby sun lounger, his hands behind his head. "So, tell me all your news. How's work going?"

For the first time in as long as she could remember, she could answer her dad's probing questions honestly and with her head held high. "You know, it's going really well. I'm starting to get somewhere with the chaperone role, and it's like the students are really opening up to me."

Pops strolled into the courtyard, carrying a tray of ice cold drinks. "Sounds great. I knew you'd find your feet. Nate?" He passed her dad a tumbler. "Homemade lemonade?"

Ade accepted a glass and took a long, refreshing pull of the ice-cold sour liquid. She dangled her bare feet in the cool water. Zoning out from her folks, she traced the intricate pattern of the pool tile with her finger. Its surface cooled her down and slowed her pulse. Closing her eyes, she imagined leaning back against Sylvie's chest, letting go of all her worries. She pulled her cell from her pocket and scrolled to Sylvie's name. Her photo flashed up on the screen, sending a flutter of expectation through Ade's chest.

"Hey, you," Sylvie said, sounding further than usual.

"Hi. Just checking in." Ade gave her dad a quick nod, and he shooed her pops into the riad.

"How was your journey?" asked Sylvie.

"The flight wasn't too bad; it's just a short hop. My dads have booked this amazing place. I wish you could see it."

"Me too." Sylvie sighed. "Bless them. I bet they've missed you."

"Kind of." Ade leaned back, catching a glimpse of her fathers' embrace through a mosaic archway. "I think they've been enjoying their time on this trip." Drawn into a meditative state by Sylvie's breath, she closed her eyes. "I really miss you."

"Me too. I've got all kinds of belated birthday fun planned though."

Ade could hear Sylvie's smile down the phone line. "Oh, yeah? Care to share?"

"I couldn't possibly. Not with your fathers in earshot."

"Oh, they've got their own thing going on." Ade giggled. "What d'you have in mind over there?"

"All will be revealed soon enough, Ms. Poole. Patience is a very attractive quality in a human."

"It is? I can think of more attractive virtues."

"Like what?"

"Kindness. Honesty. All the things I see in you every day."

"Stop it. I've spent a few days being roasted by Elda and the gang. I'm not used to the compliments."

"It's true though." Ade picked at the line of grout beside her thigh. "I do wish you were here. It's warm. We could lay in the sun together."

"I would like that." Sylvie hummed. "Is it warm enough to take your clothes off?

Ade checked on her parents. "It sure is. In the right circumstances."

"Tell me more," Sylvie said.

***

The sun set on their first day in Morocco, and the path through the riad's inner courtyard flickered with tea lights, each flame illuminating the way to the dining room.

Ade reluctantly wore something fancy, at her family's request, and she fidgeted where the unfamiliar fabric scratched at her skin. The table was pretty lavish for the four of them: all candlesticks, goblets, and cutlery for every course imaginable.

Tiny plates of food arrived randomly, leaving Ade mesmerized and confused by the spectacle. She inspected the texture of each dish before she committed to the taste test, passing on more than a couple of dubious-looking plates.

"Try to lean into the experience, Ade," her dad said, raising his eyebrow.

"Nate, we talked about this. Let her be." Her pops sat tall in his chair, looking ready to defend her quirks. "She's always had texture issues."

"We paid a hefty price for the chef tonight. I don't want Ade to miss out on all these culinary delights."

"I'll take her share," Steph said, her mouth full of a puffy flatbread and to-die-for hummus. "Pass it my way." She grinned, revealing trimmings of coriander between her teeth.

"I can't quite believe it's been twenty-five years since we brought you guys home in our old station wagon. You remember that, Sam?"

"How could I forget? Two car seats planted in our living room, and we both just looked at each other and said, 'What now?' Lucky we worked it out, hey, girls?" Her pops' eyes glistened with the memory. "Feels like yesterday."

"And a thousand years ago," said her dad.

They held hands. "All at once. How is that even possible?"

"Stop being so sentimental, you guys." Steph scoffed. "This is a celebration."

"Actually, it's not our birthday till tomorrow," Ade said.

"But it's our birthday eve, spoilsport. Time to get the party started." Steph plugged her cell into the portable speaker and scrolled to her playlist.

Her dad chuckled and looked at Ade. "Made any more plans yet?"

"For what?"

"Long-term job prospects. Plans for when you get home."

Ade shrugged, not wanting to get into that. "I told you about that opening at the marine center."

"What does that mean? Staying in France?" he asked.

"Maybe." Ade dug her nails into her palm. "You know, you could just give me a break for the next few days. We could enjoy ourselves without scrutinizing my prospects." She dipped her head.

Her pops shook his head. "She's right, Nate."

"Why would you want to stay in France? You're better off at home."

Steph strolled back into the room holding a half-eaten carrot stick. "Because of Sylvie, of course. K-I-S-S-I-N–"

"Can you just shut up!" Ade pushed her chair back, and the legs screeched against the tiles.

"Girls, you may be twenty-five tomorrow, but you're acting like you're seventeen. Sit down, and we can talk about this." Pops rested a hand on Ade's shoulder. "Stephanie, take your place at the table and stop embarrassing yourself in front of the nice people who are waiting on us right now."

"So you want to extend your stay in the south of France because of Sylvie, huh?" Their dad picked up his line of questioning with a scratch of his head.

"I've been mulling it over, yeah." Ade inhaled, preparing herself for the onslaught of questions. "I'm serious about our–"

"Relationship?" their Dad asked, the angle of his brow softening. "I liked her a lot. The question is, do you like her enough to put the brakes on the rest of your life?"

"Would it be putting the brakes on though, Dad?" Ade asked.

"Sounds more like taking the training wheels off from where I'm sitting." Steph guffawed into her baba ghanoush.

"Stephanie, please. I'm trying to have a serious talk with your sister." Dad frowned. "You think Sylvie feels the same? I mean, would she welcome you sticking around?"

Ade imagined the weight of Sylvie's head resting against her chest. "I think so. We've talked about it." Ade fudged the fact that she and Sylvie had talked about her going home rather than staying.

"Your dad and I will support you no matter what happens, honey."

Her fathers' eyes met, a deep understanding, built across the decades they'd spent together, passed across the busy dining table.

"Pops is right. If you think Sylvie is worth hanging around for, you should stay. We'll make it work." He smiled, a glint in his eye betraying the depth of his love for everyone at the table. "First things first: you need to work out how to extend your work visa."

"Does this mean I don't have to rush home either?" Steph threw an olive in the air and caught it between her teeth.

"Stop fooling around. You're coming back to start your nursing internship by this summer. No excuses."

Steph folded her arms. "But what if I find the love of my life in some mysterious European town, and I fall head over heels?"

"We can talk about it when it happens. In the meantime, your flights are booked." Dad raised his glass. "To family. Happy birthday to our baby girls."

Ade joined in with the toast, grateful for his U-turn, but his blessing was only part of the solution. The bigger challenges were how she'd secure a job after this academic year and whether Sylvie would welcome her staying in France. One thing was for sure: she couldn't wait to tell her. Maybe she was ready to plant roots somewhere other than her dads' backyard after all.

Chapter Forty

THE OVEN BEEPED. *NO*. The microwave. The fire alarm? With the forceful chirping inside her head, Sylvie opened her heavy eyelids to complete darkness. It took a couple of seconds to seek out its source: her cell. "Hello." Sylvie rubbed her face, clearing the sleep clinging to her eyelashes.

"You're listed as Madison Montgomery's emergency contact. I need you to come down to University Hospital. She's being admitted from the emergency room."

"What's happened?" Sylvie swung her legs from under her comforter and switched on the lamp, drenching her room in a light too harsh for the early hour.

"Madison's hurt herself. She's stable though and ready to come home."

Jesus. "Can I speak with her?"

"Not right now. She's having some dressings done."

"I'll be there as soon as I can. Wait, who am I speaking with?" Sylvie asked.

"Nurse Lopez. Madison is in ward five."

Sylvie swallowed the rising panic in her throat. Ade had warned her about Madison's state of mind, but she'd hoped it wouldn't get worse.

This was a first in her teaching career, but she could handle it. She drove to the hospital in a daze, carried by the adrenaline of the situation. After pushing through the main doors, she attracted sideways glances and stares. The clothes she'd managed to throw on looked like she'd been woken up in the middle of a nightmare, which was absolutely accurate. She had no time to worry about her own appearance. The only thing that mattered was that Madison was okay. She weaved her way through a maze of corridors to a holding ward and braced herself. The nurses' station was a flurry of activity, but she caught someone's attention. "I'm here for Madison Montgomery."

"Are you family?" the nurse asked.

"I'm her professor at the university. She's an international student on a year abroad."

"I got that from the lack of French," the nurse said. "She's almost ready to go home. We just need the doctor to sign her out and provide her with some follow-up. She's going to need a referral to a mental health practitioner."

"Has she said what happened?"

"She didn't need to. There were multiple lacerations to her lower arm. One was fairly deep, so she panicked and called someone. Any closer to an artery, and she could've bled out." The nurse's kind eyes met Sylvie's. "We see it pretty often. She called, thank goodness."

Nausea swirled in Sylvie's stomach. This could have been so much worse. Behind a clinical white door lay the vulnerable shape of Madison, balled up under a hospital blanket, hiding away from the world. Sylvie sat next to the bed, not wanting to wake her yet. She wondered what could have pushed this perfect-seeming young woman to the brink of her emotions. Was it the pressure of university? Being away from home for so long? Who knew what these kids were up against. So many of their troubles played out inside their heads and scarred their hearts.

Madison turned and groaned. "You didn't need to come. I told them I was fine."

"They had to call someone, and I'm on your list, so here I am." Sylvie feigned a smile. "How are you?"

"How do you think?" Madison stared at the ceiling, dry spittle crusted around her lips. "Are they letting me go home yet?"

"We just need to wait for a doctor to sign you out and get you some more support." Sylvie ran her hands through her bed hair. "Did you want to call your parents?"

"No," said Madison, inspecting her freshly dressed arm. "They don't want to hear about my problems."

Sylvie opened her mouth to object but closed her mouth. She didn't have a clue what Madison's relationship with her parents was like. She couldn't base her assumptions on her own experiences. "Is there anyone you want to call?"

"Is Ade around? Isn't she my emergency contact?"

"She's in Morocco for a few days with her sister. It's their birthday." But God, Sylvie wished she was here.

"Nice way to spend your birthday, I guess. Good for her." Madison met Sylvie's eye contact for the first time. "Thanks for coming."

Sylvie attempted a brave face.

"Ade's been good to me these past few weeks." Madison's gaze flicked from side to side. "I don't mean about the faked attendance cards. She's just been really helpful with my schedule and listening when I need her."

Pride settled in Sylvie's heart. It was no surprise to her that Ade had been a support to Madison, but she'd clearly made more of an impact than she realized.

After the doctor discharged Madison, Sylvie drove her back into the city.

"Can I come in and see you settled?" Sylvie asked, not willing to take no for an answer.

Madison gave her a look which suggested she'd rather eat her own vomit, but she allowed Sylvie to follow her into the shared apartment. The winter dawn was still tucked below the horizon, shrouding the place in darkness, and her housemates slumbered in their beds.

Madison slumped on her couch and drew a blanket up to her chin.

"Is there anything I can get you?" Sylvie hovered, desperate to be useful.

Madison shook her head, her lip trembling.

"I don't have to leave, if you don't want me to." Sylvie sat opposite, grasping at her training for the next thing to do. "Do you want to talk about it?"

Madison's gaze dropped. "It wasn't as bad as they said."

"What wasn't?"

"The cut. The bleeding. It would've healed on its own. I just panicked."

Sylvie sat forward. "You did the right thing. It's going to be okay."

"Is it? Because I can't stop. I try not to, and then something in my brain takes over, and I'm just not in control of my hands."

Sylvie was out of her depth here. She fixed her face, careful not to reveal any sign of the shock, panic, and confusion that was coursing through her right now. "No one is judging you. We're all here to support you."

Madison shook, tears falling down her mottled cheeks. "I've let everyone down. I promised Ade I wouldn't do it again."

Sylvie inhaled, not wishing to deny Madison's feelings but desperate to protect her from any shame. "You haven't let me down. And you haven't let Ade down."

"What am I going to do?"

"You're going to get some sleep right now. When you're feeling a little more human, we can talk about the next steps. You have an appointment with a doctor who's a specialist in this field, so that will help."

"What's Ade going to think? I promised her I wouldn't hurt myself." Madison cowered and pulled the blanket to her chin.

"Ade will understand that you're feeling vulnerable. She's on your side, Madison." Sylvie straightened. "I don't want you to make promises to people, okay? We're here to help you, but you don't owe anyone any promises."

Madison's eyelids dropped with fatigue, so Sylvie tucked her in and said goodbye. If only she could take all the distress and loneliness, wrap it up in a box, and throw it in the river. But life wasn't that simple. Madison had her own demons to face, and Sylvie had to wish Ade a happy birthday without destroying the mood.

She made her way back to her apartment and brewed fresh coffee, her broken night's sleep making itself known.

Her cell vibrated on the counter, and Ade's name lit up on the black screen.

"Happy birthday, you," Sylvie said, with as much lightness as she could muster.

"Thanks. It'd be better if you were here."

"We can both agree on that." Sylvie looked to the ceiling, wishing she was anywhere but in the city right now.

Her thoughts wandered while Ade filled in the blanks with details of her trip.

"You okay over there?" Ade asked.

"I'm fine." She swallowed back the emotion in her throat. "I'm just tired."

"Did you have a late night without me?"

Sylvie couldn't hide the truth. Ade would find out sooner or later and it was best that she heard from Sylvie rather than one of the students. "I was up in the night at the hospital with Madison."

Sylvie ran through the sequence of events.

"I can't believe this," Ade said.

"I'm sorry, Ade." Sylvie paced her kitchen. "She's home now, and there's nothing that won't heal, physically. But emotionally, she's in a mess."

"I know all of that. I've been supporting her these past few weeks," Ade said, her voice strained.

"Hey, I didn't want to tell you on the phone, especially on your birthday. But it happened, and it's for the best that you know before you come back into work. There'll be all kinds of risk assessments and reports to write up."

"Are you angry with me?" Ade asked.

"No." Sylvie sat down. Her nerves were frayed; she'd spent half the night at the hospital, and now she'd clearly upset Ade while she was supposed to be enjoying her birthday weekend. "I'm not angry with you. Why would I be?"

"I did a report. I made a referral before I came away. I did everything I was supposed to." She cleared her throat of what sounded like a sob. "I should've been there."

Sylvie silently acknowledged Ade's regret. "Hey, this isn't on you. Madison is an adult. Albeit a young one. She's struggling, and you did everything you could have done." The silence hung between them. "You did everything I would've done."

"Then why are you angry?"

"I'm angry with the world, Ade. It's tragic that our young people feel so much pressure to exist, to thrive, to be someone they're not, especially when they call their parents for help, and they don't come." Sylvie closed her eyes briefly. "I just wish you were here, so I didn't have to miscommunicate with you over the phone."

"I still should've been there."

Sylvie pushed down the frustration at Ade's lack of experience with students. "You can't be there for them the whole time. That's not the job."

"But what if they need you?"

"You can't help being away. I was here. There's always someone else to pick up the slack. That's the main thing."

"You don't think I could have coped?" Ade asked.

Sylvie held the phone away from her ear. "That's not what I said. When did I say that?"

"You didn't. It's just how I feel, I guess."

Sylvie ached to be with her. To smooth this over and rewrite Ade's inner monologue. But she had enough on her plate dealing with Madison's crisis. "Listen, I need to focus on Madison right now. Let's talk again when you've had time to calm down and digest the situation."

"But I should be there for her instead of being here at this stupid villa in the crazy heat."

Sylvie paused. "This actually isn't about you, Ade. It's about the well-being of one our students."

Ade hung up. Had Sylvie said too much? It was obviously a shock for Ade to hear the news and be so far away and out of control. She kicked herself for not handling it better; she should've waited until Ade was back from her trip. But juggling the emotional crisis of one person had been enough today. Ade would calm down once she had time to process what had happened. But a little part of Sylvie resented always having to be the grown-up.

Chapter Forty-One

ADE WASN'T ANGRY WITH Sylvie; she was furious with herself. Just when she thought she was adding value to her students' lives, she'd missed the biggest signal of all: one of them needed help. She paced around the perimeter of the courtyard as the sun rose. Her parents and Steph hadn't yet shown for breakfast, so she had the place to herself for all the ruminating she wanted.

She'd wanted to impress Sylvie and show her she was capable of something other than clearing out animal tanks. She bit her lip. Sylvie was so right; this wasn't about her. It was about Madison. So why couldn't she shake the failure from her shoulders?

Her pops strolled out onto the veranda wearing a silk robe. "Happy birthday, angel."

She ignored him.

"You okay there, Ady-baby?"

"You know, I don't really care for that nickname." The label was diminishing, making her smaller than she was, less able than she should be. It certainly wasn't helping this morning.

Her pops smiled. They replayed this argument every few years, but sooner or later the name would pop up. She'd always be the baby of the family.

"You don't need to look after me anymore. I'm a grown adult." She kept pacing.

He gave a hearty rumble of laughter. "Oh, yeah? Since you turned twenty-five, you've got it all figured out, have you?"

He probably didn't mean to provoke further hostility, but Ade's balloon of frustration and guilt was almost at bursting point. "I don't care what you and Dad think. I don't need a chaperone or a parent to be constantly checking in on me."

Her pops sat at the ironwork table and set down his coffee. "What's all this about?"

He gestured for her to sit, but she didn't want to. She was angry with herself and not managing it well. "One of my students did something stupid last night and hurt themselves. They had to go to the fucking hospital."

He nodded. "I can see why you'd be distressed by that. Are they doing okay?"

"They're fine. She's fine. Madison." Ade swallowed the tears. Why was she crying? She wasn't hurt.

"You have some responsibilities for taking care of Madison?"

"Yeah, it's like my only job this year, but I'm here, sunning myself around a mosaic poolside with you guys."

"It's tough when something happens that's not in your control," he said.

Ade paced up and down a couple more times, then dragged her toe against the dusty floor. "I think I knew, deep down, that she was in trouble. I made a referral for counseling before I left."

"So you did what you could."

"It wasn't enough to stop her from ending up in the emergency room."

"Is that what happened?"

"That's what Sylvie told me. But I don't know all the details, Pops, because I'm not fucking there!" She crumbled, holding her face in her hands.

Her father came to her side and pulled her into his chest. "I'm here. Come on."

"I don't know what to do, Pops."

"There's nothing you can do, realistically. You're here, and she's there, presumably with other people rallying to support her."

How could I be here when Sylvie's having to cope with this alone?

"Ade? You still with me?"

She nodded, refocusing.

"You need to come to terms with how you feel about what happened. It's a shock. You obviously feel angry at yourself. Maybe at Madison too." He squeezed her tight. "You might also feel a bit sad and worried about her."

"I do." Ade blinked away a tear. "I got mad at Sylvie when she called to tell me."

"Okay, well, you'll need to repair that too. I get the impression she'll forgive you."

"I hope so."

"Things don't always go to plan, Ade. Everyone's human. We just need to be able to talk it out."

"Do you think I'll be able to head back on an earlier flight?" she asked.

"Well, that seems like something practical we can look into." He flicked the screen of his cell and started to type. "Steph might not be ready to go yet. You'll be okay traveling alone?"

"Yes." No question. She wanted to get back and make amends with Sylvie and talk to Madison. If that meant negotiating an airport at either end, then so be it.

"I'll go wake your dad."

"No, wait. Let me. I need to tell him what's going on." The familiar fear of failure gnawed at her. Part of her wanted to just leave without an explanation, but that would cause fireworks for her pops, so she may as well be a grown-up about it all and fess up. She paused at the door to their bedroom and listened for signs of life.

"I heard your footsteps, Adelaide. You're about as stealthy as an elephant." He opened the door fully and marched out to the kitchen. "Happy birthday my heavy-footed child. What is it, honey? You look beat."

"There's been an incident back on campus. One of my cohorts was taken to the hospital." She froze, waiting for signs of her father's impatience.

"Gee, that sounds awful. What happened?" He poured coffee

into a short mug and rubbed his eyes.

"She hurt herself. It was pretty bad. I mean, she's okay; she's not dead or anything." Ade swallowed. "I feel like I might want to be there for her."

Her dad glared over his steaming cup. "You want to cut your birthday trip short?"

"I kinda feel like I'm responsible. Or if not responsible, in a position of responsibility." She wasn't making sense. This was what he did; he stared until she got tongue-tied and then they fought. "I need to support her through this."

Her dad stroked his chin. "You know what? You're right. And I'm proud of you for wanting to go back and do what you can."

Ade blinked. "Really?"

"Yes. I think you're actually showing up for this kid, and that's a great thing."

"I wasn't expecting you to say that."

He tilted his head. "What were you expecting?"

"Some drama about me having to leave. Maybe criticism that I'm not even able to commit to a family holiday?"

"Well, give me some credit here, Ade. I'm seeing this for what it is: you doing your job. In fact, you're going above and beyond in my book."

Huh. That meant a lot coming from him. "Thanks."

"Is that what your pops is doing right now, rebooking your flight?" He looked over at her pops, hunched over his laptop. "He'd do anything for you. So would I, Ade. I mean it."

He planted a kiss on her forehead, and it pulsed for a while, like he'd branded her with his love.

***

Steph hadn't wanted to leave. In fact, she begged to hang out with their dads for the remainder of their trip before she headed to Italy to continue her gap year.

Once her pops had dropped her at the security gate, Ade had journeyed back to Montpellier alone, repeating her playlist over and over. Just when she had her anxiety under some kind of control, it bubbled right back up to say "hi." She jumped out of her skin every time the plane bumped through a cloud. Steph had told her on the way over that it was perfectly normal, but that didn't stop her heart racing with every jolt.

Somehow she made it through arrivals and got in a cab. There was no way she had the bandwidth for public transportation.

By the time she finally reached the corridor leading to Sylvie's office, her nerves were fried. She eased the tension from her shoulders just a fraction, then sprang upright, alarmed by the sound of raised voices. She dithered in the hallway, trying to make out who was talking. It was Sylvie and Paul.

Ade hadn't warned Sylvie that she was coming, and now it seemed like she was interrupting something. Creeping closer, she strained to make out what the argument was about. She didn't want to eavesdrop, but it sounded like they were talking about Madison, and she needed all the facts before she visited.

"Are the risk assessments up to date?" Paul asked.

"You know they are, Paul. I don't take these responsibilities lightly, despite them being thrust upon me without my input."

"And was a referral made to well-being?" he asked.

"I double-checked earlier, and yes, Ade handled that before she went on leave."

"That's something. We can't let this get out of control, Sylvie. The last thing we need is a safeguarding investigation."

"There's nothing to investigate. The girl hurt herself in her own room. We can't be with them the whole time."

"You know the media doesn't see it that way. Neither does the international board. They sent us those kids to look after."

"We are looking after her. As much as we can, given that she's an adult." Sylvie sighed. "You know, I'm an academic. I'm not an expert in student liaison or HR. If I had a little more support, perhaps I could do more."

"You have the pastoral worker. What's her name? Adelaide?"

Sylvie didn't respond.

"Is she not up to much?" Paul asked.

"She's doing her best. I'm not sure why the Monterey team chose her as a chaperone, to be honest. She's a brilliant scientist. But she's a scientist."

Ouch. She usually loved Sylvie's style of straightforward communication, but she had really gotten right to the point there. Did she not think that Ade was good enough for this job? Sylvie's doubt twisted in Ade's chest. She shrugged her backpack and turned, scraping the wall.

"Ade?" Sylvie appeared at the open door. "What are you doing here?"

Ade blinked, working out which questions were more important: the thousand firing inside her mind or the one Sylvie had asked aloud.

"Ade? Are you with us?"

"I came back to support Madison," Ade said, unable to look Sylvie in the eye. "I guess I'm doing more harm than good."

"Not at all. Please come inside." Sylvie's face fell, and she raised her eyebrows in Paul's direction. "Can you give us a minute?"

"Of course," he said, approaching the door. "Let me have that incident report by five, please—from both of you."

Sylvie collapsed at her desk and put her face in her hands while Ade hovered at the edge of the room, a torrent of questions racing through her tired brain. What was the report Paul needed? And what did she have to do with it?

"You heard that, didn't you?" Sylvie asked, finally looking up.

"I did."

"I didn't mean it. I was just trying to highlight to Paul that international exchanges need resourcing properly. You can't do it on a shoestring."

"Is that what I am?" Ade asked, not understanding the analogy.

"No, you're not a shoestring. But you're not..." Sylvie sighed deeply, "you're not that experienced in supervising students or leadership. They sent you over here with a mixed bag of emotionally fragile youngsters and left you to it."

"I have you," said Ade, her stomach suddenly hollow with worry.

"But that's just it. This isn't my day job. I'm leading a completely different discipline. It's just not okay that we've both been left to flounder without the right support in place."

"But you said I wasn't up to the job."

"That's not what I said. You can remember what I said, word for word. I was suggesting to Paul that he'd fallen short of his responsibilities, not you."

Confused, Ade recalled what she'd overhead. Maybe Sylvie was right, but it hurt thinking she was inadequate. Of all the things she craved, it was Sylvie's approval. Not her dad's, not Stephanie's; it was Sylvie she wanted to impress. "I should go. I wanted to get to Madison."

"Wait, please." Sylvie rose with her arms outstretched. "I'm so glad you're home. We need to celebrate your birthday."

Ade didn't feel much like celebrating. "Doesn't seem right."

Sylvie briefly cast her gaze to the floor. "I really missed you."

Ade shuffled on the spot. She'd missed Sylvie like nothing ever before, but the sting of her comments hadn't faded. If she could talk her down so casually, what else was she thinking? Was this the reason she hadn't wanted to take their relationship so seriously? Because she wasn't really that into someone like Ade? "I missed you too. I really did."

"Will you come to my apartment when you're finished at Madison's?"

"I'll see how late it is." Ade turned and left.

It was petty, but she couldn't just shrug off the criticism. Sylvie had a point: she wasn't qualified, and this job was a push way out of her comfort zone. The Monterey faculty knew it. So why did it hurt so much that Sylvie held up that mirror? Had she expected Sylvie to see the best in her, to see her potential? She couldn't even see it herself. How could Sylvie see past her faults when they were so glaringly obvious to everyone else? This whole trip had started as a chance to prove to everyone that she was more than just a lab rat. But now, she'd just confirmed all their assumptions. And that hurt. But the tiny tear in her relationship with Sylvie hurt even more.

Chapter Forty-Two

"I FUCKED UP, ISA." Sylvie poured another glass of wine.

"If Ade's stormed off over something like this, then maybe she does need to grow up. It's not even about her."

"It's not her fault that one of the students had a mental health crisis. It happens all the time. You know that." She dragged her spoon through her crème brulée. "She'd done everything I would have done."

"She'll come around, won't she?" Isa asked.

"I hope so. I left her to it last night, thinking she needed to calm down. But she hasn't been in contact today. Should I call her?"

"Yes. Absolutely."

The regret sat heavy on her heart as she recalled Ade's expression. Sylvie had been frustrated at Paul, and a tiny part of her had wanted to show how much of the heavy lifting she'd been doing these past few months. But her explanation had framed Ade as lacking, when she was anything but.

"Call her, Sylvie. You're used to being honest with people." Isa huffed, obviously tired of her own bit-part in the saga. "How is the girl doing anyway? The one who hurt herself."

"She's doing okay. I called her last night, and she seemed much brighter. She starts therapy tomorrow."

"They worry me, these young people. It's all they do when things get too much." Isa's concern hung between them.

"People have always hurt themselves, Isa. It's nothing new," Sylvie said. "It's a way of, I don't know, feeling something other than what's in front of them."

"I know the psychology, but I wish they'd find another way." Isa screwed her nose up.

"There are plenty of ways to numb the pain. I'm not sure any of them are preferable." Sylvie's own coping mechanisms wouldn't have landed her in the emergency room, but maybe she was one of the lucky ones. Ade wasn't so fortunate. She'd obviously been stewing on the whole thing, berating herself for what she did and didn't do. Sylvie had to make contact with her tonight. She had to make Ade see how sorry she was for hurting her.

"I'll get the check this time," Isa said, as if she'd read Sylvie's mind. "Why don't you head off and see if you can find that handsome young thing and get her firmly back on speaking terms?"

"Thank you, I will." Sylvie delivered three kisses on Isa's cheek and made for the door.

Winter had gripped the city. The branches of the treelined promenade were barren, robbed of their twinkly lights and not yet ready for their first flush of blossom. It was the darkest, dampest month of the whole year, and Sylvie could feel it in her bones.

Even the familiar square that Ade's apartment overlooked seemed empty and dull. Piles of trash had gathered on the breeze, strewn across the place like no one cared. A bulb had blown in one of the street lamps, and it was darker than usual. She looked up at Ade's window, where the light shone to signal she was home.

By the time she'd climbed the steps to the top, she fought for her breath. Ade waited by the open door, her expression neutral, like they were meeting for the first time back at class. "You didn't call," Sylvie said.

"I had to think." Ade stared at her socks.

"And now?"

"I need someone in my life that I can count on, someone who isn't going to say things behind my back," Ade said, her arms folded. "I get enough of that from my dad when he holds me up to some standards he hasn't explained yet and tells me I'm not good enough."

Sylvie had seen the pressure that Nate had put on Ade. He

wanted her to succeed, but that level of perfection came with a long way to fall. She reached for Ade's hand. "I don't need you to meet some unknown expectations. And I *am* someone you can count on."

"It hurt. The casual way you spoke about me with Paul hurt me."

"I know it did. I'm really sorry." Sylvie dipped her head, wishing she could take it all back.

"Sorry you said it or sorry I heard you?"

"Both." Sylvie rubbed her temples, pounding from the exertion of the stair climb. "I'm sorry I hurt you. You mean more to me than..." Could she say what she meant? The realization hadn't been a sudden one. Ade had crept into her heart and made a home for herself. *I won't lose you because of one throwaway comment.* "You mean more to me than anyone I've ever had in my life. Forgive me for being careless with my words and careless with your feelings."

Ade blinked, her face still blank. "That's a nice thing to hear."

Sylvie smiled. "Can I give you a birthday present?"

"Well, it's kinda not my birthday anymore, but if you insist."

She stepped into Ade's space. "I really do insist."

Sylvie had missed Ade's body. She stroked the tiny hairs at the nape of her neck and leaned in to where Ade's lips had just parted. Sylvie rushed to seal their embrace, and their bodies melted together, a breathless meeting of heaving chests. Did Sylvie crave Ade's body or her forgiveness? Either way, right now, Ade was the only woman in the world. Sylvie's body filled with want, and she needed her lips against Ade's skin.

She'd never been one to give into her desire, always holding back, waiting for the attention. But now, she'd strip naked and show her everything to Ade just to win a second of her attention.

With her core on fire and evidence of her desire between her legs, Sylvie reached for Ade, hoping for a release to her aching center. If only Ade would touch her, it would ease the guilt and pain and they'd be united again. Ade seemed to sense her need as Sylvie's body curved against her. She touched Sylvie without a single word, holding her gaze. Her fingers popped every button on Sylvie's shirt to reveal her goose-bumped skin, shivering with anticipation. "I need you." Sylvie burned for Ade's mouth on her. She pushed up her hips to meet Ade's hand, but she moved away, not giving in that easily.

A smile flickered across Ade's lips.

"Are you going to make me wait?" Sylvie asked. She would beg to rest in Ade's arms if she had to. An addict, yearning for her fix, she melted into Ade's embrace and waited for the next move. Transfixed, Sylvie looked up to Ade's softened gaze and almost drowned in the whirlpool of her eyes. Her heart skipped a beat. *Is this what love feels like?* The pounding of her pulse was almost deafening.

Ade lightly skimmed Sylvie's breasts, balancing her strength and her precision, her hands exactly where they needed to be to completely undo Sylvie. This time around, Ade didn't ask what Sylvie wanted; she knew it by heart. Her amazing brain had it all mapped out. She trailed her finger over Sylvie's ribs to the edge of her underwear.

"Take these off," Ade said.

Sylvie closed her eyes, needing to be taken there against the wall. "Please," Sylvie said. "Touch me."

Ade smiled with a glint in her eye, the promise of what was to come, and her touch landed with a gentle tenderness. Ade met the thrust of Sylvie's hips and caught the moan from her lips with a kiss. Sylvie tensed in Ade's arms. She'd give up everything for her, follow her to the ends of the earth...maybe even to California.

Ade broke away and looked into her eyes, almost into her soul. *Is this it? Is this what people mean when they ache for another?*

Ade laid Sylvie down and, still fully clothed, stood at the tip of her toes. Sylvie widened her eyes, daring Ade to take her. She knelt at her feet and took Sylvie's ankle in her hand, kissing the length of her foot. Her worship was almost enough to make Sylvie come, but Ade continued her quest, planting her lips along Sylvie's calf, tracing a path with her fingers until she reached where Sylvie was more than ready for her.

Ade opened Sylvie's legs. Ade's lips parted, betraying her own desires.

"I can't wait any longer," Sylvie said, her body rising as she begged Ade to take her in her mouth.

Ade grinned. "I'm in charge today."

Sylvie relented, a willing, aching plaything with no real thoughts except how Ade could satisfy her need for pressure. With Sylvie on the brink of crying in frustration, Ade finally landed the barest of kisses right at the top of her thigh. She followed it with the softest stroke and returned for a second and third time until Sylvie melted into her mouth.

Ade's stream of kisses brought Sylvie to the peak of her desire. She looked down, her heart about to burst with affection, before Ade placed her tongue exactly where it was needed. Sylvie writhed against the warmth of her mouth, with every tender motion in sync with Ade.

"I want more," Sylvie said, willing to beg for everything she needed right then. No one had ever read her body this way. She'd never willingly allowed herself to be unscripted and understood. "I love you," she said as Ade carried her to the peak of her climax.

A flicker of uncertainty passed over Ade's face. She inhaled and eased off holding Sylvie at the plateau of pleasure before she deepened her stroke and gripped tighter so Sylvie couldn't back away from the intensity of her touch.

It was all too much, and then it wasn't. Sylvie was ready to crawl away until she craved more of everything Ade had to give. Sylvie rode another wave of ecstasy, willing Ade to go faster and deeper inside, to touch parts of her that had never been reached. If this was what the future had in store, Sylvie was there for it, no matter what tried to get in the way.

Chapter Forty-Three

ADE TIPPED HER CHIN up, drawing her new confidence right to the top of her body. She hoped Fernando at the marine center would see the change in her. Gone was the cowering, mumbling Ade who sat in the corner and hid from company. Here was capable, strong Ade ready to take on the next job.

Worry nibbled at her stomach. What if he didn't need her anymore? What if he'd found her work lacking? She banished the insecurities from her mind and strode through the lab toward the manager's office.

"Ade, it's great to see you. I was glad you reached out." He sat back on his swivel chair and offered her the seat opposite. "What can I do for you?"

This is it. Her chance to change the trajectory of her career, and maybe more. "You spoke to me about a job opening. I'm interested."

"Straight in there, Ade. No small talk. Just how I like it." He tapped a few times on his laptop. "Marina. Cool name for a lab technician. She's going on maternity leave in eleven weeks, maybe sooner if things start to happen. You never know, do you? It's like an octopus. Things just happen when they happen."

Ade replayed his monologue in her mind. "Sorry, was there a question you needed me to answer?"

"Can you start in three months and do some handover with Marina in the meantime?"

Three months would take her to Easter. "I'd have to carry on at the university for a little longer to make sure the students from Monterey finish what they need to do and get home."

"We can work out the details." He searched under a pile of papers on his desk. "I have the job description and the salary details here somewhere... I can sponsor your visa for another year."

"You don't want to interview me?" Ade raised her eyebrow.

He grinned. "Let's be honest with each other, Ade. Do you think you could tell me more about yourself in an interview than I've already seen in the past four months that you've actually been working here?"

Relief washed over her. She hadn't wanted to face any questions she'd not prepared for or worry about how she looked or what her body was doing that she wasn't conscious of. "No, I can't tell you any more about myself in an average one-hour interview than four months of your observation."

"Let's settle it then." He extended his hand, and she shook it.

Ade skipped out of his office but couldn't leave without saying hello to some of her favorite residents. She gravitated toward the deep sea tanks, itching to tell someone her good news. "How're you doing, fish? Looks like I'll be sticking around a little longer." The angel fish floated away. "Sure, you go tell your friends."

She looked up to Greg, holding a clipboard above the tank's temperature gauge.

"I didn't know you'd be in today." Greg flashed his widest smile, looking genuinely pleased to see her. "Can I show you something? The new sand dollar cells have replicated."

His enthusiasm was catching. Ade scrambled off the floor to witness his creation. "This is fantastic, Greg. You should be proud of yourself." Even she could tell that she sounded like the mentor no one predicted she could be.

"Did you say you were sticking around? Did I hear right?"

Ade wanted to share this with Sylvie before anyone else, but he'd asked her straight out, and she couldn't lie. "I'm going to be taking over as lab tech from Marina."

"Does that mean you won't be working with us anymore?" Greg asked.

"Of course I'll be sticking with you guys. I don't start for another few weeks, and I'll work something out so we can juggle everything." She'd need to convince Sylvie for that one to work. She hadn't actually mapped out the logistics of taking on another job.

"But you won't be coming home with us?"

Was Greg disappointed? It seemed bizarre that any of the students she'd traveled out with last September would actually miss her. A couple of them had barely acknowledged her all year. But Greg was different. "We still have a few months left until you go home." Back in September, Ade had figured she'd crash out by reading week. Now she'd signed for another year. Her cell phone vibrated in her pocket. "I'd better go. Stick with it, Greg. You're doing a fantastic job."

Outside in the parking lot, Sylvie leaned out of her open window. "Did you get it?"

"I'm not sure that's the right term, but he offered me a job." Ade matched Sylvie's expression, beaming across the empty lot. She eased into the passenger seat and took Sylvie's cheeks in her icy hands. "I'm glad I can stay with you." She couldn't be anywhere else. The idea of walking away from the one person who made her feel whole and understood was unthinkable.

"Let's go celebrate," Sylvie said.

"Wait. I have a little plan for you." Ade fastened her belt. "Drop me off in town and meet me at your apartment in an hour."

By the time she was done, dusk was beginning to spread its wings over the city, but the day had been blessed with winter sun and a relative warmth. Sweat beaded on Ade's upper lip as she jogged across to Sylvie's apartment block. She wiped it with her sleeve, wanting to appear put together and cool.

Her arms ached with the unwieldy package she carried, a collection of moments and memories of her and Sylvie's time together. The butterflies in her tummy swarmed. Why was she nervous? Sylvie would love this reminder as much as she did.

Once through the main entrance, she made her way up to Sylvie's front door and fixed her face into a casual smile.

"You're back." Sylvie welcomed her inside. "What was all the secrecy?"

"I wanted you to have this." Ade thrust the box in her arms, then fidgeted wildly.

"What is it?"

"Nothing is wrapped, so it's all just there." Ade pointed awkwardly.

Sylvie tilted her head. "I don't understand."

"The postcard is from the beach where we first really talked. After we met at the marine center that day. It's a good memory." Ade pulled another object from the box. "This is the ticket stub from the movie theatre you took me to." Her words stuck in her chest. This was an awful idea. *She must think I'm a psycho for keeping all this trash.*

"This is a napkin. From the night of the recital?" Sylvie grinned. "You kept all this stuff?"

"I know it looks crazy, but these are all the things that have made me happy this past year." The list had been getting longer since the long days of September; everything that Sylvie had brought into Ade's life made her smile. "I was keeping it to show my folks when I got home. Then I had the idea of sharing it with you."

Sylvie shook her head. "This is my conference program from Paris."

"I know. You came back buzzing from that, and it opened my eyes to how much you have to say about the world and our place in it."

Sylvie turned over the postcard of the beach at Palavas. "To tomorrow and whatever history it brings." She wiped at a falling tear. "Ade, that's beautiful."

"I've thought so many times that the present is the best place to be, and that it's best to forget the hurts of the past and the worries about the future. But you've shown me that hanging onto a few memories, however trivial they might seem, can be precious." She took Sylvie's hands in hers. "And the future interests me more than ever. I want a future with us in it."

"You know what, Adelaide Poole?" Sylvie kissed her. "I'm here for that future."

Sylvie's kiss anchored Ade. She didn't need the world to understand or accept her when she loved herself. With Sylvie, it all became possible. She grew taller to shake life by the hand, rather than shrink from its scrutiny. A tear of utter joy traced a path down her cheek. This was love. This was everything.

Epilogue

One year later.

SYLVIE STEADIED HER FEET, breathing in the cool air. Behind her, San Francisco's blocky Exploratorium stood tall and imposing on the waterfront at Pier 17.

From behind, Ade wrapped her arm around Sylvie's waist, and she relaxed, appreciating the support.

"There must've been a thousand people in there." Ade squeezed. "You blew them away."

Sylvie swallowed the sour taste in her mouth, still dry from spent nerves. "It never gets easier."

"But you get better. Every damn time." Ade kissed her earlobe with a familiar tenderness.

That never got old, and the sensation rushed through her just like it had the very first time. "Thank you for coming with me." She turned to face Ade and kissed her.

"I wasn't going to miss the chance for a trip home."

"I know. But air travel and big crowds aren't exactly your thing." Sylvie cast her gaze to the ground.

"But *you're* my thing." Ade tipped her chin and drew a stray lock of hair away from Sylvie's eyes.

"I saw you out there, in the audience."

"Oh, yeah?" Ade smirked. "I was trying to keep my usual low profile."

At the podium, Sylvie had focused on the one person that could get her through the speech of her life. "I just kept reminding myself that we'd practiced over and over, just you and me in our little apartment. If I could block out the rows of people and the bright lights, it's just you and me."

"Sounds like my every day." Ade took her hand. "Watching you up there on stage is pretty strange. It's like all I want is you near me. Far away Sylvie messes with my head."

"I get that," Sylvie said, squeezing her hand tight.

"But I looked around today in the auditorium, and I see what you do to people. People nod when you talk. They scooch forward in their seats and hang on your words, like they crave their meaning as much as I crave every day with you." Ade held her hands. "I know your legs are shaking, and all I want to do is hold you and take everything away. I know the tremor in your voice is because you're scared of how the world will judge what you say. And I get that more than anything." She cleared her throat. "But I also know that every word that comes out unrehearsed is gold. You're the wisest person I've ever met. You see the world as it's meant to be. All its flaws and failures."

Sylvie swallowed the tears of adoration threatening to flow.

Ade stepped backward. "Even though I've never dreamed about a time beyond today, I want you by my side forever."

Sylvie laughed. "When we first met, you didn't believe in forever. Or before. Just right now." Her hands grew clammy. "Will you ever marry me?" she asked. "I know you don't really believe in marriage. Maybe I don't either. It's so rooted in the ownership of women as objects. But when I think about a life that doesn't include me as your wife and you as my, whatever, I can't..."

"You done?" Ade took Sylvie's cheeks between her palms. "I will marry you," Ade said, as if she was ordering another coffee.

The world stopped.

Sylvie was capable of being loved and loving someone. It wasn't just for books and movies. "I want you here in my heart." Sylvie said. "Today, tomorrow, and forever."

~ THE END ~

AUTHOR'S NOTE

Hi there, I just wanted to say a big thank you for reading *Here in My Heart*.

I hope you enjoyed it. If you did, I'd be thrilled if you could leave a quick review on Amazon or Goodreads. Reviews mean the world to new writers.

You might want to check out the first in this series, *Here You Are*. You'll spend more time with romantic artist Elda and sexy barrister Charlie. Can these two strong women heal past wounds to find love?

Thanks for your support. And happy reading!

www.jofletcher.com
Follow me on Instagram, TikTok, and
Facebook at JoFletcherWrites

Other Great Butterworth Books

The Here Together series by Jo Fletcher
Here You Are *(Book one)*
Can they unlock their hearts to find the true happiness they both deserve?
Available on Amazon (ASIN B0CBN935ZB)

The Heart Remembers by Ally McGuire
One wedding. One ex. And a week that might just lead to forever.
Available on Amazon (ASIN B0F932F8LZ)

The Sister Act by Helena Harte
She's faking it for one sister...but is she falling for the other?
Available from Amazon (ASIN B0F4KSVCZ9)

Sapphic Eclectic Volume One to Six edited by Nyx & Willows
Because everyone deserves love.
Available free from the Butterworth Books website

Change in Time by RJ Nyx
Book Two in The Extractor trilogy: Working in the past is hell on your future.
Available on Amazon (ASIN B0DWG24C66)

Racing Hearts by Sydney Lear
When love takes the wheel, there's no hitting the brakes.
Available from Amazon (ASIN B0DZP9X3G2)

Driving Me Barking by JP Preston
Sometimes the one who got away never really left.
Available on Amazon (ASIN B0DWG1LLXN)

Escape in Time by RJ Nyx
Book One in The Extractor trilogy: Working in the past is hell on your future.
Available on Amazon (ASIN B0DSJFDZ7R)

Ship of Dreams by Brey Willows
Two rival captains, one deadly mission, and secrets that could set the skies ablaze.
Available on Amazon (ASIN B0DRW1X75N)

Unwritten by Helena Harte
No strings is fun 'til it unravels.
Available from Amazon (ASIN B0DGQFFHYB)

Chucking Putty at the Queen by Simon Smalley
A heartbreaking, humorous, and courageous exploration of being authentic
Available from Amazon (ASIN B0DGGBV22W)

The Promise by Addison M Conley
When the world keeps pulling you under, who do you reach for?
Available on Amazon (ASIN B0DDY9FH6Z)

Back to Back by Jo Fletcher
When Fred and Ruby's worlds collide, can love rise from the rubble?
Available on Amazon (ASIN B0D6M499K2)

Heart of the Storm by Ally McGuire
Sometimes a storm is just what you need to clear the skies ahead.
Available on Amazon (ASIN B0CYTSQXWW)

Sanctuary by Helena Harte
Passions ignite and possibilities unfold. Welcome to the Windy City Romance series.
Available from Amazon (ASIN B0D4B42RRW)

Brave Enough to Love by Valden Bush
In a dance between truth and sacrifice, can they rewrite the rules of love?
Available on Amazon (ASIN B0CQP8PMVB)

Dead Ringer by Robyn Nyx
Three bodies. One killer. No motive?
Available on Amazon (ASIN B0CPQ8HFK7)

Medea by JJ Taylor
Who will Medea become in her battle for freedom?
Available from Amazon (ASIN B0CK2FB7GW)

Virgin Flight by E.V. Bancroft
In the battle between duty and desire, can love win?
Available from Amazon (ASIN B0CKJWQZ45)

Fragments of the Heart by Ally McGuire
Love can be the greatest expedition of all.
Available on Amazon (ASIN B0CHBPHR6M)

Stunted Heart by Helena Harte
A stunt rider living in the fast lane. An ER doctor who can't take chances. A passion that could turn their worlds upside down.
Available on Amazon (ASIN B0C78GSWBV)

Dark Haven by Brey Willows
Even vampires get tired of playing with their food...
Available on Amazon (ASIN B0C5P1HJXC)

Green for Love by E.V. Bancroft
All's fair in love and eco-war.
Available from Amazon (ASIN B0C28F7PX5)

Call of Love by Lee Haven
Separated by fear. Reunited by fate. Will they get a second chance at life and love?
Available from Amazon (ASIN B0BYC83HZD)

Where the Heart Leads by Ally McGuire
A writer. A celebrity. And a secret that could break their hearts.
Available on Amazon (ASIN B0BWFX5W9L)

Stolen Ambition by Robyn Nyx
Daughters of two worlds collide in a dangerous game of ambition and love.
Available on Amazon (ASIN B0BS1PRSCN)

Cabin Fever by Addison M Conley
She goes for the money, but will she stay for something deeper?
Available on Amazon (ASIN B0BQWY45GH)

Breakout for Love by Valden Bush
They're both running from their pasts. Together, they might make a new future.
Available from Amazon (ASIN B0CWHZ4SXL)

The Helion Band by AJ Mason
Rose's only crime was to show kindness to her royal mistress...
Available from Amazon (ASIN B09YM6TYFQ)

That Boy of Yours Wants Looking At by Simon Smalley
A riotously colourful and heart-rending journey of what it takes to live authentically.
Available from Amazon (ASIN B09V3CSQQW)

Of Light and Love by E.V. Bancroft
The deepest shadows paint the brightest love.
Available from Amazon (ASIN B0B64KJ3NP)

An Art to Love by Helena Harte
Second chances are an art form.
Available on Amazon (ASIN B0B1CD8Y42)

Let Love Be Enough by Robyn Nyx
When a killer sets her sights on her target, is there any stopping her?
Available on Amazon (ASIN B09YMMZ8XC)

Dead Pretty by Robyn Nyx
An FBI agent, a TV star, and a serial killer. Love hurts.
Available on Amazon (ASIN B09QRSKBVP)

Nero by Valden Bush
Banished and abandoned. Will destiny reunite her with the love of her life?
Available from Amazon (ASIN B0BHJKHK6S)

Warm Pearls and Paper Cranes by E.V. Bancroft
A family torn apart by secrets. The only way forward is love.
Available from Amazon (ASIN B09DTBCQ92)

Judge Me, Judge Me Not by James Merrick
One man's battle against the world and himself to find it's never too late to find, and use, your voice.
Available from Amazon (ASIN B09CLK91N5)

Music City Dreamers by Robyn Nyx
Music brings lovers together. In Music City, it can tear them apart.
Available on Amazon (ASIN B0994XVDGR)

Scripted Love by Helena Harte
What good is a romance writer who doesn't believe in happy ever after?
Available on Amazon (ASIN B0993QFLNN)

Call to Me by Helena Harte
Sometimes the call you least expect is the one you need the most.
Available on Amazon (ASIN B08D9SR15H)

What's Your Story?

Global Wordsmiths, CIC, provides an all-encompassing service for all writers, ranging from basic proofreading and cover design to development editing, typesetting, and eBook services. We specialise in helping self-published authors get their books into the world but also help authors find a traditional publisher or agent.

Another part of our work is charity and community focused, delivering writing projects to under-served and under-represented groups across Nottinghamshire, giving voice to the voiceless and visibility to the unseen.

To learn more about what we offer, visit: www.globalwords.co.uk

A selection of books by Global Words Press:
Desire, Love, Identity: with the National Justice Museum
Aventuras en México: Farmilo Primary School
Times Past: with The Workhouse, National Trust
Young at Heart with AGE UK
In Different Shoes: Stories of Trans Lives
Our Pride: with Nottinghamshire Healthcare Trust

Printed in Dunstable, United Kingdom

67419833R00178